BENEATH THE SURFACE

A Novel Inspired by Real Events

ANTHONY MURPHY

ISBN: 979-8-9902125-9-6

Printed in the United States of America

Dedication

הַלֵּל לַיהוָה אֱלֹהִים ,יֵשׁוּעַ הַמָּשִׁיחַ ,רוּחַ הַקֹּדֶשׁ ,וּמַלְאֲכֵי הַצֶּדֶק

Hallel la-Adonai Elohim, Yeshua ha-Mashiach, Ruach ha-Kodesh, u-Mal'akhei ha-Tzedek

Praise The Lord God, Jesus Christ, the Holy Spirit, and the Angels of Righteousness.

It is through Thee that the drive, motivation, persistence, and progress of all works are made possible. AMAWAN (Faith).

To everyone with a goal, a dream, or a vision—pursue it wisely and with all your heart. **Never relent. Never give up.**

To my loving grandparents, who instilled in me countless morals, principles, and values—you always believed in me and never gave up on me. Rest in harmony and peace.

Author's Note:

This material was written exclusively for cinematic adaptation, personal reflection and transformative exploration. It is not intended for any other use.

This work may include language reflective of certain characters and environments. Such language is offensive and not endorsed by the author. It appears only for authenticity and context.

Contents

Acknowledgments

A heartfelt thanks to Christine. Your support and guidance have helped transform this manuscript into a tangible gift to the world.

To every person who has ever taught me something worth knowing—thank you.

To all the honorable and principled souls I've encountered on this journey through the federal penal system, from every state in the nation and countries abroad, you have each played a part in awakening the light of consciousness within me.

And finally—To the Guys… My Guys! That League of Extraordinary Gentlemen, and The Coalition.

LOVE and RESPECT!

D.O.B.: 1974

1

The Trial Begins

"All rise! The Honorable Judge Sarasota presiding!" The bailiff's command thundered through the courtroom, carrying not only authority but the unspoken promise of consequences for disobedience.

"You may be seated."

The gallery obeyed in unison, wood benches creaking under the shift. The room was packed, spectators shoulder to shoulder, their murmurs dying into silence. Beyond the heavy doors, the hallways of the federal building swelled with overflow—anxious onlookers pressed in, straining for any fragment of the drama unfolding inside.

Sensing the tension that often comes with such a crowd, Judge Sarasota addressed the room.

Judge Sarasota: "Folks, first of all, good morning. Welcome to the United States District Court for the Western District of New York. My name is Judge Sarasota, and I'll be presiding over this criminal case for which you have been summoned as jurors. The case is captioned *United States of America versus Anthony Murphy*, also known as Supreme; Terrance Stinson, also known as T-Rock; Lamont Paige; and Junior Lopez, also known as Luda."

With that, the judge delivered his preliminary instructions to the prospective jurors and began the process of *voir dire*, which continued for the remainder of the day.

As proceedings wrapped, Judge Sarasota turned his attention toward the front rows.

Judge Sarasota: "Counsel, before we adjourn, I want to speak to the family members. As I've said, you are welcome here throughout the trial, but you may not discuss anything with the jurors. I believe we have family seated in the front—again, I must emphasize: do not approach or speak to them.

"Also, while you're here, you may hear testimony that stirs strong reactions. You are entitled to your impressions and opinions, but I must ensure jurors are not exposed to any comments as they enter or leave the courtroom."

He gave a brief nod.

Judge Sarasota: "Counsel, we'll recess until 8:30 tomorrow morning. Thank you."

With that, the gavel fell, and the court was adjourned.

***

The ride from the federal building to Monroe County Jail was a relatively quick one, 4 to 6 minutes depending on traffic. I absorbed what little I could of the people during these moments. Before long, I would be back within the tangle of iron, concrete, plexiglass, disturbing volumes of noise, and an assortment of collective chaos. Questions by the score would ensue regarding the ins and outs of the court proceedings. Being the gentleman that I am, I exercised patience while attempting to explain the federal court's process.

The interest in my plight seemed genuine, but I knew it lacked sincerity. If for any reason my battle was lost at trial, I'd be on my own—a solo Samurai, save for those who stood honorably beside me in the field. I worked out to quash the building stress of the day. By the time I had showered and put some overly processed food into my stomach, it was almost lockdown.

Adequate rest came with difficulty. In addition, the echoes of voices vibrating a cacophony of inaudible syllables were constant.

My concern for the woman I loved so dearly uprooted my heart from its core. It appeared with great clarity, the burden I'd laid on her lap regarding my incarceration. I could see fear and worry in those beautiful brown eyes. Still, she made every effort to maintain her composure for both of us. Leah's bravery caused my heart to swell daily with dignity, even though the once-thick rope that bound us so closely was now more akin to dental floss.

2

Twenty-three months had passed since the day of my incarceration, twenty-seven days after the birth of my only son, Premier. My mind reeled in hostility and grief as dreams came and went erratically. In contemplation of an additional indictment for multiple counts of weapons trafficking just the day before, I finally awakened worse for the wear than when initially going to bed.

When those gates buzzed open at 6 am, all activities became a blur—shower, grooming. The U.S. Marshals were calling the mainframe to expedite the arrival of my three co-defendants and me at central booking ahead of schedule. Mostly, all those I shared familiarity with wished us well. What else could be said? Shoulders squared and head high, we took the elevators to Central. Each instant I heard the rattling of or came in contact with those steel shackles, I subconsciously reverted to glimpses of movies projecting the harsh and vile conditions of the American slave trade. It was always mostly a vast majority of indigenous captives of African or Latino/Indian descent. Some of us were more poorly treated than others. The manacles would not only rub off layers of skin but could easily damage your tendons supporting the ankles or wrists. Every movement came with the risk of injury. The greatest damage, though, was the imprint it left upon each individual mind of the incarcerated. Before long, the shackles were in place and the convoy was en route. At the Federal Building, the court was called to order.

Judge Sarasota: Note the presence of counsel, the defendants, and our prospective jurors.

The jury selection process continued and was concluded. The jury was sworn. The Court presented its preliminary instructions to the jury.

Judge Sarasota: Before we recess in a couple of moments, I want to go over some things. First, I am going to address myself to the spectators. Now, it is my understanding that there are both family members of the defendants and potentially family members of friends of those who purportedly were victims of violence. I'm going to say this once. You're all welcome to be here, but only as long as everyone observes the proper rules of decorum. That means I don't want either side talking to the other. I don't want anyone talking to themselves. I want you here doing what you have an absolute right to; that is, listen. And that goes for both sides. Why am I saying this? I have a selfish goal. Whatever side you're on, I want you all to walk away saying, "That was a fair trial." I'm not singling anyone out now, but I will if I have to, and the Court Security Officers are keeping me advised of any friction, and if anyone becomes unruly or obstructive or does not respect the rights of the other side, I will not hesitate to bar you from the courtroom. If I have to, I will.

Enough said. I trust everyone will conduct themselves like an adult. If that unlikely event does happen, I have advised the Court Security Officers to advise me.

"Is the government prepared to begin?" asked the judge.

"Yes, Your Honor. The United States calls Sean Tucker to the stand," the Assistant United States Attorney Shirkin announced.

Loud murmurs rippled through the courtroom at the mention of the name, a low tide of disapproval etched into every face in the gallery. Jurors shifted uneasily, eyes flicking from one another to the bench. The judge's gavel cracked against the wood in sharp bursts, calling for order that refused to settle.

From the bullpen, Sean shuffled in under federal custody, his bulk swaying in a tight navy-blue Yates County jumpsuit. Why he'd chosen to take the stand didn't matter anymore. What mattered now was retribution—whatever the verdict.

After the oath, he lowered himself into the witness chair. The wood groaned in open protest beneath the weight, the sound hanging in the charged air like a dare.

Courtroom Deputy: Would you state your full name and spell your last name, please?

The Witness: Sean Tucker, T-U-C-K-E-R.

Judge Sarasota: Good morning, Mr. Tucker. What I'm going to ask you to do is speak into the microphone so everyone can hear you. Also, try to speak slowly and clearly because our stenographer, Mr. Span, is taking down everything that's said. Listen carefully to the questions you're asked, and answer only those questions.

If you're asked something that calls for a "yes" or "no," answer "yes" or "no." Unless, in fairness, you feel you cannot answer it that way—if that's the case, tell the lawyer asking the question, and I'll decide how it can be answered. Okay?

Sean Tucker: Okay.

Judge Sarasota: Folks, as I indicated with the previous witness, Mr. Tucker is in custody, and that's why one of the marshals is behind him. Please proceed, Mr. Shirkin.

Mr. Shirkin: Good morning, Mr. Tucker. Do you know a person named Anthony Murphy?
Sean Tucker: Yes.

AUSA Shirkin: Did you see him when you got out of prison in 1997?
Sean Tucker: Yes.

AUSA Shirkin: Do you see him in the courtroom today?
Sean Tucker: Yes.

AUSA Shirkin: Where is he, and what is he wearing?
Sean Tucker: (points to Murphy) He's seated to my right, wearing a shirt with brown stripes on it.

AUSA Shirkin: Let the record reflect the witness has identified Anthony Murphy.

Judge Sarasota: The record will so reflect.

AUSA Shirkin: Did you know whether Anthony Murphy had a nickname?
Sean Tucker: Supreme.

AUSA Shirkin: And did you have a nickname?
Sean Tucker: Divine.

AUSA Shirkin: Divine?
Sean Tucker: Yeah.

AUSA Shirkin: Back in 1997, where did you have occasion to see Mr. Murphy?
Sean Tucker: I saw him at his house.

AUSA Shirkin: And do you recall where his house was?
Sean Tucker: On Parker Place.

AUSA Shirkin: Is that in Rochester?
Sean Tucker: Yes.

AUSA Shirkin: During 1997, when you were out of custody and into 1998, how frequently were you seeing Mr. Murphy?
Sean Tucker: Like once a week, twice a week.

AUSA Shirkin: Do you know somebody named Trisha Thompson?
Sean Tucker: Yes.

AUSA Shirkin: And did you know her in 1997 when you came out of jail?
Sean Tucker: No, not when I first came out of jail.

AUSA Shirkin: When did you first meet her?
Sean Tucker: In the winter of '98.

AUSA Shirkin: And do you recollect where you met her?
Sean Tucker: I met her at Supreme's house.

AUSA Shirkin: Do you know someone who goes by Nafis Afrika?
Sean Tucker: Yeah.

AUSA Shirkin: When, if you recall, did you meet Nafis Afrika?
Sean Tucker: In early '98.

AUSA Shirkin: And where did you first meet?

Sean Tucker: In front of Parker Place.

AUSA Shirkin: Was this the location where Anthony Murphy lived?
Sean Tucker: Yes.

AUSA Shirkin: Did you happen to see Nafis Afrika in the company of Anthony Murphy?

Sean Tucker: Yes.

AUSA Shirkin: During that same time period?
Sean Tucker: Yes.

(There was a pause in the proceedings.)

AUSA Shirkin: Mr. Tucker, I'm showing you what's been marked as Government Exhibit 1B. Can you identify what it is?
Sean Tucker: A picture of Nafis Africa.

AUSA Shirkin: Your Honor, I move to have the exhibit…

(Defense counsel interjected prior to AUSA Shirkin's request being completed.)

Defense Counsel Howard: Your Honor, can we approach?
Judge Sarasota: Yes.

(A brief bench conference took place off the record.)

Judge Sarasota: Thank you, Counsel. Based on our discussion, the objection is overruled. Government Exhibit 1B is received.

AUSA Shirkin: Do you know a person named Lamont Barton?
Sean Tucker: Yeah.

AUSA Shirkin: Did you know Lamont Barton to have a job?
Sean Tucker: No.

AUSA Shirkin: Did you know Nafis Africa to have a job?
Sean Tucker: No.

AUSA Shirkin: During the late 1997 to early 1998 time period, did you know what their source of income was?
Sean Tucker: No.

AUSA Shirkin: Do you know someone named Terrance Stinson?
Sean Tucker: Yes.

AUSA Shirkin: Do you see him in the courtroom today?
Sean Tucker: Yes.

AUSA Shirkin: And where is he?
Sean Tucker: Sitting right in front of me, wearing the yellow shirt.

AUSA Shirkin: May the record reflect he has identified Terrance Stinson, Your Honor?
Judge Sarasota: The record will so reflect.

AUSA Shirkin: Did you know Terrance Stinson had a nickname on the street?
Sean Tucker: Yes.

AUSA Shirkin: What was that?
Sean Tucker: T-Rock.

AUSA Shirkin: When you came out of prison, did you begin to work?
Sean Tucker: Yes. Not immediately, but I did find work.

AUSA Shirkin: What were you doing?
Sean Tucker: I began working at a nursing home, performing housekeeping.

AUSA Shirkin: Approximately what time period was this?
Sean Tucker: From early '98 to late '99.

AUSA Shirkin: During that same time period, were you engaging in any illegal activity?
Sean Tucker: Yes.

AUSA Shirkin: What were you doing?
Sean Tucker: I was selling drugs and robbing people.

AUSA Shirkin: Let's start with the drugs. What type of drugs were you selling?
Sean Tucker: At first, I was selling pot. Later on, I moved to crack.

AUSA Shirkin: Crack cocaine?
Sean Tucker: Yes.

AUSA Shirkin: How soon after your release did you begin selling drugs?
Sean Tucker: Six to eight months later.

AUSA Shirkin: You said that you were also robbing people?
Sean Tucker: Yes.

AUSA Shirkin: I'm going to direct your attention to late April of 1998. Did you have occasion to attend any ceremony related to Lamont Barton?
Sean Tucker: Yes, I attended his wake on West Avenue.

AUSA Shirkin: Prior to attending that wake, had you engaged in any robberies?
Sean Tucker: Yes.

AUSA Shirkin: Did you engage in robberies prior to Lamont Barton's wake?
Sean Tucker: Myself and Lamont Barton.

AUSA Shirkin: During that time frame, were you in contact with Anthony Murphy?
Sean Tucker: Yeah.

AUSA Shirkin: Did he ever speak to you about what he was doing during that time period?

Sean Tucker: He was basically doing the same thing I was doing.

AUSA Shirkin: What was that?

Sean Tucker: He was doing robberies, too.

AUSA Shirkin: Did he ever tell you with whom?

Sean Tucker: Nafis.

AUSA Shirkin: Nafis Afrika?

Sean Tucker: Yeah.

AUSA Shirkin: After Lamont Barton's wake, did you engage in another robbery?

Sean Tucker: Yes.

AUSA Shirkin: When was this, in relation to the wake?

Sean Tucker: Seven to ten days later.

AUSA Shirkin: How did this event get planned?

Sean Tucker: Mr. Murphy called me and said that he had something. I asked him what he had. He said somebody named Fuquan.

AUSA Shirkin: Did you know Fuquan at the time?

Sean Tucker: Yeah, I knew him.

AUSA Shirkin: How did you know him?

Sean Tucker: We grew up together.

AUSA Shirkin: What was Fuquan's line of business?

Sean Tucker: He sold drugs.

AUSA Shirkin: Did you know him to be in any other occupations?

Sean Tucker: No.

AUSA Shirkin: How do you know Fuquan to be in the drug business?

Sean Tucker: I knew people he socialized with, and I'd seen him sell drugs before.

AUSA Shirkin: What type of drugs did Fuquan sell?

Sean Tucker: He was selling cocaine.

AUSA Shirkin: Powder?

Sean Tucker: Yeah.

AUSA Shirkin: During this time period, when Mr. Murphy contacted you after Lamont's wake, what else did he tell you?

Sean Tucker: Just mentioned Fuquan—that he'd been over there a while—and that the connect came over.

AUSA Shirkin: What do you mean by "connect"?

Sean Tucker: Fuquan's supplier. He was pretty sure it was in the house.

AUSA Shirkin: What do you mean by "it"?

Sean Tucker: The drugs or money. Perhaps both.

AUSA Shirkin: Where did this conversation take place?

Sean Tucker: He started by phone when he told me to come through. Supreme doesn't like to talk over phones. I met him in front of One Parker Place.

AUSA Shirkin: Besides you and Mr. Murphy, was anyone present?

Sean Tucker: No.

AUSA Shirkin: Did he tell you anything regarding Fuquan's location?

Sean Tucker: No. I already knew where he laid his hat. I had another friend who lived the next block over and used to see Fuquan coming and going from time to time.

AUSA Shirkin: Who was the other friend?

Sean Tucker: Rakim.

AUSA Shirkin: Was Rakim somebody Anthony Murphy knew?
Sean Tucker: Yes.

AUSA Shirkin: How do you know that?
Sean Tucker: I've seen them in the same company.

AUSA Shirkin: During that time period, did you know the business Rakim was in?
Sean Tucker: He was selling coke and crack.

AUSA Shirkin: After you spoke to Mr. Murphy about targeting Fuquan, what happened?
Sean Tucker: We moved on him that same day.

AUSA Shirkin: Who was there?
Sean Tucker: Nobody was there, surprisingly.

AUSA Shirkin: Who were you with?
Sean Tucker: Mr. Murphy.

AUSA Shirkin: How did you get there?
Sean Tucker: We drove a rental car.

AUSA Shirkin: Do you recall the address that you went to?
Sean Tucker: No, but it was off of Ridgeway Avenue, close to Marshall High School.

AUSA Shirkin: In the City of Rochester?
Sean Tucker: Yeah.

AUSA Shirkin: What did you bring along?
Sean Tucker: Two crowbars, tape, and a duffel bag.

AUSA Shirkin: Why a duffel bag?
Sean Tucker: I know that Fuquan wore a vest. He often carried a gun or would have one in the house.

AUSA Shirkin: Let me stop you there. Do you mean body armor?
Defense Counsel Hood: Objection! Leading, Your Honor.
Judge Sarasota: Sustained.

AUSA Shirkin: What type of vest are you referring to exactly?
Sean Tucker: Kevlar or Teflon bulletproof vest.

AUSA Shirkin: Anything else?
Sean Tucker: We knew he had drugs or money in the house—perhaps both. I needed the bag to carry it out, not to look conspicuous. In the bag were the crowbars and duct tape.

AUSA Shirkin: And the purpose of duct tape?
Sean Tucker: For when I peeled the plaster from around the window panes, I could then just remove the window.

AUSA Shirkin: What would that serve?
Sean Tucker: I would then be able to reach my arm inside to unlock the door and go inside.

****

Pressing the pause button. I could see him trembling like a big bowl of gelatin. Blindfolded, he couldn't see, but his ears revealed why he was here. Heavy perspiration soaked his shirt instantly. Trouble had found him. The kind that even the devil didn't want in hell.

Since his most acute sense was sound, I pondered for a while, deciding to utilize this avenue to jar his psychological state. Sean and I were both upstate together. He had a keen knowledge of the sound of metal on stone. Several pieces of steel, large and small, rested on the table nicely and comfortably on a thick white apron. Accompanied by shelves loaded with other supplies, a small microphone connected to a large speaker was aimed in his direction. I began sharpening a piece of metal that was already sharpened. The microphone picked up that sound as it bellowed out a gross melody of grinding steel upon a wet stone. It was enough to make the hair on my arms stand up. Surely, his imagination was fast becoming a cohort of opposition. I was his sole ally, which, ironically, was his complete nemesis. Sunshine was a forgone memory. Now, only darkness reigned.

I've heard before that there's a thin line between genius and insanity. How much truth exists in the saying remains a mystery. What's known is that it takes a certain degree of intelligence to form such a line. Balance, like the scales of justice, is essential in the lives of all. Unfortunately, true justice will often evade the downtrodden and oppressed. Not this time.

I'd broken a sweat while engrossed in fine-tuning the blades. Any butcher at a quality market would be pleased with such instruments. Many of the cleavers were heavy and capable of severing bone upon deliberate impact. Rolling my shoulders and stretching my neck, I began to envision how much of a good day it was going to be.

I took a drive out to the quiet countryside of Medina, New York, to visit someone I'd once been close to years ago. Dave raised livestock, trading and selling meat on fair terms. After catching up, I bought two calves, about six months old. In the cab of my pickup, the pair mooed and cried in protest as I eased them into a large kennel. Along for the ride were two freshly shorn lambs, their pink skin still warm from the shearing.

By the time anyone at the scrapyard realized I'd slipped away, I had already said my goodbyes to Dave and was headed back toward Rochester.

2

Iron and Blood

Fretting over being tailed by anyone wasn't a concern. I was like a phantom to most civilians. Prior to being held hostage myself, I no longer had any known enemies. Still, out of habit, I observed my rearview mirror and the surrounding company on the road while traveling. I was a totally different person from two decades hence. So was the case with most who had known me. There would always be the exception, I presume, of those who crossed a man in a manner deemed unforgivable.

In the catacomb beneath the secondary building of a scrapyard at an undisclosed area, the guest of honor remained seated. Above his blindfolded head was a perforated metal ramp which leveled off into a loft of sorts. Made of the same material, bright lamplight spilled through overhead in small circles upon all beneath.

Big Boy seemed to have soiled himself. The smell was nauseating. Taking one of the knives available, I cut roughly up both legs of his pants, severing the waistline on both sides. Lancing his skin along the way, you could hear him yelp each instant the tip of the blade made contact. All attempts at talk proved futile. The gag, made from a sock found in an alley, sufficed quite well.

"Shhh, lil' buddy," I whispered, pinching both of his hog-like jowls with caring hands. "It's going to be okay. Just not for you."

I fought to pull the cut garments off the target. I hosed him down with cold water, watching as he trembled and attempted muffled screams. Before bringing the farm animals inside, salt was poured into each wound on both legs.

Squirming more than a maggot in trouble, the poor boy appeared as if he wanted to respond in gangster-like fashion. I'd about had enough of the suspense. Taking the filthy sock from his mouth, he coughed. Being the gentleman that I am, I retrieved a water-filled artificial teat used for feeding orphaned mammals.

At the touch of the nipple to Divine's parted lips, he recoiled in either disbelief or disgust as sharply as the chair he was bound to would allow. Perhaps it was the smell of fresh latex that toyed with his psyche. I tried again, only to meet renewed resistance. I picked up the hose and sprayed him in the face and mouth. Coughing and gagging were followed by a few vulgar retorts. His emotional response was in no way progressive. It displeased me to gag this guy again. At catching the scent of that foul sock, Divine tucked his chin into his rolls, turning his face defiantly side to side.

"What do you want?" he blurted. "If I ain't dead yet, it must be something you want! There's no need for this! You want money? Drugs? Tell me what it is so I can make it happen!"

Desperation was beginning to settle in. Just as quickly, a flash of anger rose from beneath my surface. I cut his wet shirt off while his breath became panicked. Despite seasoned eyes, I was taken aback to witness that this dude had his nipples pierced. More disturbing was my learning that Sean had a particular bedroom fetish. It appeared he preferred to self-suckle.

Looking at my watch, I saw it was 2:37 p.m. I needed to wind this up shortly.

"Shut up! I do not wish to hear you," I said sternly. "There is a new hierarchy here, and guess what? You are at the bottom! If you make another outburst, I am going to do terrible things!"

There was no response. Reestablishing my composure, I resumed speaking.

"You will be monitored until my return. I must go for now. There are a few more of your types I need to run down. Too bad you can't join the hunt. Ha, ha, ha! I do have a sense of humor. You'll see."

I turned on a fan before leaving. Tonight would prove to be cold and dismal. Releasing the pause button on the digital recorder, the direct testimony of Sean "Divine" Tucker resumed.

AUSA Shirkin: Did you plan on entering Fuquan's location that way?
Sean Tucker: Yes.

AUSA Shirkin: Did you take anything else along for use?
Sean Tucker: No.

AUSA Shirkin: What happened once you arrived at the target destination?
Sean Tucker: We climbed the stairs to the top-floor apartment. I knocked. No one answered the door.

AUSA Shirkin: Was it a single-family home?
Sean Tucker: A two-family. Fuquan lived upstairs.

AUSA Shirkin: Did you know whether Fuquan was or wasn't present?
Defense Counsel Wolfe: Objection.
Judge Sarasota: Grounds?
Mr. Wolfe: Speculative.

Judge Sarasota: Sustained. Lacking a foundation for such knowledge.

AUSA Shirkin: Did you want to know whether someone was at the residence?
Sean Tucker: Yes.

AUSA Shirkin: So, how did you find out?
Sean Tucker: I looked around the house and the side street for his vehicles. Didn't see any. Then I went to knock on the door.

AUSA Shirkin: What happened next?
Sean Tucker: We entered the apartment, began a search.

AUSA Shirkin: Did you take anything?
Sean Tucker: Yes.

AUSA Shirkin: What was taken?
Sean Tucker: Cash.

AUSA Shirkin: Do you recollect the amount taken?
Sean Tucker: Like $240,000. It was in the bedroom.

AUSA Shirkin: Did you find anything besides the money worth taking?
Sean Tucker: Nah. There didn't appear to be any drugs there.

(There was a pause in the proceedings.)

AUSA Shirkin: Mr. Tucker, do you know anyone named Trisha Thompson?
Sean Tucker: Yeah.

AUSA Shirkin: In relation to finding the money at Fuquan's residence, when did you next see Trisha Thompson?
Sean Tucker: Supreme's house at One Parker Place. I came over and she was there.

AUSA Shirkin: And what was she doing while there?
Sean Tucker: She was upstairs, beat up and tied to a chair.

AUSA Shirkin: Did you talk to her?
Sean Tucker: No.

AUSA Shirkin: Did you talk to anyone about how she'd been tied up and beaten?
Sean Tucker: No, I just seen— I didn't see her beaten until after the fact.

Defense Counsel Wolfe: Objection.
Judge Sarasota: Sustained.

AUSA Shirkin: Are you aware of when Trisha Thompson may have moved away from Rochester?
Sean Tucker: Yeah.

AUSA Shirkin: Did you ever see Trish after she moved?
Sean Tucker: Yes, I seen her up in Albany, NY.

AUSA Shirkin: Was this the last time you came in contact with her?
Sean Tucker: I used to see her afterwards, back in Rochester.

AUSA Shirkin: Do you know someone named Ronald?
Sean Tucker: Yeah.

AUSA Shirkin: Did you know him personally?
Sean Tucker: Yes, I did.

AUSA Shirkin: Who was this person, Ronald?
Sean Tucker: He was a dude I knew from the north side. A hustler. We interacted from time to time over the years.

AUSA Shirkin: What business was he in?
Sean Tucker: He was selling weight. Smaller quantities of crack ranging from an 8-ball up to an ounce.

AUSA Shirkin: Did you ever have a conversation with Anthony Murphy about Ronald?
Sean Tucker: Yeah.

AUSA Shirkin: To what extent was this discussion?
Sean Tucker: Preme told me Trish had a jux—

AUSA Shirkin: A what?
Sean Tucker: A lick or robbery.

AUSA Shirkin: Could you repeat that word, please?
Sean Tucker: A jux.

AUSA Shirkin: What does this mean on behalf of everyone present?
Sean Tucker: A jux is a term for robbery.

AUSA Shirkin: What did you guys do after talking?
Sean Tucker: We sought Ronald out. Went to his place.

AUSA Shirkin: How did you get there?
Sean Tucker: By car.

AUSA Shirkin: Whose car?
Sean Tucker: Preme's. He drove a rental car.

AUSA Shirkin: Who was in the rental car with you?
Sean Tucker: Just Preme and me.

AUSA Shirkin: Where did the two of you depart from?
Sean Tucker: One Parker Place.

AUSA Shirkin: What did you bring along for the job?
Sean Tucker: We had gloves, ski masks. That was it.

AUSA Shirkin: Why the gloves and masks?
Sean Tucker: To avoid leaving any prints behind. The masks were to obscure our identity.

AUSA Shirkin: After reaching Ronald's place, what did you do?
Sean Tucker: I walked up to the driveway until I came to the side door. I knocked.

AUSA Shirkin: Do you recall when, as in what time?
Sean Tucker: Afternoon, around 1 PM. No one answered my knocks. Preme then the basement windows.

Defense Counsel Wolfe: Objection.
Judge Sarasota: Sustained.

AUSA Shirkin: Was it a house or apartment building?
Sean Tucker: A single-family home.

AUSA Shirkin: Did you devise a plan on what you'd do when you got there?
Sean Tucker: Not really, no.

AUSA Shirkin: After Mr. Murphy went into the backyard, when did you see him next?
Sean Tucker: He went through a window. I next see him opening the side door to let me inside.

AUSA Shirkin: What did you do?
Sean Tucker: I went inside.

AUSA Shirkin: What happened next?
Sean Tucker: We checked the house room by room to see if anyone was home. Once the house was cleared, we began searching. It wasn't until I reached an upstairs bedroom did I found anything of value.

AUSA Shirkin: What did you find?
Sean Tucker: In the top drawer of a dresser, there was $24,000; all $100 bills. There were also a few diamond rings on top of the dresser.

AUSA Shirkin: What did you go there to find, initially?
Sean Tucker: Drugs and money.

AUSA Shirkin: Did you take the money?
Sean Tucker: Absolutely.

AUSA Shirkin: During this time period, did you own a gun?
Sean Tucker: Yes.

AUSA Shirkin: Did you have it with you when you went to Ronald's place?
Sean Tucker: No.

AUSA Shirkin: Did Mr. Murphy own a gun around this same time frame?
Sean Tucker: Yes.

AUSA Shirkin: Did he have one on that day in particular?
Sean Tucker: Not that I am aware of.

AUSA Shirkin: How did you know that Mr. Murphy owned a firearm?
Sean Tucker: It was common knowledge. I'd seen it before on his person or whenever we got together.

AUSA Shirkin: Were you on parole upon your release from prison?
Sean Tucker: Yes.

AUSA Shirkin: For how long?
Sean Tucker: Seven years.

AUSA Shirkin: Are you presently on parole?
Sean Tucker: Yes.

AUSA Shirkin: In the year 1997, did you ever have contact with law enforcement?
Sean Tucker: Yes.

AUSA Shirkin: What was the nature of this contact?
Sean Tucker: I was pulled over while driving.

AUSA Shirkin: On how many occasions did this happen?
Sean Tucker: Once on Jefferson Ave, another on Genesee Street, and the last was behind my apartment building on West Main Street.

AUSA Shirkin: Were you a licensed driver?
Sean Tucker: No.

AUSA Shirkin: Whose vehicle were you operating?
Sean Tucker: On all occasions, it was one of Preme's cars.

AUSA Shirkin: Why were you driving the car?
Sean Tucker: I asked to borrow some transportation.

AUSA Shirkin: And he said yes?
Sean Tucker: Yes.

AUSA Shirkin: Were you alone during these police stops you've described?
Sean Tucker: On one of those occasions, I was with Terrance Stinson.

AUSA Shirkin: T-Rock?
Sean Tucker: That's the one.

AUSA Shirkin: In Murphy's car?
Sean Tucker: Yes.
   (There was a pause in the proceedings)

AUSA Shirkin: Do you know an individual by the name of Smiley?
Sean Tucker: Hmm.

AUSA Shirkin: How did you meet Smiley?
Sean Tucker: The first time we met was at the barbershop on Clinton Ave. I'd say about 1989. He used to hustle around the neighborhood selling drugs in the Conkey area.

AUSA Shirkin: When you were released in 1997, did you have any dealings with Smiley?
Sean Tucker: Yeah.

AUSA Shirkin: If you recall, where was this?
Sean Tucker: It varied. Smiley and Preme were running a few speakeasies, gambling spots. They changed locations often. Had a lot of houses at their disposal.

AUSA Shirkin: Do you know a person named RZA?
Sean Tucker: Yeah.

AUSA Shirkin: How did you come to know RZA?
Sean Tucker: I was introduced to him through Preme.

AUSA Shirkin: What year was this?
Sean Tucker: '98.

AUSA Shirkin: How did this introduction unfold?
Sean Tucker: Basically, Preme stopped by his house to drop off some smoke. I was riding with Preme, so that's how we were introduced.

AUSA Shirkin: Where did RZA live?
Sean Tucker: On a dead end behind Country Sweet on Lake Avenue.

AUSA Shirkin: How would you describe him?
Sean Tucker: Puerto Rican or Dominican, long curly hair, 6'2".

AUSA Shirkin: Do you know how Mr. Murphy knew RZA?
Sean Tucker: No. Only that they've known each other for a long time.

AUSA Shirkin: Would you say they were friends?
Sean Tucker: Very much so. More like brothers. Preme was very protective when it came to RZA.

AUSA Shirkin: Why so protective?
Sean Tucker: I recall them talking about an incident where some guys tried to rob RZA during a home invasion. There was a shootout. RZA killed three of the robbers and assaulted at least one other person. He was held in police custody for two days. On day three, they released him, and he has never served another day since.

AUSA Shirkin: Who told you that?
Sean Tucker: They both did, but on separate occasions. Preme and RZA had waged a silent war against any who they believed was connected with or closely related to those involved. They were hunting down all of the males over 18.

Defense Counsel Wolfe: Objection.
Judge Sarasota: Sustained.

AUSA Shirkin: Rob who?
Sean Tucker: RZA.

AUSA Shirkin: When was the last time you met RZA?
Sean Tucker: He was at Preme's house at 2 Parker Place.

AUSA Shirkin: What were Preme and RZA doing upon your arrival?
Sean Tucker: They were in front of the house, connecting a boat trailer to his pickup truck.

AUSA Shirkin: Whose boat?
Sean Tucker: They both had boats. Preme had two. I think RZA had three or four.

3

Eyes Behind the Mirror

I put great care into my behavior and actions. The fact is, someone is always watching—for the good, the bad, or the indifferent. People have done it since before time was measurable. Even when no one was in plain sight, my intuition kept whispering unease.

Several miles ticked onto the speedometer as I roamed the southeast side of the city. I drifted through streets, avenues, and cul-de-sacs I'd never known existed, expanding my understanding of Rochester's urban landscape. Even in my heightened paranoia, I found beauty—fleeting glimpses of the geography that I couldn't ignore.

A slight depravity momentarily crept over my being. Exposure to such an ornate environment certainly tilted my mind in a favorable decrement. I could sense the abundance. Not the material substance, but the sources from which the opulence is derived.

It felt inviting and welcoming. Though I wasn't in a position to linger, a smile or two found my eyes, which were kindly reciprocated. It wasn't long before I passed Cobbs Hill. Turning left behind the reservoir and reaching Twelve Corners, I again entered a maze. Eventually, it spilled out onto Atlantic Avenue. I worked my way back to familiar territory. If someone were tailing me, I'd soon identify them.

Downtown was bustling with activity. The working world was in sync with its daily 9-5 program. Similar to how Morpheus explained the modern world as Neo knew it in "The Matrix." That was, of course, before his eyes were completely opened. There were things undetectable by an unfocused eye. Timings so subtle that coincidences and *deja vu* would become commonplace. Flowing with traffic, I picked an underground garage beneath Midtown Mall to park and exited the vehicle.

It was imperative that I pay homage to a fallen comrade whenever I'm in this mall by visiting All Day Sunday. The name of this boutique truly reflected the consciousness of the ownership as a universal family. Great builder and destroyer, Almighty Shabazz of the lost tribe, evoked an ardent presence amongst his loved ones. There was no mistaking his essence. My brother's assassination will never be forgotten.

Surely, history has proven that a well-manicured lawn abets the exposure of snakes. Even when severed, a snake's head is very capable of deploying a strike, and if venomous, death may result. Obliteration is the only solution. Indeed, Shabazz's understanding of such birthed an angelic state. He was the grim reaper to all serpents.

"Peace, great mind!" I said, exchanging a right-handed embrace and hug with Bazz's younger brother, Malik. The seven was sharp. Even though he was attending business school, Malik had long been capable of running the entire establishment. I should've been taking more notes from his book. There was a jewelry department to the left of the entrance. Anything from platinum to various cuts of diamonds was available for purchase.

Many selections of urban clothing were strategically arranged further in the rear of the store, closer to eight dressing rooms for convenience. To the right were a variety of spiritual upliftment books such as *Spirit of a Man* by Iyanla Vanzant, and history like *Destruction of Black Civilization* by William Chandler, to name a couple. A plethora of fragrances and custom incense were at hand. At least six to ten staff members were available at all times to assist any interested customer.

I soaked it all in with sweeping glances. "G, who do I need to see about getting my ears pierced and some high-quality coal?" I asked.

With a wave of his hand, he indicated the jewelry department. Before Malik departed, I asked, "Lord, I need a big favor."

"What you need, G?"

"Let me know if you see any unusual grafted activity around your entrance. I think I'm being followed."

"Why, Equal!" He went on his way.

Another customer had come by then. I waited patiently, watching Leah interact with a smart degree of professionalism. It was very difficult for me to divert my attention. Impressive. Gawking at any woman is never good in my opinion.

Since I was exposed, when asked, I told the truth. "I really like your mannerisms. You were very kind and professional. It's easy to see how disarming your smile and voice are. I'd like to buy some earrings already."

She contained a laugh behind such a beautiful smile and offered me a seat at the piercing station. Relishing in Leah's complete presence and proximity is understated. Our conversation was light and airy. I was instantly attracted to her. The attraction was unshakeable, and I feared it would grow. Ultimately, I decided on two piercings per lobe. She began prepping the necessary instruments.

"This is a painless procedure. All you have to do is relax," she said.

"Says the extreme beauty who's intoxicatingly redolent," I responded as Leah leaned close, sterilizing my earlobes with an alcohol pad.

"Spreading the butter on really thick, aren't you?" Leah said with a hint of humor.

The truth was that if she had been a spider, her web had already entangled me. I unknowingly walked into those fine strands of silk.

There was a mechanical sound reminiscent of an active handheld paper puncher immediately after she counted to three. An unwanted tear involuntarily streamed from my eye toward the ear just pierced on the right side. Leah wiped it away. Hence came the second piercing. Following it, another large tear. She captured it before it reached its resting place, tracing the tear's route to the source.

Studying my face for answers, Leah asked, "Are you in any pain?"

"No. Everything is as you said it would be—painless." I smiled.

Moving to my left side, Leah repeated the process, and again the tears came.

"I've done this hundreds of times and never seen anyone tear up when pierced."

"Maybe it's some sort of sign?" I suggested.

"Sign? What kind of sign?"

"I was hoping you had the answer. Did you know your name is

biblical? Old Testament, to be precise."

"I see there's more to this book than the cover," Leah replied.

"A page or two," I said. "But I don't think I have anything on you. You're special."

"Oh boy. If I had a nickel for every one of your compliments…"

"Well, you'd be on your way to wealth. I don't fling compliments on a whim. My words are rooted in truth, which gives them life. I can't believe how much you've gotten out of me—we just met." I looked into her eyes.

Her smile could have melted the Sandman's heart into molten glass.

"Thank you. That's very sweet."

"Now you're the one pouring it on thick," I said. "Didn't I mention my interest in a couple of sets of earrings earlier?"

She had my undivided attention. It was as if we weren't in her workplace at all—it felt more like a date. All I noticed was Leah. I needed to find something that would open the door to her heart.

"Hey!" Leah said in a hushed tone. "Let's get you squared away before I get in trouble."

"I'll take full responsibility for anything in advance."

She regained her professional composure, giving me instructions, and I agreed to comply in order to prevent infection. Reluctantly, I paid my bill. Turning to Malik, the Lord just sailed without commenting. I nodded in agreement.

"Lord, I've been doing the knowledge of what you asked. Everything appears culture," Malik said.

"Thank you, G. I'll come through again soon. Give my love to the family. Peace."

Glancing in Leah's direction, she was busy attending to two customers. It seemed as if I were never there.

Eight days had passed since I had my ears pierced. Eight days that felt more agony. There were times when I didn't know what to do due to my preoccupation. I could see Leah beyond the thick glass display as I strolled toward her workplace. Three customers held her attention as they either browsed, selected, or asked questions concerning a particular piece of jewelry. Since I knew literally every single person there except Leah, much conversation was shared and many smiles exchanged. I purchased clothes and books. The staff operated on a commission-based income. Helping others as well as myself while supporting the family business couldn't have been any better.

Noticing there were no customers at Leah's station, I made a beeline toward her, bags in tow. She checked my ears, ensuring there was no sign of infection. I shuddered at her touch. Unbeknownst to me, a few coworkers had teased her about my interest, but she brushed it off. Before leaving, we exchanged a polite farewell. I took three steps, then stopped, turned, and walked back to her.

"Every time I see you, my days get brighter. No matter what I'm doing, thoughts of you prevail. Have a nice day."

I left quickly, giving her no chance to reply.

Walking until the looming escalators obscured any view of my position, I could see Leah busy at work. The flow of customers seemed endless. Knowing I'd be in Toronto for the next week or so, I had to make a lasting impression. Brainstorming, I went upstairs to a greeting card shop and found a really nice card—one that was completely blank on the inside. It had to be my meaningful thoughts that she pondered. No one else's.

After purchasing the card, I took the stairs to the first floor. Settling amid several tables at the food court, I began to construct the following:

"Of all pieces to entail the game of chess,
A certainty of certainties remains. Many see it as a game
of mental warfare, just how is it not —war with love, a hint of the
same?
Soldiers expended within the field, bishops are commissioned
with insightful angles deployed by slight gestures of hand.
Knights upon nags cantering cavalierly secure
flanks of ominous ranks approaching the throes of its enemy.
In between two castles, the King is torn,
one being his subjects engaged in battle,
the other— a Queen whom he sentimentally adores."
Crown Your King.

I allowed the ink to dry and folded the card, replacing it inside its envelope. Writing Leah's name on the front, I strolled over to the florist shop near the Broad Street entrance. I purchased a dozen long-stem roses with instructions for delivery, card included. The two women making the delivery were giddy with excitement at my idea. I trailed at a distance as they pinpointed Leah, giving her the card and flowers. She kindly accepted with a smile and placed her gift behind the counter. In the blink of an eye, she resumed work. Leah's lady coworkers were ecstatic with queries. Pleased with the results, I turned towards the parking garage. Merging into the evening traffic, I popped in an Isley Brothers CD. The beautiful City of Toronto awaited me.

4

Bloodlines and Loyalties

The drive to the scrapyard was uneventful. So was the hunt. No luck finding any pestilent, crossbred humans today.

"Morning, bud. Sleep well? Let's take a gander at you."

A quick check of the fat man's shackles told me everything was still secure.

"Please! Please! Please!" Sean's voice cracked with desperation.

"Hold on." I yanked the fan's plug from the wall. "Between that hum and your chattering teeth, I couldn't make out a word."

"Th-th-th-thank you!" he stammered.

"Don't thank me yet. In situations like this, there's no gain without sacrifice. You should know that. It's common sense."

I crossed to the wall, plucked a thin, silvery strip of material from a shelf, and grabbed a Styrofoam cup. Back at the desk, I peeled away the sheet covering his bulk from the shoulders down. From a thermos the yard staff had left, I poured steaming coffee into the cup. It was still hot enough to send a curl of steam into the air.

"This is a solar blanket," I told him. "The slightest movement will trap the heat. You won't be cold for long. I'm about to put a cup to your mouth—it's semi-hot coffee. Drink it. Warm your bones."

I let him inhale the steam first. Then, slowly, I tipped the cup to his lips. He drained it in a few gulps.

"Thank you… ah… thanks," he murmured.

I set the empty cup on the table and hit the record button on the digital recorder. Time to begin.

"Let's get to the pancakes, scrambled eggs with cheese, and fried beef sausage of the matter," I said. "Talking about food's making me hungry—shouldn't have skipped breakfast. Anyway, I figure you've pieced together why you're here. That tape should've given you a clue. Someone wants you alive. I thought about what you said last night—it's the only reason I didn't call the man who put the contract on you this morning. This is your shot. I don't care about the reasons. My reason is money."

I took a pull from a bottle of water, let the pause hang.

"So, I'm going to ask some straightforward questions. Keep your answers short. Your existence depends on it. Are we clear?"

"Very," Divine said.

"You asked last night what I wanted—since death hasn't come for you yet. So… what do you have for me?"

Big Boy's breathing turned heavy, the truth winding around him like an anaconda's coils.

"My time's valuable, Sean. What do you have for me?"

He said nothing.

"Okay then." I shoved back my chair and rose to my feet. "May the pain you endure be harsh and unending, your torment infinite. Ezekiel, chapter eighteen, verses twelve and thirteen."

"I can get you two hundred and fifty grand—right now," he said, his voice cracked and desperate.

"Keep talking."

"There's a woman I deal with… lives in Manhattan Square, Building Eight, fifteenth floor, apartment seventy. Works eight to four, Monday through Friday. Name's Lisa. She's got a daughter, about ten. The cash is inside the cushion of a bench at the foot of her bed—matches the set. Cut the seam, lift it, you'll see it. No one's home during those hours. Keys are on my keychain. Take the money. Just… let me go. Please. I'm begging you."

I found the keychain, walked over, and stood behind him. Peeling the blindfold halfway down, I asked, "Which keys?" He pointed them out. I pulled the blindfold back into place.

"Pray all is as you say."

Before he could finish a word, I was halfway up the stairs with the keys and the digital tape in hand. Three of my men—handpicked for this—listened to the recording three times, committing every detail to memory. Without a word between us, the plan began to form.

Two cars. Less than an hour. They'd be inside that apartment, peeling back the cushion, claiming the prize.

Once the self-serving intelligence was passed on, I headed back down to the basement. Sliding into my chair, I studied the man in front of me. Whatever trace remained of the person I once knew was gone.

"The validity of your assertion is in the process of confirmation. Providing your wisdom is fertile, your release may be practically solidified," I assured him.

From the moment I delivered the news, Sean held his breath the instant the words left my mouth. Forty, maybe forty-five seconds later, a long exhale escaped him—like a weight sliding off his shoulders.

I couldn't help but be glad for his relief. Even after all the spineless things he'd committed, there was still a faint light in this one-way tunnel.

Deep in his soul, he knew that karma would pay a visit eventually. This token that Sean was on the verge of receiving quickly gave cause for immediate self-evaluation. The simple truth is, he could be in a much worse situation.

Imagery is a powerful thing. Divine sensed that small speck of light growing larger. Increasing respectively as the sun would at dawn, beginning its rise into a clear eastern sky. He could picture the warm rays coursing over his skin. Peace of mind had been found. Guiding him farther and farther from the terror that sodomized his being involuntarily. Relocation was his only option. Of course, this was all speculation.

Father Time didn't adhere to anyone's schedule. It appears that only the sensuous curves of an hourglass are shown with limited favor. A solid object rapped three times on the floor above my head. Standing impulsively, I climbed the steps in response to the summons.

Upon my entry into the kitchenette, a solitary soul sat, intently studying electrical engineering materials. An outstretched finger marshalled my observation to an iPhone resting on the near end of the table. In a synchronized fashion, short, brief vibrations vied to command attention. I picked up the device. There were two text messages.

The first message lit up on my screen: *Bingo!*

A second followed: *En route with prize. The COS wants to stay longer—thinks there's more.*

I texted back: *Tell them, be safe.*

Within the web of my own personal thoughts, I had to admit how much I was going to enjoy the month ahead of me. For all of the reasons, this creep broke the bond of trust years ago. Trust could not exist in the here and now. Justice is the reward or penalty for one's ways and actions. Justice for the one downstairs surely would soon make manifest.

I looked at the man whose focus was absorbed by the documents beneath his glasses.

"Big love my G, what's good?" I asked.

"NE. Wanted to get in the field this morning. That's all."

The Jab was a stiff one. The impact—solid.

"Indeed. There will always be another opportunity. Everyone doesn't have the stomach that you possess, Banks. If I have to dismember this clown downstairs like a side of beef, we—you and I—will do so harmoniously. Just like any other time we work to beat our best record, for we know it's the nature of The Business."

"I'm still debating whether it would be best to slow-roast this joker alive over an open fire for twelve hours or stew him overnight in one of those vats on the property. The dogs would love it either way. Stewing would certainly soften the bones, making it easier on the shredder. Cleaner too, with all of the meat cooked off. Speaking of food, have you eaten yet?"

"No. I was waiting to see what the business is first," Banks replied.

"Well, I'd better get to it. The guys need to walk into some good food when they return. You want something specific?" I asked.

"Do you." he answered. Instantly, I went to work.

The aroma of home fries, cream cheese omelets, pan-seared Italian turkey sausage, and toast filled the room. It was proven. The speed of smell travels through air currents, just as sound does, though not as fast. Everyone on the premises, able to move on their own accord, made way to the kitchen. Banks was joined by Shorty and by Bull. Stien G came through the door carrying a gym bag. He was wearing that sinister smile. I was glad to see him under any circumstances. His presence was always a blessing.

"That went smoothly, P. I enjoyed the sights of the city also," said Stien in his usual philosophical manner.

"I'm glad it did. Now you can enjoy some breakfast." I made him a plate and placed it on the table.

Shorty, who was engrossed in his meal, broke from his temporary reverie. "We have to go back out west when the sun sets. Folks ain't seen such hospitality like this in decades, Big love."

"Never too much! Enjoy your meal and the rest of the day. I need to go downstairs," I said.

"TP, wait until we're done eating at least," Shorty responded quickly.

"I feared you were fiendishly determined, but it may be worse," he stated, rather solemnly, though the others laughed knowingly. He continued, "The smell of blood, pure fear, and a man's screams do not coexist well with great food."

Nodding consent, I joined my brothers in this moment of goodness. All of us here grew as individuals with certainty. During our times together as a collective, like now, is when our spirits soared toward the galaxy, and no force could stop us.

Dusk settled in over the Rochester skyline. I didn't want to see it for one reason alone. It was an indication of Shorty and Stien's departure. I knew I'd be with them wherever they went. Each time we traveled our separate roads, my heart felt less full. Knowing from experience how Shorty hated goodbyes, I refused to let him depart like a shadow in the night.

Gym bag in tow, we met at the kitchen table once again. "The two of you are forgetting this."

An unzipping of the bag revealed the $250,000 vacuum-sealed package taken from earlier.

"This is a gift and a token of gratitude. I'm sure y'all will figure out how best to use it. As you can see, the COS came back heavy. By the time I'm done with old boy, if he knows six more people of greater material than him, we'll have that too before next week this time," I said with a serious smile.

"TP, family. I was going to leave this to pass, but my heart is heavy with concern. This is love talking, so I need you to hear and feel the wisdom at hand.

"There are falling stars that we can see descending to Earth when the night sky is clear. I believe they fall for two reasons. Either the destiny was too heavy to bear, or it was encumbered by outside influences acting as fetters, causing such a decline. What people very seldom see are the stars among us, ready to defy gravity and rise to the heavens. You are a star, Preme. Bright as the sun itself. But there is a burden upon you. One that has plunged you into hell to walk among demons."

"I can't help you with this weight. The necessity for you to purge is the only thing that will set you free. Kill all your demons and rise.

"We have a new mission. A righteous endeavor. Your light is necessary to help us all navigate the path to Growth and Development. The wheels on the locomotive are moving. I can't afford to have you miss this train. Feel me? You and Khaki rid yourself of everything that haunts you in this wretched city. The devil and his company have no place in heaven. There are 720 steps to the top of the mountain. All of which will be accounted for. While our heads are held high with dignity and integrity to the North, we'll never falter. Our destination is always East. There can be no regrets for all we'll sacrifice in order to achieve. The next gathering is in three weeks in Englewood. Love."

We embraced. Just as moonlight is shrouded by thick clouds, leaving darkness in its wake, my comrades had departed, Chicago- and L.A.-bound.

5

The Queen's Welcome

Tops Supermarket, Pittsford, NY. My cart was half full when the phone buzzed in my pocket.

"Hey, beautiful. How are you?"

"Hello, stranger." Leah's voice had that playful edge.

"I thought you'd left the country. No messages? What's going on?"

I smiled, scanning the aisle for pasta sauce. "At the supermarket, stocking up for dinner. Just saw your messages."

"Eight of them," she shot back.

"I'm feeling neglected. What are you cooking?"

"First—my apologies. You never deserve to feel neglected. I had to deal with a few things at the scrapyard. But tonight? Tell me, my Queen—what shall I serve?"

"Surprise me," she said, almost daring me.

"All right, love. Bath will be ready as usual. Later."

The call ended, but I could still see her smile.

I finished the shopping with a purpose, knowing exactly what kind of reception I wanted at home. Like every meal I made for her, this one would be built on more than flavor—it would be built on intention.

At 3:39 p.m., I stepped inside, three bags dangling from my hands. The quiet of the house met me like an open canvas. I showered fast, scrubbed my hands like a surgeon, and stepped out with a plan. Dinner wasn't just dinner tonight.

The most tedious part of cooking, at least for me, is the prep. To many famous chefs, the greatest gift they've ever been given is a good sous chef—someone who works with the precision of a general on the battlefield. In that role, attention to the smallest details is everything, and a thick skin is non-negotiable.

I grew up under the care of the most loving grandparents in the world. From them came a treasure chest of lessons, but one in particular never left me: *Always put your heart into what you do. Love—especially love—should be the main ingredient in any food you prepare for others. The quickest way to someone's heart is through their stomach.* That was Grandma's creed, and it's been mine ever since.

At 5:15 p.m., I began drawing a bath—scalding hot water, bath soap, scented oil. By now, it was second nature, like tying my shoes. I shut off the faucet, satisfied with the steam curling into the air, and returned to the kitchen to tie up any loose ends.

By 5:30, I heard the familiar hum of Leah's car pulling into the drive.

I met them at the door with a smile—the queen and the prince of the castle. Quan streaked past me like a comet, laser-focused on trading his school uniform for a few more minutes of daylight before the sun dipped.

One kiss became two, and two became eight. Leah laughed, holding me at bay long enough to slip inside and shut the door.

"Wow. It smells amazing in here. What's cooking?" she asked.

"You told me to surprise you," I said. "I'll tell you all about it later. For now, your bath is waiting. And if you want me to bathe you myself, just say the word."

"I'm sure you wouldn't mind," she teased, that familiar smile tugging at her lips.

"The thing is, if you do, you'll probably end up in there with me… and bubbles will be everywhere."

I laughed internally at this truism. The fact of the matter is, we really knew how to push each other's buttons. Every day, I felt like I hit the lottery. Even the days when we didn't see eye to eye. The love in my heart—so light, yet so solid—kept me grounded whenever I felt the urge to float amongst the clouds.

"Okay. Let me know when you're done so I can rub you down. I'm going to set the table. Want me to help you undress?"

I didn't wait for a response. Heading back to the kitchen, I could hear her giggling.

Close to half an hour had passed since Leah had taken refuge in her steaming bath. Hunger nudged me to peek through the slightly open door. She had drifted off, looking so serene and beautiful I couldn't resist kissing her forehead. She startled awake.

"It's only me, sweetie," I whispered. "Let's get you out of this tub so I can feed you."

Though she didn't need my help, I offered my arm as she stood. In the steam's glow, her body reminded me of an hourglass, all curves and shimmer. I wrapped the towel around her shoulders, drawing her gently to me.

She stood at five feet seven inches tall and weighed one hundred forty-eight pounds, give or take five any given day. With a six-pack, short curly hair, and features easily comparable to the extraordinary Lynn Whitfield, Leah was my slice of caramel heaven.

On the bed was another beach towel. Next to it sat a foot tub on a small bench filled with hot water. Individual containers of 100% cold-pressed olive oil, shea butter, and mango butter swayed slightly. Leah climbed onto the bed with a sigh of comfort.

"What's your flavor?" I asked.

"I'm leaning towards mango."

Removing the towel she was wrapped in, I completed the drying process from head to toe. Just as quickly, I'd disrobed and was as nude as an orca. Afterwards, I began massaging in the heated mango butter, starting at her feet and working my way across her soft, supple skin.

Biting along in fashion, futile warnings insisting my cessation of such foreplay were counter-demanded as she turned to face me. Finally, I completed the rubdown. Though my lips shone and tasted of mango, it couldn't compare to this meal we were about to receive.

Adorned in a paisley-printed silk robe and furry slippers, the majestic woman led me by the hand into the kitchen.

Stopping on a dime, Leah exclaimed, "Dang it! I've got to change and go get Quan."

"I'm already dressed. I'll go."

I was out the door in an instant. Quan was not far from the front, his laughter guiding me easily. Following the excitement in his voice proved simple enough. As I approached, every pair of eyes—about twenty in all—locked onto me. If I hadn't known better, I might have thought I'd trespassed into the secret world of these little people.

Waving my hands in both greeting and truce, I called, "Quan, your mom sent me to come get you. Time for dinner."

His look of disappointment could've killed and buried me all in one motion.

"Ahhh, Preme, can I stay out a little longer? It's still sunny, and I'm not even hungry. I probably will be by the time we finish this game," he answered.

"Is that what you want me to tell your mom?" I asked.

"No!" Quan stared with sudden understanding and began advancing in my direction.

"You have twenty minutes. I can cover you, but no longer. By then, you all will have finished the game."

He flashed a quick smile, revealing where two of his upper front teeth had fallen out but were already being replaced.

"Okay!" he said.

I turned toward the house to dine with my special lady.

The steel door closed with a notable silence. Removing my shoes, I walked directly into the kitchen to wash my hands. Glancing right, toward where Leah was sitting on the couch, I could feel her eyes searching me.

"Babe, come take a seat so I can cater to you."

"Where's Quan?"

"I gave him twenty more minutes to finish his game."

"Is that right?" she queried, one eyebrow raised.

Walking to Leah, I took both her hands into mine. With some urging, I managed to get her to stand. As she did, she stepped into a tender kiss and a long hug.

"I couldn't bear the look on Quan's face when I told him it was time to eat. I apologize if my actions offended you."

"I'm not. That little boy has you wrapped around his finger, that's all."

"You might be right. In the meantime, come with me," I said, escorting Leah to the dining table by her hands.

Folding an apron in half, I laid it on the guest end of the glass dining table. I enjoyed transferring pots and pans to this makeshift serving station—it always seemed to engage everyone present, creating a festive environment.

"What's all of this, Sweet?"

"Your surprise. Hand me your plate, please."

The chicken was so tender that a spatula was required to keep its integrity. Removing a lid from one of the pots and setting it aside, I let the steam escape upward. Once clear, I began to serve dinner while explaining the dish.

"This is Cornish game hen, seared skin-side up in the broiler and browned in olive oil, shallots, and capers. The white sauce consists of chardonnay, heavy cream, and a hint of oyster sauce. I livened things up with shiitake, portobello, and morel mushrooms."

"You know what mushrooms do to me," Leah said.

"I'm counting on it."

"Don't say I didn't warn you."

"Time is moving too slow for me to witness the work of this holy trinity!"

With the poultry plated, I removed the next lid.

"Here we have sautéed asparagus with fresh lemon and garlic in truffle oil. This pot contains basmati rice—we discovered it at the Asian market the same day we bought the durian fruit. Lastly, beneath the aluminum foil is roasted acorn squash with allspice, raw brown sugar, and butter at its center, cooked in its own skin."

Leah's eyes glistened in the soft kitchen light, full of emotion.

"No man has ever treated me this well. I'm sorry," she said, wiping her eyes with a napkin.

"Tears of joy, right?"

"Yes, very much so."

"There's no need for an apology, my love."

I retrieved two frosted glasses from the freezer and filled them with cranberry juice. Placing the drinks on the table, I embraced Leah from behind, kissing her cheeks and drinking her tears.

"You deserve the best," I whispered.

She smiled and went to the window.

"Quan!" A pause. "Quan!" Her voice carried over the distance.

"I'm coming, Mom!"

Moments later, he flew into the house.

"Go run some bath water and take a bath. Afterward, come eat."

Quan spun on his heels and set to the task.

"Sweet, you have such an extraordinary gift. I've never experienced cooking like yours. Have you ever considered opening a restaurant again?" she asked.

"Many times. The question is where? There's a lot of money to be made here, but is this the place to plant roots?"

Leah let the thought linger, allowing herself a few days to digest the question before raising it again.

6

Price of Betrayal

The stairs creaked slightly under the weight of each step taken. Sean turned his head in my direction as if he could see through his blindfold. The stench of human waste was immediate. I grabbed the water hose, adjusted the water from cold to warm, and snatched away the solar blanket. Powerful streams of water punished his skin, hitting nicks caused earlier by the knife. Tilting him to one side, I sprayed his buttocks and chair. With the bulk of the filth washed down the drain, I opened a bottle of bleach and drizzled its contents over the tiles. After a quick spraying of the floor, it smelled much better.

Once he was covered again with the solar blanket, I found myself a seat at the table. I made an effort to find comfort.

"Okay, someone went to the location you gave me. Turns out what you said was true. That's the good part. The bad part is you don't think your life is worth more."

"I never said that, sir," Sean blurted.

"You also haven't said otherwise. If you don't, I am going to honor my previous agreement. To get out of this, you will have to pay what you weigh in order to stay... alive, baby. It doesn't need to be your money. It can be your plug or the one who puts you on those licks. Don't be concerned with who's taking the loss. Material is replaceable. Your life isn't."

A still quiet filled the room. Minutes ticked away, seeming longer than most. Fear had overtaken him entirely. I was counting on it. Fear, such a wonderful tool. It was once told to me that *fear is the most effective tool in God's arsenal. It's why the church created hell.* Given some thought, to live in constant fear is hell.

"I could make some calls to get more money," Sean volunteered.

"No calls. I need addresses and any information worth utilizing. This is a no-brainer. Considering all that work you did to get those dudes you testified against locked up just to get ten years in prison, surely you will cooperate to save your own life."

While waiting for some feedback, my anger began rising like molten lava in the hyperactive volcanoes of Hawaii. Consumed by rage and other volatile emotions, I sprang to my feet. The chair flew into the wall, knocking an item or two from the shelves. Almost instantly, I was standing before Sean. In one swift motion, I chopped the fat man across his trachea with the side of my right hand.

His choking and gasping were loud and heavy.

"B-A-N-K-S!" I screamed.

"What's the business?" came the answer from over my shoulder.

Jolted by the response, I must've hopped six inches in the air after being startled. "Your assistance is needed. Could you grab some duct tape and a sturdy, clear trash bag, please? Thank you," I said.

A few seconds later, Banks returned with the items. I went to work, cutting away a portion from the sealed end—enough to fit over Divine's head.

When he finally realized that he was being fitted with plastic over his head, panic set in. Careful to maintain the blindfold's position, I took a steady hand despite my inner aggression. Duct taping the loose ends of the cut portion of the bag to Divine's neck—several times around—created a dead end from which water could not escape. Murmurs and pleas came from the hostage, solidifying his eagerness to talk. Talk, he most certainly would. Now wasn't the time.

"We're going to take a trip to the water park," I said to no one in particular. "Grab that water hose, G. Cold water, please."

Banks complied and handed it to me. Holding the open end of the bag gathered in my left hand, I put the nozzle inside and pulled the trigger with my right. Approximately a gallon or so of water was collected. It was time to break the monotony of kind patience and have a little fun.

"G, you are about to bear witness to one of the four elements of this planet. The power of water," I said.

Momentarily deaf to all the fat man had to say, I raised my left hand high above his head. With it came the plastic bag and the level of water gathering at its base. All hysteria broke loose within Divine. The fury I was about to unleash would be cold—harsher than the winter waters of Lake Ontario.

Cresting at Sean's eyebrows, the water immediately filled with bubbles, followed by unintelligible sounds. Why this dude attempted to literally talk when submerged defied reason. Panic—that very close cousin of fear—settled in like a well-fed newborn anticipating a good night's sleep. Ten seconds later, I lowered the bag to let poor Sean catch his breath.

A storm of hard coughing and gagging pursued. Snot billowed from his nose, and he began to drool. He sobbed, begged, and pleaded.

"Those tears aren't genuine!" I insisted.

Divine's reply didn't come quickly enough. Water rushed into his open mouth as I raised the bag. Straining against shackles that wouldn't yield, sounds came from somewhere deep within that no man is supposed to make.

Twenty seconds.

I lowered my hand. Vomit gushed forth and into the water. Sean's breathing was labored. In a high-pitched tone, his voice rang out, "I'll talk! I'll talk! I'll talk! Please! I'm sorry! I'll talk!"

The sobbing ensued. This was the authentic music of an individual quickly broken and shattered like cheap glass. Over the course of the next few applications, terror would find its place. I raised my hand. The contents of his stomach swam around his face.

It was time he heard my voice. To have a complete comprehension that my voice paralleled the worst of the worst nightmares.

"They say the harshest pains are painless… that if enough torture is endured, the crucified becomes insanely close to the Maker's light," I said.

Twenty seconds. I lowered the bag. The coughing fit broke, replaced by another rush of vomit. The sobbing amplified, but I had on mental earplugs. Up went the bag. He had begun screaming for help. I managed to hear it beyond the water.

"Have you seen the light yet? Have you felt enough pain? I doubt you have. Your plight must continue. I must prepare you for hell!"

I held up the bag for twenty seconds more.

Sean was utterly defeated—broken in body and spirit. His apologies spilled out in a jumble, from past robberies to testifying in federal court. It sounded more like a confession than a plea.

"Time for another swim, buddy."

"I'll tell you everything I know! Please! Please! Please!" His voice cracked into hysteria.

"I need to make sure you're telling the truth."

I lifted the bag. The water inside had grown murky, thick with debris—disgusting to look at, worse to smell. His body jerked and trembled, the convulsions sharp and strange. Still, I needed to know who sat at the top of the food chain.

Twenty seconds.

"Seen the light yet? Or do you need more guidance?"

"I see it! I'm sorry! Sorry! Sorry! I won't do it no more! I'll tell you everything. Please! Mhhhhhhhhh! Ah! Ahhhhh! Ahhhhhhh! Ah! Ahhhhhhh!"

By my count, we were making progress.

Without warning, I raised my left hand. Sean gasped, dragging another mouthful into his lungs. The screams cut off, replaced by a ragged, choking cough. His body shook in sharp, seizing tremors.

I held the bag a few seconds longer before lowering it, watching for signs I might need to bring him back. With effort, he steadied— breathing hard, but breathing.

I slipped a rubber band around the bag where my hand had been, leaving a four-inch gap for air.

The digital recorder was ready. I hit record and set it on the chair facing him.

"There's a hungry pack of wolves roaming the woods," I told him. "The bigger the plate, the brighter your fate. Now… give me everything you've got."

***

AUSA Shirkin: What type of boats?

Sean Tucker: They were fishing boats. Really nice ones. I think they were called bass boats.

AUSA Shirkin: Do you know where these boats were purchased?

Sean Tucker: Not exactly. Probably at an auction. They spent a lot of time going to auctions.

Defense Counsel Wolfe: Objection.

Judge Sarasota: Sustained.

AUSA Shirkin: Where is 2 Parker Place in relation to One Parker Place?

Sean Tucker: Directly across the street.

AUSA Shirkin: I'm sorry, let's backtrack for a minute. What is dro?

Sean Tucker: It is a very high-grade of marijuana that is basically grown hydroponically.

AUSA Shirkin: Okay. Did you discuss anything while at Preme's house on this particular day when RZA was present?

Sean Tucker: Yes.

AUSA Shirkin: What was discussed?

Sean Tucker: Preme and RZA were hashing out details concerning a potential score.

AUSA Shirkin: What do you mean by score?

Sean Tucker: A jux—a robbery.

AUSA Shirkin: Did Preme and RZA discuss any of the details while you were present?

Sean Tucker: Yes. They said they were going to take the boat out on the bay to do some fishing until nightfall.

AUSA Shirkin: Where? What bay?

Sean Tucker: Irondequoit Bay. They had scuba diving gear in the boat as well.

AUSA Shirkin: What was the scuba diving gear for?

Sean Tucker: I asked the same question. I was told that once dusk set in, they would be timing how long it would take to swim underwater to a mansion on the waterfront. That there was no other way in from land.

AUSA Shirkin: Did anyone say who was being targeted?

Sean Tucker: No. I asked. They said it didn't matter.

AUSA Shirkin: What happened next?

Sean Tucker: I was invited to go with them for the dry run and to test my diving skills. I declined because I'm not much of a swimmer.

AUSA Shirkin: So you didn't go with them?

Sean Tucker: No. They left to go to Irondequoit. I went on about my business.

AUSA Shirkin: After that day, when did you next see either Preme or RZA?

Sean Tucker: About four days later.

AUSA Shirkin: Where did you see them?

Sean Tucker: At RZA's house behind Country Sweet on Lake Avenue.

AUSA Shirkin: What were they doing?

Sean Tucker: Preme was cooking all sorts of seafood—king crabs, prawns, scallops, and some pasta.

AUSA Shirkin: Why did you go to RZA's house?

Sean Tucker: That evening during the 5 o'clock news, the newscaster spoke of an armed robbery in the suburb of Irondequoit, outside Rochester.

AUSA Shirkin: What made this robbery any different than the next or any other?

Sean Tucker: It was the description of the robbery that was distinctive.

AUSA Shirkin: How so?

Sean Tucker: The place robbed was the Sea Breeze Amusement Park. There were two perpetrators. What was reported to authorities was that they were wearing dark-colored wetsuits. Culver Road is the only avenue of commute by vehicle or anything on wheels. According to detectives leading the investigation, there were no vehicles seen on traffic cams or other video surveillance coming or going during the feasible time in question—between midnight and 2 a.m.

AUSA Shirkin: So, to be clear, for the jurors' understanding, the suspected robbers were wearing wetsuits?

Sean Tucker: Yes.

AUSA Shirkin: This report also said the suspects didn't exit the crime scene by car?

Sean Tucker: Correct. These two details are what grabbed my attention.

AUSA Shirkin: Why is that?

Sean Tucker: I recalled the scuba gear, and that RZA said the jux wasn't approachable from land.

Defense Counsel Wolfe: Objection, Your Honor. Speculative.

Judge Sarasota: Approach.

Two AUSAs stepped forward for the government, joined by four defense attorneys representing the defendants on trial. The judge and prosecutors switched off their microphones for a private conference at the bench.

The court stenographer, barred from hearing the exchange, could not record the discussion between the judge, the government, and the defense—despite courtroom procedure requiring that all open court proceedings be transcribed.

When the sidebar concluded, all parties returned to their respective positions. Direct examination of Sean Tucker resumed.

AUSA Shirkin: Do you recall what news station you watched this report on?
Sean Tucker: Yes. Channel 10.

AUSA Shirkin: Do you remember which month of 1999 this robbery could have been committed?
Sean Tucker: August.

AUSA Shirkin: May I have a moment, Your Honor, to confer with AUSA Wesley?
Judge Sarasota: You may.

There was a brief pause in the proceedings as the two prosecutors quietly discussed an issue. As AUSA Shirkin spoke, AUSA Wesley took notes. As the conversation ended, AUSA Wesley folded the paper, handed it to an assistant to the U.S. Attorney's Office, and the assistant gathered her briefcase and purse before immediately exiting the courtroom.

AUSA Shirkin: Thank you, Your Honor.
AUSA Shirkin: Did the news report mention whether anything was taken?
Sean Tucker: Yeah. It was only said that a large sum—an undisclosed amount of cash—had been taken just prior to the AMSA pickup later that morning. (The witness raised a finger on his right hand in the air, as if requesting permission to speak.)

AUSA Shirkin: Yes?
Sean Tucker: Yeah. My father was head of security at Sea Breeze. He screened and hired every individual under his employment. Since he'd landed the security contract with Blue Cross Arena in downtown

Rochester, a select pool had previously been at his disposal. I was told by a cousin of mine who worked at the amusement park that more than $300,000 in cash was taken.

AUSA Shirkin: $300,000?
Sean Tucker: Over $300,000.

Murmurs rippled through the crowd of spectators. The judge rapped his gavel to regain control.

Judge Sarasota: Ladies and gentlemen, I need you to keep things orderly and not act as a distraction to all parties involved. Mr. Shirkin, please proceed.

Mr. Shirkin had spent the last several seconds rubbing his head with his left hand. He couldn't imagine what he'd do with $300k-plus. It infuriated him that the defendants lived so cavalierly, taking what they desired on a whim. He had to make these jerks pay at any cost.

AUSA Shirkin: Yes, Your Honor.

(A note was passed from AUSA Wesley to Mr. Shirkin.)

AUSA Shirkin: Did Preme or RZA ever mention any involvement with the Sea Breeze heist?
Sean Tucker: No. They fixed me a plate. We ate and drank and smoked. These guys never spoke about anything after it was done. If I had inquired, I might not be here now.

AUSA Shirkin: Do you recall a time when you, RZA, Preme, and T-Rock met together after the Sea Breeze robbery?
Sean Tucker: Yes.

The chair in which the witness sat continued its agonizing protest against what it presently bore, its creaks and cries at times loud enough to distract from Sean's testimony.

AUSA Shirkin: Approximately, during what month did the four of you meet?

Sean Tucker: September.

AUSA Shirkin: Why did you meet?

Sean Tucker: Initially, Preme called me. He told me to swing through.

AUSA Shirkin: Did he say why?

Sean Tucker: No. That's why he asked me to come over to his place. He didn't trust electronic devices. He would never use them for any purpose but making contact.

Sean, throughout his testimony, continued to stare menacingly at the four men on trial. He often wore a smile and giggled or snickered while testifying, as if this ordeal the defendants were fighting—and his part in it—was a harmless prank.

AUSA Shirkin: After you and Mr. Murphy had made contact, what happened?

Sean Tucker: He said to come over.

AUSA Shirkin: Where did you meet him?

Sean Tucker: At his house on Parker Place.

AUSA Shirkin: Which house on Parker Place are you referring to?

Sean Tucker: Two Parker Place.

AUSA Shirkin: Did you go inside?

Sean Tucker: Yes.

AUSA Shirkin: Who was present?

Sean Tucker: Only Preme and RZA. I was person number three.

AUSA Shirkin: When did the next person arrive?

Sean Tucker: T-Rock didn't arrive until I drove over to his place to pick him up.

AUSA Shirkin: So, to be clear, you left 2 Parker Place after you'd arrived to go get T-Rock?
Sean Tucker: Yes.

AUSA Shirkin: Whose car were you driving?
Sean Tucker: I drove my own car.

AUSA Shirkin: Where did T-Rock live?
Sean Tucker: On Thurston Road.

AUSA Shirkin: Did he know you were coming?
Sean Tucker: Yes, I called him once en route.

AUSA Shirkin: What did you say?
Sean Tucker: I told him, "Yo… I got somethin' for us. Be ready."

AUSA Shirkin: When you arrived at Mr. Stinson's residence, what happened?
Sean Tucker: I pulled into his driveway and flashed the high beams twice.

AUSA Shirkin: Do you see Mr. Stinson today in the courtroom?
Sean Tucker: Yes.

AUSA Shirkin: Will you please identify Mr. Stinson for the record?
Sean Tucker: He is sitting at the defendants' table, third from my right, wearing the white dress shirt and black tie.

Sean pointed with his right arm and index finger toward T-Rock. The witness chair protested beneath the man's weight, its shrieks audible over the trial spectators' expressions of disgust. As Sean pointed out, he boasted a smile wide enough for pictures at the 6th-grade graduation. The expression of utter disbelief on T-Rock's face told it all. He didn't see that coming.

7

Concrete Confessions

Toronto, Ontario, is magnificent for lack of better words. It is an environment that's befitting the most complex and fastidious of people. I'd have to admit, there's not a cleaner metropolitan city in my travels thus far, with the exception of Montreal. Outside of the native countries themselves, Toronto offered some of the finest restaurants I've ever known. Coupled with the beauty of diverse ethnicity, this jewel was arguably the most multicultural city in the world.

The city was chock full of ongoing events, activities, and nightlife. Sports fans had the Toronto Raptors, where Rochester native John Wallace made his debut in the NBA. There's also the Blue Jays and the Maple Leafs, just to name a few. One of the most prolific realities experienced was that this city projected very little violence. It was pleasant, seductive, and had a personality of its own. A city easy to fall in love with. Definitely a wonderful place to live. A remarkable home.

With all of Toronto's splendor, it failed to distract my thoughts of Leah. She seemed to be the lodestone drawing me mentally by the second. Somehow, my stay in Toronto concluded two days early. I found myself on the QEW heading east in a hurry. Depending on traffic, four hours would get me to my destination.

Text messages arrived on my phone asking about my whereabouts.

I did know that breaking my prior engagements would prove disappointing. Stopping at the Trinity Donut shop in St. Catherine's, my stomach lured me inside. After purchasing a pint of milk and a few fresh pastries, I returned to my vehicle. A multitude of apologies on my behalf were extended to those I may have disenchanted. With concrete assurances to improve our next meetings, we decided to reconvene via phone at midweek for schedule confirmation.

I was humbled and grateful. Gifts would find their way to each person's workplace. I had to show them my appreciation. In truth, I had an urgent set of circumstances in need of tending. It refused to be neglected. My lot is constituted by matters of the heart. The Rainbow Bridge border crossing was a sight to behold. Depending upon where you were in this vicinity, the view of Niagara Falls proved breathtaking. It was a lovely sight. I sensed that such a precious moment like that was supposed to be shared with someone special. I was en route to see her.

It wasn't until approximately 6 pm that I finally strutted into 'All Day Sunday. Morphing from pensive and stern to all smiles, I greeted everyone. The weight of the outside world happened to levitate itself from my shoulders. Walking counterclockwise around the boutique afforded many angles of Leah while working. Her beautiful, brown, observantly sly eyes were giraffe-like in nature. Slightly hooded and protected by the longest of lashes, I yearned for her closeness.

Once I had decided on a few sets of Maurice Malone tank tops and boxers, I handed the money to Ziggy. Promptly making my way to the jewelry department, I waited until all customers had been attended.

"Good evening, Miss Leah," I said, looking directly into her eyes. "You look stunning."

"Thank you, and good evening. Correction—it's Miss, not Mrs."

"Even better. I stand corrected. I had every intention of buying some jewelry. Except for..."

"What is it?" she inquired.

"The finest jewel present, I'm sure, is not for sale. Also, you're all I seem to be able to focus on," I admitted.

Maintaining a professional poker face, she asked permission to examine my piercings.

The second Leah arrested my earlobe between her forefinger and thumb, I flinched. Caught totally unaware, her face filled with concern.

"Are you okay? That's not supposed to hurt."

"It doesn't. Your skin is so soft that my knees almost gave out," I said, pretending to study some earrings through the glass display.

Leah stood motionless for a few seconds, her eyes twinkling like stars in my peripheral vision.

"Thank you for the flowers and the card. It was a very nice gesture."

"What flowers?" I asked with a blank expression.

"I know it was you. You were gone just long enough to figure it out."

"There must be some misunderstanding. Whoever sent it surely has impeccable taste in women—just my humble opinion."

Leah's caramel complexion was growing scarlet by the second.

Shabazz's father had made his presence felt. I greeted him warmly as he decided to maintain close proximity. Perhaps the old king was curious to see where my interests lay—in the jewel, or the jewelry. Women sense when a man desires them, and Leah's keen observation of my every move betrayed her.

"Miss, would you be so kind as to show me that set of earrings, please?" I asked, indicating.

"Certainly," came her reply.

Leah opened the sliding doors of the display case. Touching the item I had selected, she met my eyes for confirmation. Securing the slide, she placed the jewelry on the counter.

"Here you have a pair of marquise-cut yellow diamond studs. The collective weight is 2.76 carats, set in 18k gold. As you may have noticed, this cut is prized for its ability to capture light even in low-light conditions. If you purchase these, may I suggest screw backs?"

Leaning closer as if to inspect the earrings, I whispered, "I love it when you talk to me that way."

"You're going to get me in trouble with the boss."

"No, I won't. Trust me." My voice returned to normal.

"In your opinion, if I were to purchase another set of diamonds to complement these, which would you recommend?" I asked.

The lovely lady led my eyes to a pair of half-carat stones cut and set in the same fashion.

"Thank you for such a lovely presentation. You had me at the first kiss," I admitted.

"Kiss?" She lowered her voice, sternness settling in. "Sorry, wrong girl."

"No, you're wrong. Your spirit kissed mine—with lips as irresistible as the ones on your face."

"What?" Leah said, startled.

"Forgive me. Sometimes I talk under my breath. I was asking for the price on the initial pair of earrings."

"The retail value is $10,500."

I looked at Leah, and she forced a smile that reached my depths.

"Okay. If I get these right now, what's my price?"

"Give me a second." She held up a finger and conferred quietly with the boss. Upon returning, she said, "How does $9,000 sound?"

"I'll take both sets."

"Cash or credit?"

"Cash."

I unveiled a stack of hundreds and passed it over to Leah. Wetting her fingers on a sponge, she counted the bills twice, checking for authenticity. I remained silent until the count was complete.

"You might want to insure your merchandise," she said.

"That's a great idea. I hadn't considered it. See? You're already making me better."

With the boss pleased by the close of the sale, cash in hand, Shabazz's old king disappeared into his office. Leah's smile was no longer contained—it flashed vibrantly.

"In whose name would you like this insurance?" she asked.

"Yours."

The reply gave Leah pause, as though she had just seen me for the very first time. Her hushed inventory aroused a slight awkwardness inside of me, so I broke the silence.

"I don't know how I let you get your hooks so deep into flesh. I'm ready to fill out an application just to be close to you."

"I'm at a loss for words."

"There's not much that needs saying. All you need to do is crown your king."

I took her hand, tracing its outline with my fingertip.

"When will I see you again?" I asked.

"When would you like to?" she countered.

"Since two days before Kwanzaa."

"I beg your pardon?"

"The day you pierced my ears, darling woman."

Understanding, Leah wrote her number on the back of a business card and slipped it inside the bag with my purchase.

"I'm working until nine tonight because of the holiday schedule. I should be settled by ten, maybe ten-thirty. Call me around then."

A time check revealed ten minutes to seven.

"I'm missing you already," I said, making her burst into laughter.

Bidding farewell to everyone, I departed the establishment elated, genuinely happy, and thrilled.

8

Echoes in the Dark

There was a total of seven people lined up for the take-down. The personal reasoning behind the selections was irrelevant. What was pertinent was the accuracy of such facts. According to the information received, at least two million will be accessible. Things were beginning to look up very quickly. It brought joy to my heart to put those who didn't come across plates like this that their dedication and loyalty truly deserved it.

I was mentally preparing myself to put Sean to question again. By design, every detail needed confirming—sometimes the second pass shook loose more than the first. Maybe more fruit would drop from the tree. Maybe not.

Then Banks rolled in a fully charged car battery and a set of jumper cables, and I felt a quick, almost electric jolt of satisfaction. Tools like that have a way of keeping people honest. For some, only the looming shadow of real pain—or worse—makes sense. Those who can't self-correct get persuaded by other means. What was about to happen was one of them.

With multiple routines practiced and exercised, we had executed scores of kidnappings over the last two weeks. None of this work was about money. That was merely a by-product—one that would be used constructively, not reinvested into the drug trade.

I tapped Banks on the arm, motioning him aside. Once we were out of earshot, I leaned in.

"I'm thinking of tweaking the plan. Forget the lambs and calves—we're having a cookout. I know exactly what to do with those ewes. The Latin brothers will go wild over whole roasted pigs." I nodded, sealing my own agreement.

"What's the business?" Banks asked.

"My fault," I said. "I want to break his will completely. But I'll need a big favor from you."

I explained what I needed in hushed tones so as not to be overheard.

Banks' face hardened. "What? Absolutely not. Out of the question. That's way out of my lane—above or below my pay grade, however you want to spin it. I'm not doing it."

I laughed like I'd never heard anything more hilarious. His chest was filled with indignation, but he soon realized no harm had been intended.

"You're tripping, G. Any one of the sisters upstairs can handle that assignment," I countered.

The fat man in restraints trembled at the outburst between us, though we paid him little attention.

"I didn't mean you, per se. We must utilize our channels. Whoever you send can also pick up some goods from the market to kick off this cookout later. From here on out, I want to start using those hockey masks. It will have a greater impact if this parasite sees what's in the next few applications."

"I'm on it," Banks said.

Before I could give thanks, he was on his way upstairs.

Taking time to don the hockey mask, I came over to remove the blindfold. First, the trash bag around Sean's head needed adjusting. Unwinding the rubber band, I tightened the bag at his neck again to prevent spilling the contents.

With time, his eyes adjusted to the light and his surroundings. I waited patiently. There was no rush for this fool to see what he had gotten himself into.

Time has proven that some decisions a person makes are temporary, while others could prove long-term or even permanent. Sean had made some bad decisions—choices that could not be undone. He would have to live with it, at least for as long as was allowed.

A few of the men working on the premises helped to bring the collapsible steel bear cage downstairs. We dissected the perforated makeshift ramp overhanging Divine. With the bear cage restored for use, he would shortly be transferred to his new residence. As long as he saw us donning masks, Divine held onto a glimmer of hope in his eyes. Kidnappers wearing masks usually indicated, in the perception of the captive, release at some point. Once their goal was accomplished, all parties could walk freely with no expectation of revenge or retribution—provided that all kept their mouths shut.

For Sean, it would be a little different. He would always wonder who snatched him, whether or not they were near or distant, and if they'd strike again. Would he be capable of thwarting another attempt at abduction? Sean had a strong sense that he would get out of this pickle—especially after they collect on the seven people he'd compromised. Money talked in this world, much more than hollow words backed by fallacy. This is why he held on to hope.

All of the masked men pitied him for his delusion. They knew he wasn't going anywhere. His fate had been sealed long before, when he decided to plug into the Matrix. He afforded those agents the utilization of his being.

Through him, they longed to see what law enforcement and society would never be entitled. There was one exception: Sean was far from honest in his testimony. It's quite difficult to defend yourself against a lie when it's constructed on the fly. To catch such inconsistencies, normally, the deceiver needs to be kept in conversation. Usually, at such a time, the opportunity to separate fact from fiction presents itself.

I took care not to spill any contents of the bag around Divine's neck during its removal. The solar blanket was put to the side as well. Rolling the fully charged car battery and jumper cables closer, the beady eyes in that fat orangutan face of his evolved into a pair of fifty-cent pieces. He watched as I connected the jumper cables to the battery.

Picking up the unoccupied end of the cables, I stood before the guest of honor.

"Some people do not feel so confident about the intel you provided me earlier. I tried to speak up on your behalf, but my vote was in the minority. This process you're about to endure will either confirm all you've said or draw out any inconsistencies. Details are vital in this business," I said, touching the opposing charges together playfully. Sparks jumped willingly into the air.

"I was telling the truth. Please, please—I told the truth. You don't have to do this, man. You don't have to do it. It's all true. It's the truth. Send somebody to—"

Sean's words were cut short the second I touched the live tip of each cable to both of his pierced nipples. The description attributed to the man experiencing the electrical charge roaring through his body was horrifying. Sean's screams were not quite human but more animalistic.

His crying was like that of a crippled cape buffalo abandoned by its herd in the African wild. With the cover of darkness came a pack of hungry hyenas. Making no attempt to suffocate the defenseless beast, the hyenas—known for a bite powerful enough to break elephant bones—tore chunks of flesh from its hindquarters while disemboweling the creature simultaneously. The pack cackled as it gorged and gorged. With muzzles and fur dripping with fresh blood and fecal matter to their shoulders, the cape buffalo remained in a wide-eyed caterwaul.

"Just like the good old days," I thought to myself. There was nothing to beat the good cheer of conjuring up a person's worst fears.

Some seconds into the experiment, he was beginning to foam at the mouth. Twenty or so seconds later, the charge was placed to his piercing again. Sean no longer sounded human. When he scrawled, I mimicked his cries. His will to survive such torment was purely semantic in nature. By the fifth round of therapy, I had to stop.

"My man, you smell like bacon," I said with a smile.

"While you're regaining your composure, let's have some trivia. Did you know that during the 14th century, Great Britain—England specifically—was a reckoning power? King Edward III, of the House of Lancaster, was known throughout Europe as the Lion of Lancaster."

I studied Divine's eyes to see if he was coherent.

"Born in the year 1312 of their Lord, as they said back then, he lived for sixty-five years. Surely, you must know all great and powerful kings were so as a result of those he, meaning the king, surrounded himself."

I returned the jumper cables to the cart and disconnected the other end from the battery. Pacing the floor, I resumed the one-sided colloquy.

"Can you imagine how cunning, shrewd, and ruthless the king's council would have needed to be for him to maintain and advance his kingdom? There were spies everywhere. Payments and bribes arranged. Merging of royal bloodlines to ensure peace and prosperity, where only the destruction of war's wake would echo. Oftentimes, opposing families of influence and wealth to the King were framed in the courts for treason—or any number of crimes punishable by hanging. All their wealth and land would be taken and redistributed amongst the dukes and earls loyal to the Crown.

"Some were obliterated literally. For example, say at a family banquet, every attendant who drank of the wine perished by poison. Perhaps all who would remain of any house in question were young children. They, of course, would be governed through the proper channels by appointed guardians, ensuring expectations were met. Diplomacy was always the first step. Butchery wasn't far behind.

"King Edward III had some of the most efficient persecutors. This is where I get the term 'Put you to the question.' I imagine that's where the word interrogate was born. If I say they were brutal in their tactics, I'd be understating the seriousness of such business."

Footsteps sounded overhead, drawing closer to the stairs. I picked up the jumper cables. This time around, I connected one to each leg of the steel chair upon which Sean sat.

"I'm going to have a nurse come down and put some raw aloe on those nipples of yours. They'll heal in no time. The fellas are back. Time to put you to the question."

Sean's high, breaking screams cut through the basement like a male soprano dragged against the blade of fear itself.

***

It was as if Divine, the Brown Street Bully, Sean, was saying, "Gotcha, sucka." I couldn't wait until recess to share some choice

64

verbiage with Mr. T-Rock.

AUSA Shirkin resumed the direct examination.

AUSA Shirkin: Could you walk us through what happened after you arrived at T-Rock's house?
Sean Tucker: After T-Rock came outside, he got into the passenger seat of my car. I told him right after to go get strapped and bring a mask and gloves.

AUSA Shirkin: What do you mean, "strapped"?
Sean Tucker: To bring a gun.

AUSA Shirkin: How did you know T-Rock had access to a firearm?
Sean Tucker: I personally provided two handguns to T-Rock for personal use.

AUSA Shirkin: Provided how?
Sean Tucker: I gave him both guns from my personal collection.

AUSA Shirkin: What was the make of these handguns?
Sean Tucker: A 9-millimeter and a .45 caliber. Both semi-automatics.

AUSA Shirkin: How did you come to possess such firearms?
Sean Tucker: I would buy them from people on the streets.

AUSA Shirkin: Once you told Mr. Stinson to get his gun, gloves, and mask, what happened?
Sean Tucker: He returned dressed in black, wearing a bulletproof vest, and carrying the items in his possession.

AUSA Shirkin: He was wearing body armor?
Sean Tucker: Yes.

AUSA Shirkin: How did you know this?
Sean Tucker: T-Rock took off his hoodie once we arrived at Preme's house to get more comfortable.

AUSA Shirkin: What did you bring with you?
Sean Tucker: I had a gun, gloves, and a mask. I think that's it.

AUSA Shirkin: Can you describe the gun you carried?
Sean Tucker: A Glock 27.

AUSA Shirkin: Do you recall the kind of gloves you used?
Sean Tucker: Baseball gloves.

AUSA Shirkin: So you and Mr. Stinson went to Mr. Murphy's place at that point?
Sean Tucker: Yes.

AUSA Shirkin: When you arrived, who was there?
Sean Tucker: Preme and RZA.

AUSA Shirkin: If you would, please tell us what happened next.
Sean Tucker: Once the four of us were inside the house, we lit a blunt to smoke while RZA revealed the jux.

AUSA Shirkin: At which house on Parker Place was this?
Sean Tucker: 2 Parker Place.

AUSA Shirkin: Did you see anything unusual inside 2 Parker Place when you arrived?
Sean Tucker: Yes. There were four wigs on the kitchen counter — natural hair wigs twisted into dreadlocks, various lengths.

AUSA Shirkin: What else did you see?
Sean Tucker: Next to the wigs was a police scanner.

AUSA Shirkin: You saw these items on the table inside Mr. Murphy's house at 2 Parker Place?
Sean Tucker: Yes.

AUSA Shirkin: Have you ever seen Preme with a police scanner before?
Sean Tucker: Yep.

AUSA Shirkin: When?
Sean Tucker: All the time.

AUSA Shirkin: What was the police scanner used for?
Sean Tucker: It was used to pick up calls dispatched to 911, the fire department, ambulances — things like that. He mainly used it to get the drop when someone was calling in a crime. If a crime was reported in progress, he'd have the advantage of knowing.

AUSA Shirkin: Did you ever use a police scanner with Mr. Murphy before this particular occasion?
Sean Tucker: No.

AUSA Shirkin: Why was the scanner present?
Sean Tucker: To take with us on the jux. It had been programmed to pick up every call to 911 in the city.

AUSA Shirkin: How was it programmed?
Sean Tucker: Every individual police station citywide has its own section where calls come in. The entire Rochester Police Department would probably know about it, but mainly, the closest station would respond.

AUSA Shirkin: Where did you learn this?
Sean Tucker: From reading the manual that came with the scanner. There were other things you could get the scanner to do with a special chip, but I wasn't familiar with it.

AUSA Shirkin: Where did you get that chip information?
Sean Tucker: I heard Preme and RZA discussing it. They kept vague on that subject.

AUSA Shirkin: Who was doing the talking?

Sean Tucker: Sometimes Preme, other times RZA.

AUSA Shirkin: So, if you can, tell me what they shared with you and Mr. Stinson.

Sean Tucker: There was a large blank drawing tablet and writing utensils on the glass dining room table. Next to it was a file folder. I later learned there were pictures inside the folder.

AUSA Shirkin: Share with us how this plan unfolded.

Sean Tucker: Preme began by opening the file folder. He took out several large photos — could've been 8x10s or a little larger. They were in color. The pictures were of the corner buildings on Joseph Avenue and Wilkins Street, and the structures next to each, if anything was there. He wanted me and T-Rock to record each picture's contents to memory.

AUSA Shirkin: What were the photos for?

Sean Tucker: Across the Avenue from the bodega was a meat market. On the other side of Wilkins Street was a small credit union. There was only a small grass lot with a couple of wooden benches for sitting. It was surrounded by a rustic wooden post fence made from large trees cut lengthwise into quarters. Two spaces acted as entry and exit points at either end of the longest fence section parallel to Wilkins Street. Oh yeah — there was a transit bus stop there, too. That was the last corner. The building where the old meat market used to be was the target.

AUSA Shirkin: Who told you that?

Sean Tucker: Both Preme and RZA during the briefing.

AUSA Shirkin: Why was this location considered a target?

Sean Tucker: It was a place where guys gathered for high-stakes dice and poker games.

AUSA Shirkin: How do you know this?

Sean Tucker: I know people who used to frequent the location — gamblers.

AUSA Shirkin: When you say "high stakes," what are you referring to?

Sean Tucker: Amounts of cash. These games were hosted for higher-level drug dealers. On an average night, a person could visually see in excess of five hundred grand in plain view. Who's to say what else was in someone's carry bag or on their person?

AUSA Shirkin: And people you know who participated told you this?

Sean Tucker: Yes.

AUSA Shirkin: How did you, Mr. Murphy, and RZA know of this?

Sean Tucker: I'm not sure, but it wasn't exactly a secret.

AUSA Shirkin: So these pictures served what purpose?

Sean Tucker: To formulate a mental vision of the surrounding area and the target building itself.

AUSA Shirkin: Was there any discussion on how the robbery would take place?

Sean Tucker: Yes.

AUSA Shirkin: How was this robbery going to unfold?

Sean Tucker: While Preme was walking T-Rock and me through the photos, he set them up on half of the table exactly how the corner properties were laid out, if one were to approach from the west. RZA was drawing a three-dimensional blueprint of the target location using the drawing pad.

AUSA Shirkin: For what reason do you suppose this drawing was being constructed?

Defense Counsel Wolfe: Objection. Speculation.

Judge Sarasota: Overruled. I will allow it, so long as it qualifies within the parameters of the hearsay rule.

AUSA Shirkin: Please proceed, Mr. Tucker.

Sean Tucker: Could you repeat the question, please?

AUSA Shirkin: Sure. When the drawing was completed, did anyone explain its purpose?

Sean Tucker: Yes. RZA did. He wanted those of us who had never been inside the building to see its entire layout.

AUSA Shirkin: Were either Preme or RZA ever in the building?

Sean Tucker: So I was told.

AUSA Shirkin: When was this?

Sean Tucker: That same evening, prior to my arrival, after receiving the intel call.

AUSA Shirkin: Did anyone say how they got inside?

Sean Tucker: No.

AUSA Shirkin: Were there people gambling at the time either Preme or RZA were inside the target location?

Sean Tucker: No. It was around 8:30 p.m. when we all met up at Preme's house on Parker Place. The gambling didn't begin until 11 p.m., when the police changed shifts.

AUSA Shirkin: Why at 11 p.m., when police had a shift change?

Sean Tucker: I'm not sure. It's just what I heard.

AUSA Shirkin: Who told you this?

Sean Tucker: I don't recall who.

There was a pause in the proceedings. AUSA Shirkin walked over to the prosecutor's table, riffled through several file folders, selected one, and returned to the witness stand.

AUSA Shirkin: Earlier, you said you all were together planning the robbery around 8:30 p.m., and the games didn't begin until 11 p.m. When were the four of you going to execute the scheme?

70

Sean Tucker: According to the plan, we'd all be inside the building between 9:30 and 10 p.m.

AUSA Shirkin: How was this going to be made possible?
Sean Tucker: All of the heavy lifting had been done.

AUSA Shirkin: What do you mean?
Sean Tucker: Preme and RZA had already put the jux in motion. There were other people involved.

AUSA Shirkin: Who and how many?
Sean Tucker: I'm not sure.

AUSA Shirkin: If there were already others involved, why include you and T-Rock?
Sean Tucker: More than anything, I'd say for two reasons: precaution — because of how he's wired — and because he always made sure we didn't go without.

AUSA Shirkin: Who is the "he" you are referring to?
Sean Tucker: Mr. Murphy. He always used to say, "I want to put some money in your pocket."

Mr. Wolfe: Objection, Your Honor. Relevancy.
Judge Sarasota: Sustained.

AUSA Shirkin: What functions were you and Mr. Stinson to perform during this robbery?
Sean Tucker: First, you have to agree you're in before any information is exchanged. Once everyone gives their word, Preme usually gets straight to business. There are a few things you need to know about Mr. Murphy.

AUSA Shirkin: Like what?
Sean Tucker: Preme wasn't very trusting — even if he dealt with you. He didn't care much about parting with money; it was more a matter

of principles. If your principles aligned with his, he'd do anything for you. Anything.

AUSA Shirkin: Even kill?
Sean Tucker: Absolutely.

Mr. Wolfe: Objection! Prejudicial. No foundation!
Judge Sarasota: Sustained. Court reporter, please strike the witness's last answer from the record. Jurors, you are instructed to disregard the last question and answer.

The spectators murmured. The judge rapped his gavel repeatedly.

Judge Sarasota: Let's settle down, ladies and gentlemen. Any further disruptions, and I will have the marshals escort you from this trial. Mr. Shirkin, proceed.

AUSA Shirkin: May I have a moment, Your Honor?
Judge Sarasota: Yes.

The AUSA conferred briefly with co-counsel before returning to the podium.

AUSA Shirkin: When you said Mr. Murphy wasn't very trusting, what did you mean?
Sean Tucker: The littlest thing could raise his antennae. May I give an example?

AUSA Shirkin: Yes, please.
Sean Tucker: Preme did not trust electronics — especially phones and gaming devices. Anyone who went against that belief was kept at a distance. Another example: once we agreed to the jux, everyone's phones were collected, batteries removed, and placed inside a lead box.

AUSA Shirkin: Why was this done?

Sean Tucker: To block any signals to or from anyone's phone. From that point, our only communication was on two-way radios. Preme and RZA had access to someone's paid frequency. I never knew who that person was.

AUSA Shirkin: What was your agreed function in the robbery?
Sean Tucker: T-Rock and I were going to function as back-up for Preme and RZA.

AUSA Shirkin: Could you be more specific?
Sean Tucker: On this jux, the pieces had already been set in motion. Our role was more auxiliary.

AUSA Shirkin: When did you leave Parker Place?
Sean Tucker: We were mobile by 8:55 p.m.

AUSA Shirkin: Did you ride together, the four of you?
Sean Tucker: Yes.

AUSA Shirkin: What did you use for transportation?
Sean Tucker: A white cargo van. No windows on the sides.

AUSA Shirkin: What equipment did you bring?
Sean Tucker: Just masks and gloves.

AUSA Shirkin: Why only that?
Sean Tucker: Preme said we wouldn't need anything else.

AUSA Shirkin: So what did you and T-Rock do with your guns and his bulletproof vest?
Sean Tucker: We left them at Mr. Murphy's house — along with the wigs, drawings, and pictures. The only items that came with us were the scanner and two-way radios. It left me confused.

AUSA Shirkin: Confused how?
Sean Tucker: I couldn't understand why I'd go into a jux without my gun, knowing there'd likely be armed security.

AUSA Shirkin: Did you voice those concerns?
Sean Tucker: Yes.

AUSA Shirkin: To whom?
Sean Tucker: Preme.

AUSA Shirkin: How did he respond?
Sean Tucker: He said, "Everything we need is already in place."

AUSA Shirkin: Did he elaborate?
Sean Tucker: No, so I didn't press further.

AUSA Shirkin: What happened when you reached your destination?
Sean Tucker: We drove down Remington Street, where T-Rock and I were shown an extra getaway vehicle in case it was needed — plus two more: one on Berlin Street near Hudson Avenue and another on Thomas Street. Then we circled back to Remington and Wilkins.

AUSA Shirkin: Once there, what did you do?
Sean Tucker: RZA contacted someone on the two-way radio. After an "all clear" came back, he said he and I would exit the van, and I'd follow him to the next spot. T-Rock would follow Preme after we got there.

AUSA Shirkin: Did T-Rock and Preme arrive as planned?
Sean Tucker: Yes, within a couple of minutes.

AUSA Shirkin: Where did you meet up?
Sean Tucker: RZA and I walked through some yards to a side door at the apartment building/old butcher shop and went inside. We stood in the hallway and waited for T-Rock and Preme.

AUSA Shirkin: What happened next?
Sean Tucker: While we waited, I saw the van we'd arrived in drive past and head south toward downtown Rochester. Seconds later, T-Rock and Preme came through the door.

AUSA Shirkin: Who do you suppose was driving the van?
Sean Tucker: I have no idea.

AUSA Shirkin: Did you ask?
Sean Tucker: I knew better than that.

AUSA Shirkin: What happened next?
Sean Tucker: We moved upstairs to where the two apartments were located.

AUSA Shirkin: Tell us, what did you see?

9

The Lost Rib

Leah demonstrated to be my breath of fresh air. The voice that answered my call brought goose bumps to the surface of my skin. Our initial phone conversation must have lasted ninety minutes. Neither of us wanted to say good night. Eventually, we agreed to speak again tomorrow while expressing our forward anticipation of what the next day would bring. I could hear my heart beating in between my ears. It was loud and clear. Dudes who shared my company were glad for me. They'd heard me laugh about a thing or two, but they've never seen me smile in this manner or at such lengths.

We spoke the next morning, about thirty minutes before she went to work. I wanted her to know where my mind was. Leah seemed pleased by such consideration and asked,

"I guess it's fair to presume that you find me interesting?"

"More than I have the courage to admit at this time," I said with honest humor.

"Well, I'll be the first to say it—I'm not perfect. I make mistakes like anyone else." Her voice was sober.

"In the TANAKH, specifically The Book of Genesis, it says YAHAWAH created woman. We all make mistakes. Adam and Eve made a few in the Garden of Eden. You may be my lost rib."

There was a slight pause.

"You're full of surprises. I wasn't expecting to hear anything like that," she admitted.

"I hope I'm not running you off."

"No, not at all. What you said was insightful."

"I'm glad you think so. When will I be allowed to see this beautiful, sexy woman I'm speaking to?" I asked.

"When do you want to see me?"

"I'd come to work with you if it were possible."

We both laughed.

"I get off tonight at six p.m. How does seven-thirty sound?"

"Like it can't get here soon enough," I answered honestly.

"I'll call you when I'm leaving the mall."

"And I'll be able to tell you how many times my heart beats from now until I see you tonight."

"Boy, you're crazy. Bye." She was playful.

Crazy about you, I thought.

My schedule for the day became much tighter. Whatever it was that needed doing had to be accomplished by 6:30 p.m. Tonight was going to be one of no distractions. I showered twice, groomed myself, and dressed. I wanted this woman in too many ways to count. My gut told me that she desired me as well. The evening would reveal just how well our chemistries meshed.

I simply did not see this woman as a mere night of sensual seduction. She was indeed a wholehearted pleasure that moved my entire being from the moment we first met. I fully grasped that taking things day by day was proper. However, I'd been wired to always envision beyond the present into the potentiality of a given circumstance. If she were even half what my soul sensed her to be, a great relationship was bound to evolve. Seldom would I pursue a woman without consideration of a possible future together. On the contrary, who's to say what caliber of female seeks out a man—and why?

I was invited to Leah's home that evening. It was more than a first date. Increased depth and promise permeated the atmosphere. Come to find out, she was from the southwest side of the city. All this time, only five to six city blocks separated us. I was well positioned on both Columbia and Hawley St. Now, with Leah living on Warrick Avenue,

Rochester seemed to get instantly a little cozier.

Leah answered the door in a matching gray sports bra, boy shorts, and thick, blood-red socks. She hurried me inside to ward off the wickedly cold winds swirling about outside.

"Where is your coat?" she asked, both surprised and concerned. I was unable to resist goading her with my response.

"When I knew it was time to come see you, I stepped outside and felt no cold. Even now, it feels like lava is flowing through my veins," I said, smiling. Holding herself in a tight embrace and shimmying, I adhered to Leah's instruction, following her upstairs. My eyes regarded every silent step taken. With nicely proportioned legs and a derriere worthy of a triple take, Leah's lean waist and visible contour at the small of her back stimulated me. Once confined to the warmth of the apartment, I gave Leah a huge embrace.

I found myself quite riveted by Leah's accomplishment-driven attitude and clarity of communication. We talked for hours. As rest began to make its demands known to her body, I volunteered to make my departure. Leah insisted on my company. We retired to her bedroom. Lying with a pillow under my head, I urged our closeness. It was something I had been yearning for, seemingly for an eternity.

The scent of Leah's hair invaded my nostrils. Her soft skin warmed my neck as her face pressed close. Wrapping my right arm around her shoulders, I could hear my heart pounding steadily, drowning out all sound almost entirely. I was where I wanted to be—next to the woman I adored, beyond my perception. There was no doubt in my mind that heaven existed on earth. Every conscious person knew when he or she crossed that border. It felt as if simultaneously nothing else and everything mattered.

We talked while staring at the ceiling. While looking deeply into one another's souls, we made addresses upon each other's skin with our fingertips. I'd become intoxicated by Leah's personality, beauty, strength, and fragility. The petals of this lovely rose had multiple layers—layers of the rose's spirit, mind, and body. There I was, balancing upon the single edge of a petal, desiring to make all of the correct and lasting impressions. To be her welcoming rain in times of drought.

After suggesting that I get more comfortable, I undressed very slowly while she watched. Donning only a pair of Maurice Malone boxers, Leah rolled back a sheet and comforter, inviting me further into her sanctuary. With hands as smooth and warm as sunbathed silk, she caressed my chest and core. For a moment, Leah rested her head on my chest. "Your heartbeat is incredibly strong," she said, speaking softly. Raking her nails across my torso, gooseflesh formed in its wake. "You're the reason why."

I kissed Leah's forehead twice, and a third time. As she looked upward into my eyes, our lips ensued into a slow, sweet, and teasing kiss. It soon grew into an unleashed tsunami of suppressed passion. The surge of undercurrents increased with each passing second. Our breathing had become labored from hunger. Leah showed an insatiable desire that rivaled the potency of my own. Her lips were succulently tender, and her saliva akin to mango nectar. I became the willing hummingbird, ready to pollinate all of her useful lands.

Leah had begun to explore the geography of my anatomy—my ears, neck, collarbone, and chest. She lingered at my nipples, where she decided to nip and lavish, flicking her tongue to and fro with both a show of delicacy and force. My nature fought against the restraints of my undergarments. It felt as if my soul was being reached into, shifted, and stirred.

Her fingernails slowly dredged my inner right thigh upwards, from the knee beneath my boxer shorts. With some coaxing, Leah mounted me. It had become my time for exploration. The boy shorts she wore soon became thongs as I pulled the material into the crease of her bum. A gentle spanking, alternated with a clawing of her buttocks, fueled the inferno. Biting, tongue-tracing, and kisses found their way to her sports bra. Tasting her nipples through the thin material sent shockwaves coursing through Leah's body. As she removed her bra, gravity released the extent of her breasts' fullness into my face.

There could be no façade of delay regarding this very instant. I was overwhelmed by a yearning beyond the physical. I desired to reach into this beautiful woman's depths, becoming a permanent fixture in her world, cemented to her soul like the foundations of Paris' Eiffel Tower. Leah was the only woman to have awakened me to such a degree. Externally, I maintained a suave demeanor; internally, I was possessed, and was her possession.

In one swift motion, I reversed positions. Leah started slightly, settling on the bed with the weight of my body blending into her softness. I kissed her forehead, each eyelid, the tip of her nose, and sucked at each of her lips. Tonguing a trail to both nipples long stiffened, I was soon at Leah's pierced navel—slowly, very slowly, teasing my way to her inner thighs. As far as my neck would allow, I turned horizontally, nibbling back and forth towards her garden. I eased the tip of my nose continuously across her lightly veiled vulva, breathing deeply. Moaning a slow exhale sent vibrations into her womb.

A wisp of heat coiled upwards through the cloth of her boy shorts like that upon a hot cup of tea. Pulling at the garment with both hands and teeth, it found its way onto the bed next to us. I salivated at her nudity and release of pheromones.

Leah was wet and swollen with anticipation. Spreading her vulva with my index and middle fingers, I selfishly tantalized the clitoris for a few seconds. All control was out of the window. My fingertips caressed her breasts as I tasted her briefly and sampled again. She responded noisily, biting down on her lips. Guiding her to the edge of the bed, we stood. Wrapping my arms around her waist, I lifted Leah into the air. Instinctively, her arms embraced my neck and her legs my waist. Turning towards the wall, I spoke while biting her right earlobe.

"Now, hold on." Relocating my arms between my body and Leah's thighs, her weight was now maintained by the supine positioning of my hands, forearms, and a rigid vertebrae.

I thrust-curled Leah's weight upwards my chest. I placed my hands against the wall just above eye level. Leah began to glide down my finely oiled arms the moment I began to straighten them. She inched closer as I nibbled along her thighs. She comprehended the measurements of my intention as our eyes met.

"I want you to watch me please you," I said. I took Leah into my mouth and pressed close to her pelvis, working my tongue in all directions. I hummed with her in between my lips, watching her every reaction. Leah's eyes were closed, and she was biting her bottom lip. Her breath was hardly containable. I continued to hunger for her sweetness, firing upon her sensitivity like a spark plug. I didn't hold back.

"Tell me how you like it," I demanded, while not letting up. My voice, as were my actions, was brimming with passion.

"Let me taste it," I whispered. "I want to taste it. Give it to me."

A deep, guttural croak escaped Leah. She sounded like a different person altogether. Leah's breathing became shallower as her voice grew higher in pitch. My eyes were locked into every subtlety and sensation she exuded. Realizing how much the sound of my voice increased her stimulation, I began working from both angles. It was difficult describing the cacophony of Leah's screeching delight.

There was a sudden silence. One of her hands viced my left bicep as the other clung to the back of my neck, pulling me closer. Leah's body teased me with atypical strength. Barely audible, she murmured, "I'm going to cum!"

Two seconds hadn't passed when her womb contracted, swelled, and began spouting a warm and viscous substance onto my lips and chin.

Caught unaware, it proved daunting to remain steadfast. Her secretion poured down the crease of my chest. Wetness covered me from face to waist.

"I'm so sorry. I didn't mean to..." she attempted before I interrupted her mid-sentence.

"Did you just..." I paused, unsure how to broach the situation.

"No!" she answered, somewhat insulted. "Whenever I'm stimulated beyond my peak, that's how I respond. I'll understand if you..."

"Sweetheart, I'm good. In fact, it excites me learning I arouse you to such levels. I've never seen a woman's flower pulsate like the human heart. Prepare yourself—you have to cum for me at least three times. I'm trying to see how much juice I can get from this Georgia peach."

Before consent was yielded or granted, I was performing extensive acts of pleasure.

10

Code of Preme

Drool stretched from Divine's bottom lip to his stomach. The electrical treatment he endured had left him as spent as a large caliber shell casing. If asked his name, Divine would probably need a while to figure it out. He'd purged himself. It was okay because hosing him down would come soon enough before his transfer of residence.

Unshackling his wrists and ankles, Divine slid from the chair, collapsing to the floor. Two of the women from upstairs were appointed to hygiene duty. He was stripped of his remaining articles of clothing. The ladies began scrubbing Sean where he lay with long-handled, soft-bristled brushes dipped in a bucket of soapy water. Sean gave an impression of a juvenile walrus. If such a likeness were so, we were its zookeepers.

A cold spray from the water hose jolted the walrus into a dim momentary reality. Still not completely grasping being unshackled, I told him to dry himself off, throwing him a huge towel. Being no fan of lethargy, I touched the walrus's feet with the live jumper cables. The reaction was prompt. "Dry off!" I repeated. Once finished, I pointed to the cage. "That's where you're going." He followed my index finger, and he swallowed hard.

The cage was approximately 5'x4'x4'. It had been filled with a bed of fresh hay covered by a cotton blanket. Made of reinforced steel, the walrus had no chance of breaching its design once properly secured. Perhaps not wanting to believe that this was his new reality, he remained seated on the floor naked. A crisp smacking sound vibrated the airwaves. One of my men struck Sean across his back with a doubled-over extension cord. The viciousness of the blow sliced home.

His face displayed raw agony. Sean arced his back as a result of the biting cord. He turned towards his assailant.

Before any foolish ideas were permitted to form in his mind, I stepped in at a blind spot. The jolt of energy from those live jumper cables immobilized Sean. He fell over sideways, twitching with arms and legs extended. Replacing the cables on the cart, I grabbed Sean beneath his armpits. Dragging this behemoth a couple of yards took some energy.

Retrieving a 20-foot coil of all-purpose rope from the supply shelf, a slip knot was constructed onto one end. Feeding the knotted section through the rear of the bear cage and out its entrance, I fitted the slip knot over Divine's head and around his neck. As I adjusted the rope, Banks withdrew any unwarranted slack. "G, you will be his guide, and I will be his motivation," I said, wheeling the battery and cables a few feet closer in proximity.

"Okay, Sean. Time to go to your new home," I said in my best puppy-voice imitation. Banks kept the rope tight in his hands. Resting on one elbow, he remained still, breathing heavily—heavy, I presume, with disbelief of circumstance.

"Come on, boy. Come on. Let's go. Be a good boy now."

Banks tugged a few times at the rope. I made clicking sounds, whistled, etc. It really agitated the poor fellow. This had to be a most demoralizing defeat.

So much for chivalry. Resuming possession of the jumper cables, I turned to the subject of my query and let the show begin. Rubbing the live cables together brought forth a show of sparks, just inches from his microbiome. I touched him with both cables. He screamed a woman's scream.

"Stop it! This is not right, man! Stop it!" he said, easing away from me. I touched Divine again on his foot. The scream returned with a bit of hysteria. Further, he shuffled in the opposing direction. Again. This time, his ankles. Again. Any part of him available, I aimed at. Another jolt to the knees equaled more screams and ultimately the goal being accomplished.

Divine scurried across the bear cage's threshold via hands and knees. I gave his buttocks a charge for good measure. While closing the gate, he pleaded and resisted being enclosed. Furious, I grabbed the jumpers and touched the bed of hay. *Poof!* An ignition of flames began eating away at the hay with reckless abandon. Obviously, the idea of being burned alive wasn't appealing.

Panic set in. Screams for help followed. I simply watched him. I was emotionally devoid of Sean's well-being.

"Use the blanket to smother the flames," I said.

He reacted quickly enough. I secured the cage door with a padlock.

"Remove the rope from your neck," I ordered.

He complied.

"Are you going to continue causing problems?" I asked.

There must've been something he'd seen in the cold eyes staring from beneath the hockey mask.

"No, no more problems."

I nodded once in confirmation. Turning from my prey, I pushed the battery cart under the stairwell and disconnected the cables.

"May I have something to drink, please?" Sean asked.

Looking in his direction, I responded, "When I return, I'll have just the thing for you."

I was wearing a sincerely sinister smile beneath the mask—more disheartening than the mask itself. Meanwhile, the environment upstairs always managed to keep its pleasantry. Considering the magnitude of despair unfolding beneath ground level, whatever problems above weren't much of an issue to begin with. After a quick shower to rid myself of the smell of smoke, I decided to prepare a quick brunch for everyone. With all hands on deck, it looked like how a professional kitchen would operate. All six eyes on the stove, the oven, a countertop flat grill, and a deep fryer were in simultaneous use. Twenty minutes later, a buffet for twenty was available to enjoy.

I felt it was my duty to help maintain a sense of normalcy in the lives of those around me whose lives weren't anything like mine. True, we may have mostly come from single-family homes, often with loving environments. Still, wherever any neglect or abuse existed, we made efforts to eradicate it and fill such a void. In this moment, we shared genuine camaraderie—no exploiting or imposing upon anyone. Men and women alike.

Trisha and China Doll had returned from running errands. Three bags of fresh produce, herbs, and spices were placed inside the kitchen's pantry. I stood up from the table, removing my plate and orange juice. Setting my items on the counter, I helped them both out of their jackets. Next, I pulled out their chairs, helped them get seated, and brought hot, wet towels to clean their hands. After making two plates for the young women, they blessed their food and began enjoying the atmosphere.

We were having a really great time. These were moments to remember.

Trisha, out of the blue, asked, "May I speak freely?"

Nodding consent, those in the room had grown quiet, presuming the worst.

"Who are you gonna use the dildo on?"

The kitchen erupted with hysterical laughter. People were choking on food and drink. Doing my best not to spew the contents of my mouth onto the floor, I ignored the question until swallowing. Even though the inquiry was presented in jest, I imagined it had been gnawing at the cat's curiosity since the request was made.

Some time passed before the laughter and remarks subsided. Smiles remained etched on the faces of all in various degrees.

"Well, Miss Trisha, should any of you ladies feel the desire to experience 'The Rumble in the Jungle,' be my guest. How to address this subject in political correctness is beyond me. I hope that no one here is offended."

This time, all of the women laughed.

"We'll be having a feast later on tonight. Roasted lamb and roasted veal for those who eat it."

"What's the occasion?" asked China Doll.

"Just glad we're here with each other, alive and healthy. Knowing that this journey in particular will be behind us soon. I know some of you aren't in favor of what's being done, per se. However, you all understand the dangers of infestation and not keeping the scales of justice balanced. Despite your opinions, your loyalty is why you are here. You shall all be rewarded as a result."

Everyone present nodded in consent. The thought engine seemed to be working heavily in the room.

"Does anyone wish to accept my responsibilities downstairs in exchange for theirs? Any takers?" I asked.

There was only silence. My job was an ugly business—something most would prefer not to indulge in. Though created equally, we were from different slices of the pie. It was profound how the fruit of the same tree produced various flavors. The absolute blessing in such an analogy is recognizing its true reality. Every individual's power lies in identifying their personal strengths and weaknesses. By reaching this understanding, a foundation may be established. Roots can potentially reach deep into the earth. Trees, once mature, may begin to bear fruit. It was time to build upon my own strengths.

I massaged China Doll's and Trish's shoulders briefly, grabbed the purchase from the sex shop, and headed toward the dungeon.

***

Sean Tucker: The top stairs led to a short hallway. At the end was a window facing east toward Joseph Avenue. A front door could be seen on each side of the hallway, leading into the apartments.

AUSA Shirkin: Which apartment did you enter?
Sean Tucker: Initially, we entered the apartment on the right side. Preme and RZA gave us a quick tour of the place so that we could see it was empty. They did the same with the one across the hall as well.

AUSA Shirkin: So, the apartments were vacant?
Sean Tucker: No. I didn't say vacant—just empty.

AUSA Shirkin: Someone was living in the apartments?
Sean Tucker: I would say so. Each apartment was fully furnished. The cabinets and refrigerators in both places were stocked.

AUSA Shirkin: Did you notice anything else inside each apartment?
Sean Tucker: Yes. I observed red smears across the flooring in both apartments. By appearances, the trails began from within the apartment and led to the entrance. Someone had cleaned up, but it was a rush job.

AUSA Shirkin: Do you know what happened?

Sean Tucker: I asked RZA—while pointing toward the floor— "What is this about?"

AUSA Shirkin: And his response?
Sean Tucker: He said it's all being taken care of. No one's going to bother us.

AUSA Shirkin: What do you think happened to the people living in the apartments above the target location?
Sean Tucker: Well—

Defense Counsel Wolfe: Objection!

Defense Counsel Baker: Objection, Your Honor!

AUSA Shirkin: Your Honor, may we approach?
Judge Sarasota: Counselors, approach.

The attorneys, both defense and government, approached the bench. The judge turned off his microphone while in discussion with the lawyers. The actual defendants, the court, the stenographer, nor any spectators were privy to the discussion. Each of the attorneys returned to their assigned stations. No explanation was given for the sidebar.

Judge Sarasota: You may proceed, Mr. Shirkin.

AUSA Shirkin: Thank you, Your Honor. Mr. Tucker, do you know what may have happened to the occupants of the two apartments?
Sean Tucker: No.

AUSA Shirkin: Why did the four of you occupy these two particular apartments?
Sean Tucker: If I had to answer that question in one word, I'd say accessibility.

AUSA Shirkin: Please elaborate. Explain to the jury what you saw during this time.

Sean Tucker: Upon settling in, some four camera monitors—receiving feed from eight separate cameras—could be seen. They gave a clear view of the entire downstairs where the gambling would take place, room by room, and the entire perimeter of the building.

AUSA Shirkin: Were there any people in the gambling area?
Sean Tucker: Not at the moment. They were expected to arrive within the next hour.

AUSA Shirkin: What time was it when you made this observation?
Sean Tucker: Approximately 9:45 p.m.

AUSA Shirkin: What did you do in the meantime?
Sean Tucker: Basically, we all made ourselves comfortable in front of the TV monitors. There were two black duffel bags present in one of the apartments upon arrival—one of which had several food items: lunch meats, crackers, dried fruit, nuts, protein bars, and bottled water. The other bag had several Glock handguns, a number of extended clips, and zip ties. Next to the duffel bags was a small trash bag. RZA said, "Whatever you eat off of, drink from, or need to throw away, it goes in here. If you gotta piss, use a bottle. A dump—better hold it or shit in a bag. Touch nothing without gloves. We leave nothing behind."

AUSA Shirkin: Were there any other discussions between the four of you while you waited for people to arrive?
Sean Tucker: Very little.

AUSA Shirkin: When did the first person appear?
Sean Tucker: I'd say around ten minutes after 10 p.m. Two Hispanic guys had pulled up together. They were the first to open the doors. Both moved around the place, ensuring it was safe for the gamblers to proceed. By appearances, they either owned the place or were the security for the host.

AUSA Shirkin: What did the men do after they appeared satisfied with the surroundings?

Sean Tucker: They both began turning on all the lights, making several phone calls, speaking Spanish, and setting up the bar. One of the men turned on some music below. The volume was kept at a reasonable decibel—still, it was loud enough to render our movements indistinguishable.

AUSA Shirkin: Take us to the point where all of the players arrived.
Sean Tucker: When everyone was in attendance, the environment was festive. Drinks—alcoholic beverages—smoking weed, and food were being distributed. A few females were present with their guys.

AUSA Shirkin: At what point were the four of you going to rob the gamblers downstairs?

Sean Tucker: I didn't learn about the method until it was time to be implemented. Preme and RZA were basically waiting for everyone downstairs to settle in. As the weed and coke set the tone for merriment, T-Rock and I were given a lightweight gas mask. Preme and RZA put theirs on. T-Rock and I followed suit.

AUSA Shirkin: What were the masks for?
Sean Tucker: RZA waved me over to a floor vent in the upstairs apartment we were in.

AUSA Shirkin: What type of vent?
Sean Tucker: A heat vent or air circulation vent.

AUSA Shirkin: Continue, please.
Sean Tucker: Next to this vent was a large tank with a hose extending from its nozzle. The hose was inserted into the floor vent. The vent was then covered with a garbage bag topped with a folded blanket and a packed suitcase lying sideways.

AUSA Shirkin: What was in the air tank?
Sean Tucker: RZA said it was an anesthetic grade of chloroform. While explaining this in a low tone, he began to open the nozzle. RZA

held up a finger before speaking into the two-way radio: "Tank one activated. Engage tank two."

AUSA Shirkin: Were you told the purpose of using this chloroform?

Sean Tucker: RZA said it would take 10-15 to render everyone unconscious long enough to take the money and leave. After, he flashed a smile from beneath his mask and said, "The best robberies require no weapons, but only a sharp and willing mind."

AUSA Shirkin: Ten to fifteen minutes?
Sean Tucker: Yes. RZA turned the gas off at approximately ten minutes, or when the last person passed out. The five minutes consisted of a grace period before Preme and RZA were to "go live."

AUSA Shirkin: "Go live"? Could you explain this phrase to the court?
Sean Tucker: It's another term for going into action.

AUSA Shirkin: Did you and T-Rock go live as well?
Sean Tucker: No. T-Rock and I observed the monitors while Preme and RZA cleaned the place out. If anyone unexpected came along, it was our responsibility to apprehend and subdue whoever until the jux was complete.

AUSA Shirkin: Did you need to apprehend anyone?
Sean Tucker: No. Preme and RZA finished the task before anybody arrived.

AUSA Shirkin: How did they enter the downstairs area?
Sean Tucker: They breached the side door with some type of hydraulic equipment.

AUSA Shirkin: Why the use of hydraulic equipment?
Sean Tucker: The side door was made of heavy steel, as with its frame. Besides a locksmith, I didn't see any other way.

AUSA Shirkin: Once Preme and RZA were clear from downstairs, where did they go?

Sean Tucker: They exited the same way they'd entered and met us upstairs.

AUSA Shirkin: What did you all do at that point?

Sean Tucker: RZA spoke into a two-way radio, saying, "Assignment complete. Ready for exit." After about sixty seconds, someone responded, "Backtrack is a go."

AUSA Shirkin: Who was the person on the two-way radio?

Sean Tucker: I do not know. I was never told.

AUSA Shirkin: How long after the response from the unknown person did you leave the crime scene?

Sean Tucker: Almost instantly. While waiting for an all-clear, RZA had put the guns from downstairs in the bag with the Glocks. Preme knotted the trash we'd created and brought it along with us. The white van that we arrived in was parked on the opposite side of the street, with the keys in the ignition. Preme drove north along Remington, turned right onto Fairbridge, and took a left onto Joseph. We stayed on Joseph Avenue until intersecting with Route 104 west. From there, we took 390 south to 490 east. Preme's house was just off 490. He took the Broad Street exit, and seconds later, we were on Parker Place.

AUSA Shirkin: Did you ever learn what was taken in the robbery?

Sean Tucker: No. When we got inside the house, RZA reached inside the bag and took six $10,000 stacks out. He gave us $30,000 each. He said he would've given more, but there were other palms to bless. I wasn't complaining. By then, Preme had returned our phones, guns, and T-Rock's body armor.

AUSA Shirkin: How long did you remain at 2 Parker Place?

Sean Tucker: Not long. Preme didn't want the cargo van to linger. He also had a lot of moving pieces on his street.

AUSA Shirkin: What do you mean by "moving pieces"?

Sean Tucker: I knew he had at least one other house at the end of Parker Place. He'd mentioned before a desire to buy every last house on the dead end.

AUSA Shirkin: So, where did you go after leaving Parker Place?

Sean Tucker: I dropped T-Rock off at Thurston. From there, I went to my girl's house.

AUSA Shirkin: Do you know what came of the guns and equipment left in the upstairs apartments?

Sean Tucker: All I knew was that everything we left behind was going to get taken care of—and someone did.

AUSA Shirkin: Was it ever revealed who the other participants in the robbery were by either Preme or RZA?

Sean Tucker: No, sir. It was never spoken of again.

AUSA Shirkin: Do you know if this crime was ever reported to authorities?

Sean Tucker: Not to my knowledge. I never saw anything of it in the papers or on the news.

Judge Sarasota: Mr. Shirkin, let's take a recess at this time. Somewhere around the fifteen-minute mark, we'll return. The court is in recess.

Court Bailiff: All rise!

The man's voice traveled clearly throughout the quiet courtroom. The judge and jurors were first to depart—fourteen in total, twelve primary deliberators and two alternates. The witness was next to disappear through one of several doors leading to and from the courtroom, flanked by a pair of marshals. Secondly, the defendants on trial were escorted back into the federal holding cells. Some spectators exited the courtroom while others remained.

11

Leah's Flame

My ears were alerted to the sounds of running water making its way up from the downstairs apartment. The consistency of its cadence indicated someone taking a shower. Dawn had already taken over where night had faltered. I awakened to Leah's light breathing, tickling the skin on my chest. Her body, so close to mine that it felt as if a natural part of my anatomy.

"It is said that 'beauty is in the eyes of the beholder.'" My eyes became the sponge that absorbed all this woman's aura, beauty, splendor, and traits. She looked beyond peaceful. There seemed to be an existing smile underlying the surface of Leah's physical presence. I found myself gliding my fingertips across her soft skin like a feather, concentrating kisses where the forehead and hairline met.

Leah stirred. She produced a smile even before opening her eyes.

"Good morning," she greeted in true feminine form.

My kisses didn't subside. In between several, I managed a response. "Good mornings have become wonderful with you present," I spoke sincerely from my heart.

"That's good to know," she replied.

There was a pause before she continued. Leah looked up into my eyes. "I really enjoyed last night with you."

Leah's eyes diverted to where her fingers dallied with my taco meat. My senses told me that she wanted to say something. It had begun to pique my curiosity as well.

"What's on your mind?" I asked.

Still hesitant, she finally summoned the nerves to continue.

"My relationships normally are not the lasting ones. Mainly due to the way I climax. You didn't overreact and make a big deal about it. That means a lot to me. I feel like I don't need to hide who I am and how I feel at that moment. Thank you," she expressed profoundly.

"No thanks needed. Once I confirmed you didn't give me a golden shower, it was on," I said, smiling. "Understand this. One, I'll be coming back to the juice bar for refills. Two, it's going to take much more than turning you on to run myself away."

I lifted her chin with my left hand, kissing her lips continuously.

"Are you hungry?" Leah asked suddenly.

"Growing hungrier by the minute… on second thought, I can have you for breakfast," I added as my pulse quickened.

"Don't tempt me. Come." She requested, rising from the bed.

My eyes followed her gorgeous golden complexion. Beckoning with her hand, she eased into the bathroom and began running water for the shower. I began to rise slowly, still clearly flustered from my act of self-denial. It felt as if I were going to tear through my boxer briefs.

Leah's sweet voice permeated the silence. "Come take a shower with me. Afterwards, I'll make breakfast."

I rose to my feet and was inside the bathroom, undressing. I stepped into the steaming hot streams of water where the alluring woman awaited. The water was hotter than expected. However, I didn't complain.

After a few minutes, my body adjusted, and the temperature began easing away the cold. I shampooed Leah's hair and bathed her from head to toe. Rinsing away the soap, she returned the kindness.

"Looks like you may need some help with that," she said, pointing at my erection.

There was no falsehood in her words. I wanted her so badly.

"Is it that obvious?" I asked dryly.

Leah chuckled lightly. "Sorta, kinda."

Our caresses evolved into growing passion. Before long, I found my scrotum deep inside my potential rib. Leah wasn't just giving me sex. There was something else being shared unseen by the physical eye. She was exhibiting some of what is available to my receptiveness if given a chance. We stared into each other's eyes for long periods of time while gently colliding. Her arms and legs coiled me as vines do around the trunks of trees.

Steam consumed the surrounding space within the shower. Its heat raised our core temperatures, beads of sweat trickled down our faces, mingling with streams of hot water. Difficulty distinguishing one from the other came with one exception. I could taste a subtle salinity upon the surface of her skin. I studied her for any signs of facial expressions or teasing of the body, desiring to remain in Leah's erogenous zone. It wasn't only her body I wanted to satisfy. Her mind, spirit, heart, and soul I longed to fulfill.

February was filled with Valentine's, which had been consumed by the beginning of the year. An ensuing bond developed with each passing moment. My appetite for Leah kept growing. I wanted more of her time. Up until I was emotionally assailed by the magnitude of this woman's worth, the reality of Leah's schedule became sobering. She was a wonderful mother of a son whose name is Daquan. I enjoyed observing her parenting skills. This was one circumstance I knew better than to ever dare disrupt. All of her goodness shone through this little human being. It pleased me to learn what a good mother she'd be should we decide to procreate.

Leah was a full-time grad student at the prestigious University of Rochester. Pursuing a major in engineering, she engaged in a five-year master's degree program. The demands were high in this environment. Hence, juggling parenting, grad school, and work made the available hours in a day a premium.

I called Leah via telephone. She picked up on the fourth ring.

"Hello."

"Good evening, beautiful."

"Thanks. You're so sweet. I was just thinking of you."

"Sounds like we're both doing the same thing. What are you doing right now?"

"Just got out of the shower. Now I'm watching a movie with Daquan and putting on some shea butter."

"I've been missing you, sexy lady."

"If so, you should be next to me and not on the phone."

"I'm on my way."

"Bye."

"Peace."

I had been en route to Leah's house. After a ring from the doorbell, she could be seen ambling down the steps in her unique stride through the laced curtain covering the glass panel door. Our greeting was warm and welcoming. She led me upstairs by the hand after securing the door.

I spoke to 'Quan upon entry while discarding my boots. He replied likewise, his eyes never leaving the television.

Leah sat down on the couch with a sigh.

"Is everything okay?" I asked receptively.

"Long day at work and at school afterwards. Other than being a little tired, I'm fine. You being here makes it better." She kissed me on the cheek. Guiding Leah until she was slightly turned away from me, I began massaging her neck and shoulders. Occasionally, I'd run my fingertips through her hair into the scalp, rubbing the temples in a circular pattern. I caressed her across the forehead, down the sides of her face, and to the neck and shoulders again. Involuntarily, Leah's body pressed into mine as if an upright mattress. She purred like a kitten in a complete state of comfort. I reached downwards into the crease of her chest, probing and receiving moans and sighs. Ten minutes hadn't passed before my sweetheart was fast asleep in my arms. Da'Quan was turning around as any inquisitive five or six-year-old would to observe what the adults in the room were doing. I held an index finger over my lips, indicating not to wake his mom. He nodded, smiled, and resumed watching the movie. Leaning into the cushions of the couch, I continuously ran my fingers through Leah's short curly hair. Ten to fifteen minutes passed before she was awakened to Quan's bursting laughter.

"How long have I been asleep?" she asked.

"Not long," I said, kissing her forehead. She continued trying to ward off any fatigue.

"Looks like I'm going to be turning in early. You're so warm." Leah hugged me tightly around the waist, her nose pressed into my neck.

"Will I be sleeping alone tonight?" Leah asked expectantly.

"Not if you don't want to," I returned.

"I want you here with me every night."

"Don't tempt me any more than I presently am."

Our conversation was exchanged in low tones. Even though her actions made things clear, it gladdened me to hear Leah's verbal declaration of what she felt.

"Put your feet on my lap," I insisted.

Honoring my request, she removed her footies. Since my attempts at tickling her feet failed, I went to work firmly rubbing a foot, ankle, and calf—one side at a time.

"Oh, my goodness. Only if you knew how wonderful this feels. Be forewarned: if you keep spoiling me as you've been thus far, it'll grow into expectation."

"I guess you'd better get used to it."

"This is a first for me. OMG…"

"You mean I broke your maiden?" I asked, smiling.

She gave me an incredulous look but was deeply amused.

"No. You're the first man ever to give me a foot massage."

"I look forward to giving you a lot of good firsts."

"Oh… really?" she inquired.

"Really. Really," I confirmed.

We shared mischievous smiles.

"Speaking of firsts, there's something I need to tell you. I need more of you in my life. I'm trying to figure out a way we can spend more time together, without interfering with your goals, parenting, and work."

Leah pondered my words, her expression pensive.

"Any of the additional time we don't share, I spend on campus utilizing the terminals," Leah answered.

"How many days a week?" I asked, rubbing without interruption. The foot massage challenged her focus.

"Three to four days at two to three hours each. Trust me, I don't like it either. Right now, there's no alternative for my research," she shared.

"Hmmm." The wheels were turning as the information presented itself.

"What if you had your own terminal at home? Would it make a difference and free up some time?" I offered.

"A drastic difference. The campus is so large. Depending on where parking is found, I may have to walk another twenty or thirty minutes to reach my destination one way. Hmmm… we must find a better way. That's time taken from my loving you."

A solution was found. Pondering for a few before its introduction wouldn't hurt anyone.

"Mom." 'Quan's voice rang out.

"Yes, baby."

"Can I have some cookies and milk?"

"Can you?"

"I mean… may I have some cookies and milk?"

"That's better. The answer's no. It's too late for sweets. You just ate dinner two hours ago, little boy. If you're hungry, I'll make you a grilled cheese sandwich."

"That's my favorite! Thanks, Mommy."

"Would you like one while I'm at it?"

"Before I say yes, know this: my grandmother always said, 'To find your way into a man's heart, go through his stomach.' If you know what you're doing in the kitchen, you may not be able to get rid of me," I cautioned.

"Well, I'll be making two sandwiches for you if that is the case."

Before she stood, I returned the footies to Leah's feet. Sharing a reverent glance, she advanced to the kitchen.

12

Truth in Chains

The hay I had set aflame earlier was replaced, along with the blanket. On the upper exterior of the cage, opposite the entrance, a mount had been attached. A tripod, topped by a digital camera, stood six feet away. All of the proper connections were made for everything to work accordingly.

"By any chance, can I trouble you for something to eat and drink, please?" asked the Brown Street Bully.

"Sure—in about an hour."

I continued working methodically. Retrieving a fresh gallon of bottled water, I cracked the seal and removed its cap. A pressurized drinking tube was screwed into its place. For the finishing touches to the drinking apparatus, I reached into the shopping bag, locating a long rectangular box.

It contained a fourteen-inch replica of a human penis. To say the least, this thing looked very lifelike. Truth be told, I didn't want to touch it. If not knowing any better, the vision of someone being castrated would've been lasting. It was designed with a fluid passage through the urethra. Taking the dildo out of its box, I inserted the drinking tube into the scrotum end of the sex toy. Once secured properly, I squeezed the dildo. A light stream of water spurted from its head. Walking to the cage, the gallon jug was fitted onto the mount designed to hold it.

The vein-filled, swarthy, completed piece of meat hung topside in the cage. From the view based on the tripod's angle, it appeared as if someone was standing over Sean. The scene presumably appeared sexually motivated. Quite obviously, the Brown Street Bully didn't wear the pants in this relationship.

There, at the tip of the sex toy, was a gradual accumulation of water. It dripped onto the blanket below approximately once every ninety or so seconds. Talk about nauseating.

Divine looked on in utter disbelief and shock. He plainly could see what was unfolding, but it couldn't be reality, he told himself. I kept to the task, undeterred by his alarm.

"What is all of this?! Come on, man!"

Furor was beginning to embrace him.

"Calm yourself."

I turned on the camera. Returning to Sean, I pointed to the dildo.

"This is your water supply. All you have to do is put it in your mouth. However you do it, just don't bite it," I said.

My laughter was heartier than Santa's during the winter solstice. Once composed, I resumed speaking.

"At this time, I will go prepare your meal. Be back in a few."

Upstairs, everyone was in good spirits. I asked for Banks to upload the live feed from the basement camera in order to prep it for YouTube. He went to work. So did I. There were several moving parts within our little maze of horrors.

Too much for one man alone to run effectively and efficiently. We had many a living creature present and caged to trigger most phobias known to man, including a horde of large vermin. I carried a nine-to-ten-inch rat outside to a collapsible table. On the table were two foot tubs—one empty, the other filled with cold water, a pair of cordless beard trimmers, pliers, a shaving razor, a fillet knife, and a small cleaver.

Donning a set of thick cowhide gloves, I opened the vented plastic container holding the rat. Grabbing it under its front legs and stomach firmly, I picked up the fillet knife by the blade. With considerable force, I thumped the rodent across its head three times. The first strike of the knife's wooden handle triggered a desperate shrill. The second strike, a whimper, and the third, silence. For good measure, I broke the rat's neck and laid it on the tabletop. The beard trimmers made quick work of its coat. From there, I shaved the skin bald with the razor.

Eviscerating the rodent is a delicate process. After severing its belly lining, I cut around the anus. I pulled a length of colon free, making a knot just above the sphincter muscle. Retracing the incision, I began cutting in the opposite direction. Holding the blade's tip in an east–west direction instead of north–south greatly decreased any chance of rupturing the intestines. Slicing through the chest cavity proved easy enough. Continuing up to the esophagus, I sliced it horizontally and pulled it free. With some coaxing, the internals began oozing onto the table fully emancipated.

Pushing the entrails into the empty tub, I rinsed the blood- and hair-soiled section of the tabletop. The carcass was flushed thoroughly in the tub of cold water and left submerged. In the meantime, I cleaned the beard trimmers, fillet knife, and the remaining surface of the table. While removing my gloves, I made the short walk to the kitchen. Retrieving what was needed, I returned to the prep station.

Along with a cutting board, I brought a half cup of mandarin orange juice, Old Bay seasonings, fresh cilantro, capers, Dash, sea salt, peppercorns, a garlic clove, one each of a sweet onion, capsicum, and grape seed oil. Removing the rodent from the foot tub, it was placed on a towel and patted dry. The water was discarded. Setting the rat on the cutting board, I addressed the cleaver. Next came the severing of the rat's head, tail, and feet. Held in place on its back, I began butterflying the animal on either side of its spinal column.

I decided spontaneously to debone the flesh. Once completed, I replaced the carcass in the tub spread-eagled. Orange juice was distributed over the flesh. While allowing it to stand for at least ten minutes, I began mashing the clove of garlic with the side of the cleaver. I removed its skin and began to slice the clove and cilantro. The dry seasonings were combined thoroughly. Lastly, the grape seed oil was added to the mix. The result was an aromatic paste awaiting usage.

Pushing the paste aside, the main course was placed gingerly on the cutting board. The sea salt and peppercorns were ground and applied to both sides. Next came the massaging of the paste into the flesh and skin alike.

Taking a large cast-iron skillet into my hands, I placed it onto the grill of an outdoor fire pit. Once hot, I removed the skillet and coated it with oil. It burst into flames. Submitting the rat to the high heat of the cast iron, skin side first, resulted in absolute culinary bliss. The flames dissipated and transferred their energy into the moat. Smoke billowed upwards like that of green wood burning beneath a congested chimney. A beautiful dark-brown crust was beginning to form at the skin's edge.

Returning the pan indirectly to its heat source, I quickly peeled the onion, dressed the capsicum, and cut both julienne. Using a pair of tongs kept by the fire pit, I flipped the main course, admiring its outcome. You could hear the sound of sizzling and smell aromatic pleasantries wafting about. Everyone who was indoors was now outdoors. Their curiosity forced me to smile.

Searing four minutes skin side down and three minutes on the opposite, such an offering was well done. I transferred the fare to a heated platter. The veggies followed suit immediately into the cast iron. One hundred twenty seconds passed. The piping hot and crisp veggies were added to the platter.

"Hey, everybody," I said, walking into the building's kitchen. I sliced a baguette loaf into several one-inch pieces. Drizzling it with olive oil, I went downstairs to give the Bully his meal.

***

The Bailiff: "ALL RISE!"

The court was reconvened. Judge Sarasota entered the courtroom. His flowing black gown concealed a lean physical composition. He settled onto the bench comfortably before speaking.
Judge Sarasota: Counsel, approach the bench, please.
(There was another bench conference off the record.)
Judge Sarasota: Escort the jury in, please. (The jury entered the courtroom.) Note the presence of counsel, the defendants, and the jury. We are ready to resume with the testimony of Mr. Tucker. Mr. Shirkin, continue, please.

Mr. Shirkin: Gratitude, Your Honor. (Sean Tucker was recalled to the witness stand. Direct Examination continues.)

AUSA Shirkin: Mr. Tucker, after the incident at the gambling house, did you maintain fraternization with Mr. Murphy?
Sean Tucker: Yes.

AUSA Shirkin: Do you know someone named EQ?
Sean Tucker: Yes.

AUSA Shirkin: Did you know EQ through the fall of 1999?
Sean Tucker: Yes.

AUSA Shirkin: Did you have opportunities to visit EQ at his residence in the fall of 1999?
Sean Tucker: Yes.

AUSA Shirkin: How so?
Sean Tucker: We ran up to his house.

AUSA Shirkin: Ran up?
Sean Tucker: We burglarized EQ's apartment.

AUSA Shirkin: Who is "we"?
Sean Tucker: Me, T-Rock, and Supreme.

AUSA Shirkin: How was the idea planned?
Sean Tucker: Supreme was fronting EQ weight or large amounts of cocaine. Got EQ on his feet. He'd already known where EQ lived. At some point, something went wrong between Preme and EQ.

AUSA Shirkin: Do you recall what went on between those two? In other words, you were conducting surveillance?
Sean Tucker: I recall a time when Supreme was upset about something EQ had said. Preme had called it "a vicious slip of the tongue."

AUSA Shirkin: What did EQ say?
Sean Tucker: He had told Preme during a session that ever since Preme let him get on the team, "I could have two whole bricks in plain view,

on the back seat of his whip, ride around the city, and won't nobody touch it." That's what EQ said, according to Preme.

AUSA Shirkin: What's a session?
Sean Tucker: It's when people get together casually for drinks and smokes.

AUSA Shirkin: Was it your idea to break into EQ's house?
Sean Tucker: Yeah. At least initially.

AUSA Shirkin: Why did you introduce this idea?
Sean Tucker: Well, I never liked EQ. Besides that, I knew he had money and no longer had Preme's support. So I fanned the flames just enough for the desired result.

AUSA Shirkin: What result?
Sean Tucker: For Preme to reveal EQ's address while upset. I willingly volunteered my services to rough him up and take his plate.

AUSA Shirkin: His plate?
Sean Tucker: That means his money and drugs.

AUSA Shirkin: Oh. I see. Did Preme give you EQ's address?
Sean Tucker: Yes. But not until after much consideration.

AUSA Shirkin: What happened next?
Sean Tucker: After I'd gotten the address, Mr. Stinson and I went out to EQ's place. He lived in Greece, down past Long Ridge Mall on West Ridge Road.

AUSA Shirkin: Did you enter the property at this time?
Sean Tucker: No. T-Rock and I had to first locate the apartment. It was a huge complex called Swan Lake Apartments. The place was like a maze.

AUSA Shirkin: Once the residence was located, what did you do?

Sean Tucker: Just watched the ebb and flow of traffic in and out of the apartment complex. Tried to get a feel for the environment.

AUSA Shirkin: In other words, you were conducting surveillance?
Sean Tucker: Yeah.

AUSA Shirkin: Let's go to the time of the robbery.
Sean Tucker: From the time this surveillance was conducted—

AUSA Shirkin: How much time passed before you and Mr. Stinson entered EQ's apartment?
Sean Tucker: We moved on him the very next day after dark.

AUSA Shirkin: Was anyone at the residence?
Sean Tucker: No.

AUSA Shirkin: Would you describe the apartment complex where EQ lived for us, please?
Sean Tucker: With the exception of the complex's management center, there was a series of long tenement buildings. Each one had an upstairs and a downstairs. Exits were on opposing sides of the buildings. Each downstairs apartment had an option of a second entrance available; sliding glass doors opening onto a patio. All apartments upstairs had wood-framed balconies. There were around 40 apartments in each building, probably 30 buildings in total.

AUSA Shirkin: How long did you take after arriving to break into EQ's place?
Sean Tucker: Maybe 20 minutes. I called a few times to make sure no one was home. After, I drove around all of the parking lots in the complex to see if any of his cars were present.

AUSA Shirkin: Did you see any of his vehicles?
Sean Tucker: No.

AUSA Shirkin: From that point, when did you and Mr. Stinson break into EQ's place in order to rob him of valuables?

Sean Tucker: Immediately after.

AUSA Shirkin: How did you get inside the apartment?
Sean Tucker: We waited in the stairwell until the upstairs hallway was clear. EQ's apartment was the one nearest the west exit on my left. Once clear, we quickly jimmied the locks and entered, closing the door behind us.

AUSA Shirkin: What were you and Mr. Stinson looking for?
Sean Tucker: Money, drugs, jewelry.

AUSA Shirkin: Did you find anything of value?
Sean Tucker: Yeah. Altogether, we found six bundles of money and some jewelry. When we counted the bundles, each one consisted of $9,950.00.

AUSA Shirkin: What did you do next?
Sean Tucker: We decided to leave with what we'd found. Besides, there was no need to alarm the neighbors for any reason.

AUSA Shirkin: What did you do with the money and jewelry?
Sean Tucker: T-Rock and I split the cash 50/50. I kept the chains and bracelets. T-Rock wanted the rings and watches.

AUSA Shirkin: Did you give a cut of the proceeds to Mr. Murphy?
Sean Tucker: No.

AUSA Shirkin: Why not?
Sean Tucker: He didn't need it. He was making a lot of money.

AUSA Shirkin: How do you know this?
Sean Tucker: I seen what he was involved with firsthand. He was doing real numbers.

AUSA Shirkin: Pardon me, real numbers?

Sean Tucker: Profiting thousands of dollars on a daily basis. Preme had been trying to bring me, T-Rock, and DL into the circle for a long time. Said it was better than living from robbery to robbery.

AUSA Shirkin: Why didn't any of you accept Preme's offer?
Sean Tucker: It was because of something he said.

13

The Long Game

Leah and I spent another evening together. Each one was just as special as the first. We went out regularly, but staying in soon became the norm. Considering how my evenings were voluntarily forfeited to Leah, anything outside of her began at sunrise.

As good fortune would have it, Sunday was an off day. We were slow to rise, content in our cocoon. Somehow, we had become a true couple. When it happened, I couldn't say, but joy existed between us, undeniable and profound.

One morning, while I was making the bed, Leah came from the bathroom. She stood in the doorframe, arms crossed and ostensibly perturbed.

"Hey, pretty lady!" I said as I approached.

She retreated, arms still folded in a defensive manner. I tried again, and she withdrew. Holding my hands up in surrender, I backtracked into the bedroom.

"If I did something wrong, I apologize." I resumed making the bed and folding the comforters. She advanced to the jamb once more, making eye contact. No—she seemed to be studying me.

There was another long pause in silence. The next time I looked at Leah, she was observing her hands, fidgeting with her nails. I took a seat on the bed and leaned against the folded comforter and pillows. *Something's really bothering her,* I thought to myself. I decided to speak.

"I'm not going to be pushy. What I do know is that up until this point, we have communicated about everything together. I hope it's something that doesn't change."

"You want to know what's bothering me?" she asked, arms fastened tightly to her body. Her eyes met mine. "I think I'm falling in love with you," she confided. Leah's voice had begun to quiver and trailed off. She had no idea how long I'd clung to such emotions. I felt true elation. Standing tall, I slowly advanced to her. She stepped away, but not before I held her in my arms.

Leah's hands were against my chest. She resisted by extending both arms. I relented, taking a few steps back.

"Do you want me to leave?" I asked calmly.

"That's the point. I don't like it when you leave me!" she said with emphasis. "Come to me."

I stood in the doorway to the bedroom. Leah moved forward, perhaps one foot, and stopped.

"Closer," I insisted.

"Closer."

Another twelve inches.

"Just a little bit more."

Finally, she was standing before me.

"May I have a hug, please?" I asked.

Her hands were slow to respond, as if fighting internally with herself.

I took Leah's hands in mine and kissed each one over and over. Guiding her into my embrace, I wrapped my arms around her shoulders firmly while caressing her back.

"So that's what's been ailing you this morning, sweetie?"

She nodded into my chest.

"You're late to the party. I was in love with you after the first week we met," I said in Leah's ear, kissing her cheek and neck.

"Please, don't play with my heart."

"I'm being truthful, woman. What more do I need to do to prove it? I've been loving you. It's why I treat you as I do."

Tears began flowing down her cheeks.

"What's wrong?" I asked.

"Nothing's wrong."

"Why the tears?"

"I'm happy."

I pulled Leah closer, confessing to seeing forever in her eyes.

Time permitted our relationship to improve. All of what I longed for in a woman presented itself in Leah. She was extremely intelligent, compounded by common sense. She also possessed an optimism that was infectious. Quietly driven, she attested to be a one-woman power to be reckoned with. Beyond her beauty and personality, those qualities had to be the most appealing.

We'd spend time on campus at the University of Rochester playing love and basketball. Leah was the one who introduced me to dried mango—one of many things I'd never forget. Roughly every other weekend, we'd find our way to the movies. Often we would spend an hour or two playing air hockey afterwards. I couldn't believe how drenched with sweat we were after our battles. Spectators grew into crowds as we exchanged banter and staredowns. For every fifty games we played, I'd probably win two. To get defeated in such a way, I figured it was some mathematical advantage, perhaps geometry, in relation to her major. Leah surely viewed the table differently than I did. Just one more reason to admire the woman she was during this moment in time.

Depending upon how early our date night began, we'd cram in as many memorable moments as we could. Leah possessed commendable dancing skills, and I loved when we went dancing. Sometimes she'd opt to stay in, and we'd cook together, play Jenga, Operation, or watch movies. Other times we'd make rodeo love after baths and dinner were indulged in following a day at the office. We'd endure into the early morning hours. All I ever could see was Leah, especially on those occasions. It evolved into a complement of positive chemistry that stirred admiration among some and envy within others.

One day, Leah posed a few questions.

"Where do you see yourself, or would like to see yourself, five years from now? What are your dreams? Where are you from originally?"

"Babe, if you ask me another question before I answer the first, I'll go crazy trying to recall your every word." She giggled, and it forced me to smile.

"Okay. Sorry about that," she said. "I just want to know who you are and how you've come to be."

"Sorry isn't a description that's befitting of you. Besides, there's nothing wrong with seeking to comprehend anyone or anything clearly. The clearer the crystal, the greater the lucidity to follow."

My eyes focused on the wall, at no spot in particular. I was in the process of recall. It had been a long time since anyone asked me anything about my past.

"Before I go into my history, let me share something with you."

Leah gave me her undivided attention.

"This is an example of why I hold you in the clouds of my soul— why you're so precious to me. I've seldom met with such a spirit. It's like every passing day, you somehow reach inside of me, stirring something awake which prior to then was dormant. All good somethings. The kind that promotes reason to love you better and more wherever I find room to do so. Where you're concerned, every day I feel so lucky. This thing called love runs very deep inside of me. Consequently, I hunger to improve for you, myself, and us."

Tears streamed down her cheeks. I drank them away.

"I was born on a cold, snowy night, as was told to me. At Medina Memorial Hospital, located in Medina, NY, my tiny lungs inhaled their first breath. I was the youngest child. Unbeknownst to me at the time, I had an older brother named Eric. We were both born on the 16th of different months. As a result, he was six years and ten months my senior.

"Medina's one of those super-friendly and sleepy towns. The average population normally ranged from five thousand to six thousand people. Most activities that folks were involved in were family-oriented. Regardless of ethnicity, the best things going on revolved around church and sports. Whether it was Little League baseball, high school basketball, football, volleyball, or wrestling, everyone showed up in numbers. It appeared every single athlete in high school solely focused on making it to the Empire State Games. Occasionally, someone's parents would allow them to have a supervised house party.

"After my birth, my parents, brother, and I migrated to Rochester, NY. I imagine they were living there already. Very faintly, I could recall certain events which could be placed geographically. By the time I turned four years old, my father, Anthony Sr., and mother decided to divorce for reasons unknown. What I did know was that my mom had to find a sustainable line of employment. Considering she now had to raise and support two young boys alone, her options were slim.

"Around the time Kodak decided to hire my mom, I was learning that we, the children, would be living with our grandparents until Mom got things organized in Rochester. I was elated. My grandparents' home was the epicenter of family activity and reunions. The abundance of love, affection, and learning was consistent. It causes me to smile, reflecting upon my childhood years."

I wrapped my arm around Leah's shoulder, pulling her into me. She met with a similar eagerness in her embrace.

"I'm listening," she said.

Taking a sip of water, my memories were collected once more.

"In 1979, I attended a Head Start program. It was a slightly difficult transition for me. Being around other children, not blood-related, felt very awkward. My mom was Nanna's only child. Eric and I were Nanna's only grandchildren. Despite this, our voids were filled by extended family.

"Life was very fulfilling. Even though I didn't have adult issues to deal with at these early stages, my responsibilities were sizeable. Such willingness to assist and please my grandparents didn't go unnoticed. Chores around the house didn't seem like chores. To me, it was simply a process. Work first. Play and have fun second. I found most work fun, especially while learning from it or if a competitive challenge was somehow involved. I've always enjoyed being able to see the results of my efforts early in life. When the outcome isn't immediate or the evolution of a process is not explained well enough to be properly envisioned, my interest would more than likely wane. Am I boring you yet?"

"No, babe. I'm all ears."

I took another sip of water.

"As far as schooling is concerned, I would alternate attendance between Rochester at Nathaniel Hawthorne Elementary and Oak Orchard Elementary in Medina. It seemed roughly for every year I was at one school, the next I would be at the other. Sometimes, I'd abruptly transfer during the middle of the school year. Those circumstances were never easy to cope with or handle. In retrospect, I can see how certain types of anger and anxiety built up within me over several years.

"Each time I'd return to Rochester for any reason, I would shudder.

It was obvious in my demeanor, in my facial expressions, my eating habits. There'd always be something to do in Medina. There wasn't very much for me in Rochester. The largest contrast between the two environments was the family setting—from being involved and submersed in a social atmosphere to one of practical isolation. Since I detested wanting to stay in Rochester, I believe my mom took this as a personal insult. It may have fueled our lack of closeness. Neither knew how to fix it. Consequently, a score would pass before anything would improve."

I sighed heavily.

Leah noticed the change. She began caressing me across my chest, a notion that curbed building anxiety.

"It's okay if you want to stop. I'm able to see that's a sensitive part of your past. I'm sorry you ever felt such pain so young." She kissed my cheek.

I smiled. Somberly, I continued.

"I'm imagining I've been carrying this inside for far too long. My need to be heard is just as important as your wanting to hear. Besides, there's no better audience than you.

"I struggled to cope in the city. My mom worked a minimum of twelve-hour days. Usually, when she walked through the door, there weren't any reserves left in her. Eric and I normally had to make our own daily itinerary outside of house chores. The considerable age difference between my brother and me left us with little in common. We didn't share the same friends or similar interests. I was more of a fetter to his ankle on the best day.

"To make matters worse, the three of us weren't the only ones living at twenty-three Seventh Street. None of us were introduced formally or informally. More times than can be counted, I'd encounter the man in the white three-piece suit and hard bottoms. On other occasions, it was a couple of young children, about ten years old. I only ever saw them in the upstairs hallway. Upon stumbling across one or the other, eye contact was made. As if I could be heard or was seen approaching, I'd stand still, frozen with fear. Perhaps growing impatient with my not speaking, they'd walk through the wall, disappearing. Others could be glimpsed but would never stay at length like the man and boy.

"My complaints of such things fell on deaf ears. I remember my mom used to say, 'Did they bother you?' or 'Next time say hello,' or 'They ain't concerned about you.' She was probably right. Contrarily, I wasn't going to be initiating any conversations whatsoever. At times, I felt curious. However, my inquisitiveness did not perpetuate the necessary boldness of interaction with an apparition.

"Last summer, I drove down Seventh Street, where we used to stay. It was burned entirely to its foundation. Only remnants of the frame stood. I've always wondered if later occupants ever witnessed what I did or if it had anything to do with the fire."

Leah's cell phone began to chime. It had rung at length by the time she retrieved it.

"Hello." Her voice was so polite and sweet. "Hey, Grandma! How are you doing?"

Grandma responded.

"Of course. What time?" Leah asked. "At two o'clock. I'll be there at 1:30 p.m. By the way, Grandma, there's someone I want you to meet." She paused. "Okay. I love you. See you soon."

Leah placed the phone on the table. Her smile was infectious.

"Obviously, you know who I was talking to," she said, rubbing my chest. "Are you ready to meet my granny?"

"Indeed, I am. I've longed to share the presence with those who've helped shape you into such a fantastic and fine woman."

We embraced.

"When the time presents, you need to finish sharing your past with me. Every moment shared brings me closer to you."

"I look forward to all the closeness you can muster. By the way...love that scent you're wearing."

"Thanks. I thought you would like it," she said.

"I'll show you just how much tonight."

She laughed.

"What's wrong with now?"

"We can't be late to take your grandma shopping."

"Give me twenty minutes of hard labor; fifteen for a shower; ten to get dressed, and another ten driving. We'll be at her door with five minutes to spare," she calculated.

Saying nothing further, I scooped Leah into my arms, carrying her to the bedroom.

14

Hunted and Haunted

While Divine dined, I was busy cleaning up behind myself. The prep table and chopping board were scrubbed with soap and bleach water. The entrails were taken to one of the piranha tanks to be devoured. Within the next forty-eight hours, I planned on dressing out a few more rats in order to marinate while refrigerated. No one had actually known for certain what I'd cooked. Only that it smelled. marvelous and felt privy to special treatment.

Preparing food on the saltier side ensured an increase in Sean's thirst. He'd already begun to drink from the soup bone. It would become more commonplace as his consumption of sodium was bolstered. Pride forbade him from taking a go at it in my presence. Laughing within, I knew all of his shame would take a back seat to necessity. He would be no different than any primate in the most intimate displays at a safari.

Plans were made, implemented, and improvised. Initially, two men's teams were organized for the job at hand. Those who had little to do besides hang out, exercise, eat, and enjoy certain pleasantries were eager for a call to action. Exercising a degree of flexibility, seven teams would work simultaneously and independently of one another. All of the women in the house were called to arms. An extra set of eyes wouldn't hurt anyone, especially ones that possessed courage, good communication, and were skilled in weaponry.

After receiving blessings, everyone set out to collect their booty. For a few, the time had come to be blooded. This rite was the only passage one may take into the maze of the inner circle. There would be no worries or concerns of civilians being taken. Only the scourge of society. The rats, informants, arch deceivers, rapists, child molesters, and serial predators, whenever they've been exposed. There will never be any refuge for cancer. It must be destroyed in its tracks wherever found.

Meanwhile, open lines of communication were maintained with each individual team. Geographically aware of all locations in question, I allowed time for an inspection of Sean above any other occupant residing at the lovely establishment. Setting my watch for three minutes, I breezed down two stories, employing a seldom-used rear stairway. Upon having a visual on 'The bully', he struggled into an upright position. His plate was wiped clean. Lines creased his face on the right side. An indication of where straw contacted skin at some point during slumber.

A trail of urine reached from the cage to the floor drain. Nature remains established as an unstoppable force, from the most minute to the catastrophic. Retrieving a stiff rubber bedpan and a roll of tissue, I unlocked the dead bolt, slid the items inside the entrance, and secured the lock once more.

"Thank you," he said.

"You're welcome." I started the timer on my watch.

"My apologies. I neglected to give you these things prior to preparing your meal. Speaking of which—did you enjoy it?"

"Yes. I've never had anything so flavorful. I'd buy that dish many times over. What's it called?"

I paused, considering how best to answer. Revealing the source this soon would spoil all that was to come.

Beep! Beep! Beep! Beep! Beep! Three minutes had expired. Silencing the alarm, I accepted the empty platter and plastic fork from my guest. Backtracking toward the ancient stairwell, I stopped, turning slightly. Divine's eyes followed me, pleading.

"Your meal has many names. Depending on the country and region, the terms vary. Even in the U.S., you'll find local and native words. I've always known this dish as the House Special. In layman's terms—boneless wild *rodere*. Preparation, of course, is mine alone."

I stepped into the passage and secured the door behind me. Unbeknownst to most of society, there exists a faction within public safety tasked with inspecting properties and ensuring placement for carbon monoxide detection. This disguise was genuine enough to the observant eye; every uniform and accessory had been acquired. Few in the field were familiar with Rochester. Live video feeds enabled assessments in real time, matched against the details Sean had provided. Possessing intimate geographic knowledge of every targeted area, the lines of communication proved invaluable. And should anything arise contrary to the data previously received, the cozen would not go unpunished.

Lo and behold, all went accordingly. Unfortunately, not one pariah had been detained unawares. Something which will be addressed soon enough. For now, it was time to relax and celebrate everyone's safe return. With a substantial degree of currency at their disposal, I wanted to share a rare and sacred part of my existence. A chartered flight for everyone was arranged to Toronto. We were going live this night away like it's the last seconds of 1999.

In an act of consideration, another "House Special" would be prepared. I'd decided on a tempura-style deep fry. I decided to go with fresh-squeezed lemon. A smear of spicy Dijon brown complemented the marinade. Sprinkled generously with Spanish paprika and sea salt on both sides of the rodent, it was given a tempura bath. A large serving of steak fries and a fresh tomato-cucumber salad were finishing touches. It wasn't the million-dollar meal that his information brought to the coffers. However, the deprived, whose newfound luxury is a pile of hay, it may as well be fragois and black truffles. To everyone's surprise, the flight was shockingly brief. Thirty minutes after departure, we were landing at Toronto International Airport. One straight shot across Lake Ontario is all it took. Toronto International existed in an island setting. Uniquely designed, a single two-lane road connects the airport to the mainland, specifically The Harbor, it remains a true sight to behold.

Dusk hadn't yet settled over the city. Still, it was fast becoming alive with various illuminations that accompany each evening. Almost as a matter of duty, I instructed the driver to stop outside CN Tower. We headed into the building, paying all fares for ascension to its highest point. Laughter rivaled reluctance when entering an elevator constructed completely of glass. Fear bordered on anxiety at the rate of acceleration in our ascent. Even after multiple trips, pangs needled my core. Rising one thousand plus feet in thirty seconds is sure to have lasting effects. We all took pictures together at the Needle. A seemingly endless Lake Ontario dominated the background with awesome color.

Bypassing Planet Hollywood while exiting the CN Tower, I encouraged everyone's patience for a few minutes more. As we piled into the stretch limo, instructions were given.

"John, will you be kind enough to take us to my favorite spot on Queen Street East, please?" I asked.

"Certainly," he replied.

Witnessing such cleanliness was unique unto itself on these city streets. Everyone touched this subject at some point with grudging admiration. Fifteen minutes later, we were pulling up in front of *The Real Jerk.*

Simple in its décor, the restaurant held true to its theme. Rasta colors—red, yellow, and green—were incorporated from drapes to tablecloths. There was an upstairs section. It was either reserved for private parties or as seating overflow on those super busy days. Upon entering *The Real Jerk,* all eyes gravitated left to its main two-story wall. A larger-than-life blackboard dominated with a chalk portrait of the late, great, and legendary Bob Marley. It was a masterful piece shaded in Rasta colors. At approximately six feet wide and ten feet high, grand detail went into his features and smiling face. I could feel his presence.

Every day, a positive quote would replace the one previously positioned in reflection of Mr. Marley's life. Perhaps those were his very words. A young woman, however, greeted us with a warm smile. Once we were confirmed as a single party—large—our waitress ushered us to an elevated dining area closest to the kitchen. The waitress, Lorna, by whom she'd politely introduced herself, began arranging chairs. She next leaned heavily against a solid wooden table. It barely moved. Without being asked, two of us obliged Lorna, adjusting the tables where she desired. Her thanks betokened hints of a heavy Caribbean accent. Once seated, menus were brought tableside.

The menu proved extensive. There was a distinctive cross between West Indian entrées from Jamaica to Trinidad. Over sixty appetizers were available. Multiple drinks and juices native to the Islands were available if in season. Most of my party didn't know where to begin. It was okay. My involvement with Islanders and the culture over the years has become routine. In fact, I was often mistaken for an Islander myself.

Approximately five or so minutes later, Lorna returned with multiple bottles of water and fresh lemon wedges on a serving tray. By this time, everyone was settling and getting comfortable with accepting a new environment.

"Has anyone decided on what they would like to order?" asked the hostess.

I wanted to ask a thousand questions regarding her culture and origin. A second thought forced reconsideration, as it was being graceless.

"Yes, please. Thank you. May we have two each of the following: curry, jerk, and brown stew chicken. Two oxtails, steamed snapper, and pepper steaks. For sides, we'd like three orders of fried plantain, three orders of fried dumplings, and ten curry goat roti. Also, may I please have a soursop and passion fruit juice for everyone?" I concluded with a smile.

Lorna smiled while writing, even chuckled a few times.

"Okay. Jah know dem cook gon tizzy 'pon me."

"I'll go with you if you need me to," I offered.

She was flooded with emotion. Lorna departed to get the orders underway. In the meantime, we shared warm casual conversation while observing pedestrians and traffic through the large bay windows.

Fresh beverages were the first to arrive. Conversations were at their zenith. There were many taking place within convivial convocation. I was grateful to have introduced them to this part of the world. One by one, our orders began filling up the tables. Everything was shared among us in order to experience the complexity and variety of West Indian cuisine. Small glimpses through flavor-filled windows may take the mind's imagination on a trip to foreign lands. Places possibly locked away deep within the subconscious as experiences of our ancestors being with us together in one place in time. I've often considered such things.

"Hello… Hello… Hello, hello, hello, hello," chimed China Doll's voice, snapping her forefinger and thumb together several times.

My eyes refocused on China entirely. I sailed.

"Where did you just go?"

The multifaceted conversation continued with their eyes on a swivel. All recognized my travels, yet continued in the liveliness. A really good question had been posed. Ignoring it was not an option.

"I am here… just in deep thought. My apologies."

China was the spiritual version of a bull. Once she focused, it was hard to get out of her line of sight.

"Really?" she asked, dismayed. "I know you better than you think."

Conceding to the reality of present facts, I decided to share some of my private thoughts. A few more steaming dishes arrived in Lorna's hand. Taking a slow, deep breath, I made the decision to express my subtle disruption of our positive energy as a collective, and I waved my hand overhead. Only a brief moment had passed prior to everyone's focus adjusting to my actions.

"Thank you. Before I begin, please continue to enjoy the food while I share something with you. The food's at its best hot, and plenty more is en route."

Taking another deep breath, a sensitive topic came forth.

"Do you see that table with two chairs closest to the door?"

Everyone looked towards the area.

Roughly twenty years ago, the King of *New Jack City* was sitting at that very table. His back was to the window. He and his companion were both dressed in black, from combat boots to leather trench coats and shades. They didn't order any food, only drinks. Whatever their order of business, it was covert and seemingly held significance.

I took a long, slow sip from a cup of soursop juice occupying some small space before me. Such a clean, fresh, and lovely taste. They both had exercised a subdued demeanor. However, those subtleties were technically only hidden from anyone around them, but not from each other. Huddled over the table, it proved obvious discretion was at a premium.

I paused and took a sip of passion fruit juice.

"Eight of us were in attendance that day—pretty much in this same location we're seated presently. Our group and theirs were the only two parties in attendance. Observation didn't prove difficult with all of the natural light flowing into the restaurant. No distractions existed in order to divert my scrutiny. Once satisfied, I whispered in T-Rock's ear my findings."

I asked everyone's pardon while helping myself to a few steaming oxtail segments, gravy, fried dumplings, and plantains. To say the food was amazing is an understatement. An indulgence of such an experience is the only way one may appreciate such a Kama Sutra of culinary delights. Folding my lips inward, I sucked at them, diminishing the thick layer of collagen. Temporarily sated, I utilized water and a cloth to clean my fingertips.

"Thank you for your patience," I said prior to sharing some past events once more. "A few minutes passed, and T-Rock confirmed my suspicions. We had come to Toronto to begin the New Year Canadian style."

There were some chuckles around the table.

"Now, I'm sure all present have been curious regarding the company kept in the gallows back home. Some are there as a result of business. There are a few—including the latest 'acquisition'—ironically, all personal. It just so happened that the byproduct resulted in some good business for you all.

"Sean Tucker, aka Divine, aka the Brown Street Bully, aka Walrus, etc., sat with me at a table like ours the day we saw Wesley. We tasted the islands and drank the environment. Everything within our dietary boundaries was pretty much sampled—codfish fritters, jerk chicken wings, and coleslaw like I've never had in all my life! Right here, just as we are presently." My head sank deeply as emotions whirled in my mind like clothes in a washing machine. I took slow, deep breaths to calm myself, yet my anger was still bubbling below the surface.

I opened my eyes while raising my chin.

"I need for everyone's understanding to be paralleled, clear, concise, and unadulterated. No one's seeking sympathy. Use rationale. Support the principle. That creature in the bear cage had the nerve to get on the stand and gladly testify against me at my federal trial. He laughed while up on the stand, pointing me out. He seemed to find pleasure in such behavior. Anything I've ever said I'd do for this cat, I fulfilled. Whatever was asked was provided within a reasonable time. I'd considered buying that fool a Range for his birthday.

"Slight degrees of envy or jealousy were detected from time to time.

Who would've ever imagined the rot had grown so deeply? Back in the day, when dudes would score some bread, I'd always encourage them to flip their paper. Instead, they'd rather buy whips and chains—like we didn't get enough of that during slavery."

There was a uniform nod from the surrounding company. The storm was no longer containable despite maintaining a sturdy composure. I knew if another word was uttered, tear ducts were sure to open. The funny thing about it is, I haven't shed a tear since my arrest—besides the passing of family members. No ill will or animosity festered within the presence of this group. I'd care little if anyone presumed tears were a weakness. If any in attendance felt so, it was never revealed. Besides, this was a special group of people bursting with integrity and dignity.

"I was in love once, a long time ago. Some of you may know where I'm coming from. Others, not so much. This woman was my everything—my moon and soon-to-be earth. That's perhaps a once-in-a-lifetime type of woman. Beautiful from head to toe. Her greatest attributes, I'd have to say, were her spirit, personality, and mind. She knew how to keep me stimulated from within. That made all the difference. We shared time in this very place and would eat nowhere else but here while in Toronto. Life as I knew it wasn't evolving into something greater, purer, realer, and tangible. The foundation for such a parallel would be honesty in our aspirations and with each other.

"Moments came and went where I felt exposed and vulnerable from her keen awareness of what she saw in my eyes. Never was there an instant when manipulation came into existence. I was beyond grateful for it. Anything otherwise would've forced my eyes to see what she really had been. The soul within my physical vessel led me to another as compatible. The term most relatable, I believe, is soulmate.

"Comrades, this is not some tender 'D' pillow talk here."

Laughter erupted at the table.

"Don't think it wasn't apparent on a few of your faces. What I'm touching upon exceeds copulation itself.

"Everyone, take notice of how the human body functions. The mind doesn't have to instruct the lungs to inhale and exhale, when to relieve itself of waste, how to fight off an infection or virus, or to heal itself after a bad bruise or cut. Atoms within our molecular composition come complete with their own instructions. So it is with spirit and love when it's found. We didn't have to talk about things very much. Our involvement was fluid. Communication was exercised as a measure of our accuracy towards each other in the relationship.

"What may have been a major solidification of our bond was collective activity—going fishing, to the cinema, playing basketball, exercising, dining out once or twice a week, cooking and feeding each other at home. My personal goal was to learn all her likes and avoid any dislikes while developing the art of compromise. Not too much longer after leaving home, I'd yearn to return.

"That's when I began understanding there were unknown levels of love. Like when your significant other upsets you in the most trivial way, and later you find yourself laughing at your own behavior at its silliness. A person is truly love-struck! I can think of a couple of you here my address finds befitting."

I smiled, observing the facial expressions of all. Responses came from several, either denying or raising no contention amongst laughter.

"Remember this, all you nay-sayers, you don't have to share someone's bed to be in love with him or her."

There was a taste of silence in the air as the jewel was digested.

"Enough about me. Let's cut into all this steaming sustenance."

"Amen to that!" interposed Banks. More laughter pursued.

"What was her name, Preme?" China Doll asked.

"Pardon me?" I asked.

"What was the name of the woman you loved so dearly?"

Abrupt silence ensued after the question. A few moments passed before realizing everyone was awaiting an answer.

"Leah."

15

A Taste of Redemption

The phone rang three times before anyone answered.

"Hello," Mildred said in her heavy Spanish-Bronx accent. "Hello to you, my one and only sister!"

"Preme?!... Wassup, bro?! Where are you?"

"Hey, babe! I'm in the Roc right now. How are you doing?"

"I'm glad to hear from you. When are you coming through?"

"I might just hop on the next flight out on AA or JetBlue. You're filled with joy—I can hear it clear as day," I said. Nothing could make me happier.

"Yes, I am."

"You can tell me all about it when I get there. How's Lil Var doing? I know he's growing like a tree."

"He's good. Playing those video games he loves so much." We shared a laugh. "My n*****, I really miss you, yo. Get on the—"

There was an interruption in the background. Despite being partially discernible, I heard enough to recognize the unique sound of my partner's voice. As he entered the room Mildred occupied, I began to hear him clearly.

"I know you're not talking to another cat in my presence," Shevar said daringly.

"Yeah, this is my new man. I told you your spot was taken two months ago!" she said, followed by such a hurtful and wicked laugh.

Shevar snatched the phone from Mildred's hand. "Hello!"

Temptation overwhelmed my resistance to indulge in the trickery.

"Qué pasa?" I said. "Mildred es mi chula, papi, comprende," I stated matter-of-factly. Sensing his hostility increasing, it didn't make any sense to enrage him outright.

"Learning you're the jealous type is a first for me, Tiger!" I said.

"Tiger?! What's up, man! Ah! You had me. I felt the need to reestablish who wears the pantalones around here."

"You ain't wearing nothing but a robe right now! My robe at that— the one with all the koi on it. Stop frontin' for Preme!" Mildred bellowed in the background.

Laughter erupted at both ends of the receiver.

"When you comin' through?" Shevar, aka Tae Dow, aka Tiger, asked.

"Maybe this evening or tomorrow around this time."

"No doubt. Get here so we can holla."

"Say no more. I'll call to let you know the details. Before I go, let me speak to sis."

"Aight. One."

"One."

Mildred commandeered the phone. In the background, "You grow a lot of heart when Preme around, huh?" Shevar was heard saying.

"Go wash the dishes! I'm on the phone! Wassup, bro? It's been too long. Who got you on lock? Nothing has ever kept you away this long. When will I meet her?"

Sometimes, a person doesn't seem to possess the right to know or understand another so well. For an instant, I felt Mildred had invaded the privacy of my emotions. Without the key or combination, the vault's door was open for her perusal. Regardless of any violation I may have felt, those feelings were immediately discarded. In truth, it was only something I presume a sister—or someone very close at heart— could read.

Smiling to myself at the questions posed and thoughts of Leah, I cleared my throat.

"She's so much more than a name, and it would be my pleasure to make introductions. Her name is Leah."

"Leah. Hmm. Sounds like she's put that magic on you."

"In more ways than one. Real talk. I'm still trying to be sure about everything. I admit, she's quite a woman."

125

Mildred remained silent for what seemed a long time.

"Love's in the air. I'm glad it has found you. Know this, though: love's not only about enjoying the good times. It's how you endure the declines, turns, and loops on love's roller coaster. Everything needed to make it work is inside you. Anything you ever need or want to know about a woman, I'm here to keep you conscious."

"Thank you, Mil. From the depths of my soul."

"That's what it's going to take to make it work. Swallow pride in advance. Come see me ASAP—even if you must bring Leah. Get here. I love you, bro!"

"Never enough love. Peace."

My smile endured long after the conversation with Mil had concluded. So much so, its spillover breached the causeway of my emotional guard. By the time Leah and I met that evening, any remaining protective barrier to my heart was dismantled. We had developed an unwritten custom in our home. Something rather simple. Cater to each other. It was a simple enough practice worth establishing. Mil had been right. I'd long ago quaffed Leah's bait—hook and all. My work was also done. She had been spoiled by these very hands. I wanted to spend my life with this woman. How I'd share this idea was undetermined. Amidst a ton of hugs and kisses while bathing Leah during a hot bubble bath, we conversed.

"Babe, I may need to fly out to Harlem tomorrow."

Her eyes opened slightly in drowsy observation. Closing her lids and continuing to relax, questions followed.

"What takes you there on such short notice?"

"It entails a conversation incapable of being addressed by phone. I'm going to see Shevar and his ol' lady, Mildred. She's like my sister—we've bonded in such a rare way. I told her about you. She said that I'm in love after one minute of our talk. Mildred wants to meet the woman I'm so fond of. I think you both would get along very well. Any small chance it can be 'we' instead of just me?"

Leah continued purring like a happy cat being stroked in all the right ways. She opened her eyes. I gently dabbed accumulated perspiration from her brow.

"Not under such short notice. If given a week in advance, I'd say yes."

She was overtaken by comfort once more.

"I figured as much. It's something to anticipate. Taking you on a tour of my favorite restaurants will be enjoyable, I think, among other things. Besides, I'm really fond of your company."

I admitted to dabbing perspiration from her forehead again. She sailed—either at my show of affection or tracing her areolas, obscured by bubbles, with the soft, wet cloth held between my thumb and forefinger. I wasn't sure which. What was certain was that some of the best quality moments were shared in this house.

"Is it possible for you to come home early tomorrow? It would be a pleasure catering to you before my departure. Give you something to ponder over while I'm away."

"Is that so?"

"Yes, my educated love. In fact, I'd like you to be my professor and grade this thesis. Since it's going to require profound detailing and intimate exploration, wisdom tells me I should begin tonight."

"And the tenor of your thesis?"

"Kama Sutra."

Her eyes gave all the answers sought.

"Sweet, help me out of this tub, please? I must ensure your research is of the utmost quality."

"Yes, my Queen. Teach me what you know."

The flight to La Guardia didn't take long. Approximately 45 minutes from takeoff to landing, plus taxiing to the designated terminal. There were a few clouds in the sky. I loved observing the landscape from above. Sun rays shimmered across my face and arms. It was warmer than usual for this time of year. Upon exiting the plane, I stepped aside, raising my chin skyward, giving universal thanks for a safe trip and landing. Once completed, long comfortable strides took me across the tarmac in the direction of Terminal 16.

Before long, I spotted Shevar waiting patiently. My man possessed true Harlem sway in his bones. Donning a gray Yankee fitted turned backwards, Versace frames, Ice Burg Jeans, and a white T-shirt with gray Tiebs. Not one for too much flash, the Cuban cigar and Rolex he wore appeared modest yet tasteful. We greeted each other with a loud hand smack followed by a complete embrace. We shared small talk while walking through the airport, observing the beauties along the way. Entering the massive parking lots was like entering another world in itself. Tae-Dow had no problem finding his vehicle in such a maze. In no time, we were headed towards the first of three tolls in our exodus from the airport.

"What's goody, fam? I'm so glad you came through. I stopped on 145th and Broadway before coming to pick you up. Beef and Broccoli! Huh! Huhhh!"

"I'm cooking all the beef up my way as is. However, broccoli will suit me just fine."

"Don't spark until we clear all these tolls. Down here, they'll put them people on you for anything," Var warned.

"Say no more."

Immediately, I opened a magazine, picked up a pair of small scissors, and put them to work against the sticky, fluorescent bud. Once completed, I cleaned the scissors with an alcohol pad. I could smell a hint of vanilla while breaking the seal on the Dutch Master. Severing the cigar from end to end via box cutter, I disemboweled its contents and two exterior layers into a small plastic bag. Content with the result, the herb inside the magazine was ushered forth and rolled. The L was placed in the car door's armrest to set and cure.

"Tiger, that thing is on a diet, B."

"It ain't the size but the prize, my brother. I'm taking this one to the dome." We burst into short laughter. Traffic slowed to a crawl. In the distance, I could see the final toll looming ahead. We eased closer by the minute. Once clear, our normalcy returned seconds after passing the last of La Guardia's gatekeepers. It wasn't anything to discuss until exotic smoke filled my lungs. Tension seemed to rise from my physical being in layers as I exhaled slowly. Another pull, thus deeper, and the world around me took on a slightly different perspective. It may be explained in two aspects.

Imagine a scenario where there's an actual decent percentage of people who consistently feel they're living life underwater. Some are barely keeping their heads above water. Also, there are a few who thrive amongst the clouds. Thick plumes of smoke were released. There was a sense of profound enjoyment. My indulgence was undisturbed, and the silence for the time being was pleasing. Personal thoughts collected and scrambled by the second. By the fifth full intake on the vanilla

Dutch, my head vented from beneath the water to above it. The ascension was slow and steady in the background. Before long, water lay at my feet, and my sights were focused skyward.

Content with the continuing degree of stimulated elevation, my left hand extended, offering the L to Shevar.

"I'm good, B. Straight broccoli will have me too paranoid."

"Did you know that paranoia is one of the highest levels of consciousness? It truly helps me in the field," I said.

"Bet it does. Not for nothing, you cats up there are O.C. fam in those hills."

I retracted my arm and took another pull. Retiring the blunt to the ashtray, I reclined the passenger's seat, getting more comfortable. With concealed humor, it was time to return fire.

"You tryin' to get geographical?"

Tae-Dow burst into laughter.

"Ever consider why so many trees grow big and the grass so green in Rochester?" I queried. "Take a wild guess. For all other non-believers, The Most High has luxurious accommodations for those dying to be born again," I said in good jest.

"Jokes aside, that's why I needed you to come down—so we could talk face to face."

I opened my eyes at his tone.

"Okay. Spill." I was in the clouds.

"Once we're stationary. I've got a place in mind. You'll be hungry by then. Besides, I don't want any road distractions."

"No doubt, son! No doubt!" I responded with deliberate intent.

"I knew it all along. You're from Rochester Ave."

"BK all day. M.O.P. style," I said.

"A turn on the radio—Hot 97. I'm tryin' to hear Angie Ma's voice or a Flex mix."

"Too early for that. Angie comes on at 5 p.m., Flex at 7."

"Word?"

"Yeah. I got some fire mixtapes by Clue and Slay. Who do you want to hear?"

"Let's see what Clue do."

"Aight, fam! I knew it was something I meant to tell you! Loon got signed to Bad Boy! You remember him?"

"Yeah. Yeah. He's the one we bust down the shrimp baskets with. We had just come from the hole in the wall on the corner of 145th."

"That's him. You've got a good memory. It's been three months since you came through, and y'all only met once."

"We had a good time. I also recall that his two sisters and his old earth moved to Rochester not long ago."

"I forgot about that. We are close to your spot. After we cross the Tri-Borough Bridge—"

I interrupted.

"Make a hard right," I said knowingly.

Sammy's Reef rooted itself at the tip of the peninsula known as City Island. With only a single road in and out, divided into two lanes, anything sought after would be hard to miss. Tony's Pier rested across the pavement to the right. Certainly, it must've been an ultimate premium for such waterfront real estate. Tributaries poured into the Atlantic Ocean. Water expanded as far as the eye could see. With a desire to peer deeper into the horizon, mounted binoculars on a swivel base were available for ocean viewing—plus a small fee, of course. Parking capacity was somewhere around two hundred vehicles. Proof enough, the present calm was easily deceptive.

None of the restaurant's décor had any eye-popping effects. In fact, it felt quite reminiscent of a school cafeteria. A person could clearly see their meal being prepared. To the far right was an ice cream station, followed by hot dogs and hamburgers. Next in line was corn on the cob. Seafood followed on the bend to the steamed lobster tails with drawn butter. Completing the L-shaped service counter was the cash register and makeshift bar. We had our orders taken—six lobster tails, fried shrimp, whiting, corn on the cob, clams, and a Bronx-Harlem favorite, the Henny-Colada. Of those foreign to this combination, it's a mix of Hennessy and piña colada, stirred, served ice cold. The entrées ordered rendered a collective redolence. Once I paid for our meal, a secluded table away from all ears was selected. Salivating, an internal thanks was given to "The Exalted One". The process of separating whiting flesh from bone allowed hot steam to billow towards the ceiling. My first bite was intolerably hot. It could be felt passing through my esophagus and deep into my abdomen. Followed with sips from the colada, a coolness resumed.

"Mmm. I know you miss this, Tiger," Shevar said.

"That's a fact. Glad to be here, family. What's on your mind?" I asked, never being much of one to beat around the bush.

Tae-Dow nodded, musing more to himself than me. A long sip from his drink was ingested—perhaps one-third of it. He made a sound afterward, reminding me of someone attempting to guzzle an ice-cold 20-ounce Pepsi.

"Ha! Haw. That joint will grow some taco meat! Huh, man?"

I burst into laughter. My man could always get one out of me— even if I didn't want to laugh.

"Preme, you ain't in the Roc. This is family time, B. Turn it down and enjoy life. Matter of fact, you need to move down here. Less stress and plenty of money."

"You make a sound argument. Before I move anywhere, and you drink too much, give me the business."

"Aight. I've been in contact with some family out west. They flew down not too long ago. I never told you, but my first cousin is blowing up in Hollywood. He's been acting since a kid, and now it's paying off. The fam wants me to come visit. You were the first person who came to mind. Seems like it may be a good idea for us to take a trip. I get to visit family. You get to meet the friends of the family."

I nodded in understanding. We took moments to cut into the food before us. In some instances, I discovered myself, eyes closed, mentally far off in some distant place, enjoying this very meal. I wiped my hands on a napkin and sipped at the potent hybrid of cognac and piña colada.

"Sounds like you feel strongly about this? Considering what you've shared, I'd be walking blind using your complete judgment." I took another sip.

"Man, whew! That's fire!" I said, referring to the drink.

"If you feel good about this, we need to get there. Where are we going?" I began eating before he responded.

"City of Angels, baby! Sunshine and bikinis."

"Good times and women like fine wine. When do you want to take sail?" I asked.

"We'll figure it out before you leave. For now, let's eat."

We dined heavily, enjoying the afternoon, catching up like old times.

Later that evening, we visited with Mildred and Lil' Shevar up in the Bronx. Not long from work, Mil was relaxing. Var was doing his homework. The moment Junior heard his father's voice, he sprang to life. Jumping into his dad's arms, their smiles were genuine, loving, and warm.

Mildred set in motion at the sight of me pulling up the rear. I was met with the jolting impact of a five-foot-ten-inch, one-hundred-seventy-pound, shrieking Latina woman. I was both elated and embarrassed by the attention received. It humbled me to see her openly express her emotions. Perhaps my mom should've had a daughter as well. I will forever ponder the closeness of our relationship.

Tae-Dow lowered Lil' Var to his feet, but it didn't break the embrace he maintained around his dad's waist.

"Where's the love, baby momma?" Tae-Dow asked facetiously.

Mil ceased to smile, turned from our embrace, and spoke with complete sarcasm.

"We got beef! My brother's here now. I'll call you when I need you!" she charged, rubbing her fingers across my waves.

"It's sooo good to see you! Come sit next to me."

"Whoa. What did I just walk into?" I asked with an inquiring expression. Looking to Big Shevar for answers, his eyes diverted from mine. Sis rested her head on my shoulder.

"We have some catching up to do," she said.

Baffled as I was, my concurrence followed.

"I believe you are right."

16

The Loyalty Tax

New Year's Eve 1998

It was ten minutes to five o'clock. We reluctantly exited The Real Jerk with a bounty of carry-out. As a result of the impeccable treatment, we rendered a one-hundred-dollar tip and exchanged the sincerest greetings.

Sunset's usual gold and crimson hues were finding their way across Toronto's skyline and Lake Ontario's invisible border. The sky was alive with color and life. We cruised the busy streets bustling with both pedestrians and vehicles.

"Tonight, we'll see how y'all bring in the New Year," I said to Tony, my most recent associate.

"I can assure you my city will not disappoint. It's still very young as of yet, eh?" Tony responded over loud music.

A thick cloud, like London fog, choked the Daneli's interior. We smoked several strains of hydro with reckless abandon, enjoying all aspects of Canada's personal-use laws.

"Whatever we decide, you might want to slow down. Are you auditioning for the Canadian Grand Prix? We don't need the wrong type of attention. Every man in this truck is on parole except you," I suggested smoothly beneath cold, challenging eyes.

Tony's foot eased from the accelerator.

"Son... this spot is crazy clean. You could eat off the sidewalks!" T-

Rock blurted in awe.

"Dimes at every turn. Ice cream! Time to get my Method Man on."
I turned in the front seat, facing T-Rock.

"Method Man? What happened, Mr. Ghostface Killa? You gettin'
brand new?" I asked, smiling and feeling good.

"Come on, G. That's too technical." He laughed.

"What on Earth are you two talking about? I swear, in all my years
never heard such chat," Tony countered.

"It's music-related," I said.

"Divine!" I yelled.

The poor fellow was leaning sideways, mouth open, his head tilted
back.

"Wake up, man! You got the itis, huh?"

He took a moment to situate himself. "Yeah, men. Between the
food and smoke, there was no other option."

"You just missed a group of naked women outside. Man, mm,
mm... shoulda seen them," I joked.

"Word?!" Divine asked.

"Never happened. Point is, sponge everything up. I wouldn't sleep
through this unique experience."

Tony was on the phone while we continued watching a new part of
the world unfold before us.

"Do you guys go to strip clubs in the States?"

We all looked at each other and locked on Tony, speaking in
unison.

"NO!"

"No?" Tony repeated in disbelief. "It's a pastime for us, eh?"

"That's considered trickin' down my way," T-Rock explained. "If
you got money to give, may as well give it to me."

I laughed at his statement.

"P, where do you find this corn muffin at? I feel some type of way.
Strip club? As long as a man has some good gab, he'll always wedge a
slab."

The real jabs had been shot. I could see Tony was upset at being
called "corn muffin." Though he didn't understand its full implication,
he knew it wasn't a compliment. Raising a hand to catch Roc before he
cut too deeply, I interrupted.

"To my man's defense, ol' boy has five or six of these chicks sellin' box. His style is different, no doubt. So are the worlds we come from. Personally, I'm trying to see his world. I know what's in mine."

There was a lingering silence between the men. The radio station played tunes. Good ones. It was reminiscent of NYC stations—maybe better.

"Yo, check the billboard! We gotta go see *Life* when we get back to the town. Starring Eddie, Martin, Bernie... man, it's too many to list!"

"What's the plan, Tony?" I asked. "We're in your yard."

"It's your choice."

"Give some food, you two," I asked of my travel companions.

"*Life!*" said T-Rock.

"And you?"

"I'm with it," answered Divine. "There's a cinema not far away. Pretty decent one too, eh."

Tony picked up his phone to ring Mark and Richie.

"What's up, eh? We're going to Premier's Crisp."

He hung up. I introduced a flame to a stuffed cigar.

"Might as well float into Premier's Crisp instead of walking," I said.

In the distance, what seemed a city skyline was coming into a clearer range of visibility.

After some time, I asked, "What's all this?" pointing outwards on the passenger window side.

"That's the beginning of Scarborough."

"Is it a projects?" Divine asked. "Of Toronto, I mean."

"No," Tony replied. "It's a world in itself. A city suburb of the city, if you will."

The high-rise buildings stretched for blocks. I wondered how many people lived there.

"This is a sight seldom seen, except mostly in the boroughs. All of our projects have been torn down—too many unsolved murders, mainly," I enlightened.

"When I say the boroughs, I mean the Bronx, Brooklyn, Manhattan, Queens, and Staten Island, which make up 'The Big Apple,' New York City."

It was hard to avert my eyes from this view.

"This is an amazing atmosphere, plain and simple."

135

My thoughts were moving a million miles every four seconds. The future was unfolding in the very moment of my present. I enjoyed the foreboding within my mind's eye. My arms extended as my hands appeared to grasp and mold an inanimate object to choice specifications.

Noticing the observations of those around, I withdrew my hands lap-side. However, the vision steadfastly continued unfolding.

"That's some pretty good dro, ain't it, sport? Got you seeing things. What were you just doing exactly, sport?" T-Rock poked.

"Tryin' to do your time off me, huh? You got it. Enjoy," I said, half laughing.

"Oh, I will. Keep it up and I'll roast you all the way back to the Roc."

The entire truck erupted at that, myself included.

There hadn't been anything in my experiences throughout the lower fifty-two to prepare me for all my eyes were absorbing. I was in a great place at a great time of my life. Taking our last draws on the cigar, we exited one by one. My feet didn't seem to touch the ground. Just as I intended. Tony rolled down the passenger window. "Be sure to call the moment the movie wraps, eh. We'll need to move out. I'll time my business with yours. Say 7:30 pm." Enough was understood not to ask. Something was afloat. Whatever the case, Tony, Richie, and Mark could handle it. In a blur, the Denali pulled off. The frantic pace since leaving 'The Real Jerk' had resumed. Both parties vanished in a sea of vehicles, both parked and mobile.

Parking for Premier's Cineplex appeared more akin to that of a retail mall or Costco, for example. Pedestrians advanced in great droves. Not typical ones and pairs. Some were heading in our direction from hundreds of yards away. Life truly had the similitude to fluid water. I certainly soaked in every bit flowing amongst us. I turned to face Premier. The building was a neutral gray with its base being more of a coarse, darker sand-like texture. The roof was flat, and the structure plateaued at around 3 stories. Advertisements for more movies than I can recall were on display. It gave the dull exterior much-needed color, pop, and excitement. Life-like in size, every poster looked of consummate quality. Metal frames and plexiglass. coverings ensured protection from the elements and vandalism. The detailing was very impressive.

Eight sets of double doors allowed for entry into the cineplex. Adjacent to both sides of my position were automated devices resembling ATM Machines. I later learned a person could purchase movie tickets via credit/debit card, bypassing the otherwise lengthy lines. We entered the foyer, pushing past another set of doors. Once we purchased three tickets to see 'Life', we soon learned this monstrosity provided a total of 48 cinemas. We'd never witnessed anything as stunning. Beautiful women passed us while navigating the labyrinth of passages leading to the desired movie stations. Concessions were busy with customers of all ethnicities.

Up a set of twisting carpeted stairs was a section that looked similar to a lounge area. "Is that a bar up there?" I asked, indicating with a pointed finger. Divine and T-Rock confirmed. "Wow. No one would ever believe..."

Pop! Pop! Pop! as if a large caliber weapon is being discharged in close proximity. Chills raced up my spine at the sound. An immediate bend in the knees was instinctive. Reaching towards an empty waistline sparked greater unease. Our heads were swiveling as we stood back to back. Oddly, in these few frantic seconds, no one else registered alarm. Above the concession stand were giant replicas of individual popcorn. Large stability balls in size. Connected to thin cables extending to the ceiling, each popcorn shot twenty or so feet into the air in sync with the popping commotion. Closer inspection revealed the beginning stages of fresh popcorn being prepared. As the heat accelerated the cooking process, the Pop! sounds increased in frequency. Before long, there existed a staccato of sound. Pulse raising like an automatic weapon exchange with deliberate intent.

Once reality set in that it wasn't an attack on any movie patrons, the adrenaline surge diminished.

"I don't know about you guys, but I'm going to the bar. Time to relax," T-Rock stated matter-of-factly.

"That sounds excellent," said Divine, smiling.

I'd never been much of a drinker. However, the idea of having a drink or two did possess some appeal. We headed upstairs, finding a clean round table. A waiter promptly appeared carrying menus for three. He introduced himself and indicated to press the button centered at our table for service. We thanked Frank in unison.

Immediately, a perusal of available drinks to order tallied three hundred plus. There weren't many straight shots of anything. If so, a serving in Canada is probably one ounce by volume—quite disappointing by American standards.

"Didn't Jodeci make the soundtrack for the movie *Life*?" I asked at the table.

"No. K-Ci and JoJo from the group made a couple of tracks for it, I know. Not sure about its entirety," responded T-Rock.

"Speaking of, were you out when Jodeci moved to Rochester? I'm guessing after June of '95. I was in the belly by then. The word was out up north about them having rock star parties," I mentioned.

"I violated parole around that time," T-Rock replied.

"You know I've been M.I.A. since '92," answered Divine.

"Unfortunately, that's very true," I continued. "Divine, do you remember when we were in Groveland?"

He nodded.

"I gave you my two-year itinerary. Besides the obvious moves to get the paper, my goal was to get situated with owning real estate. Never should any one of us give a woman power enough to say, 'Get out of my house.' When you have your own, and she knows it, she'll be more considerate as opposed to haughty."

We pressed the button indicating our readiness to be served. Holding up his index finger, the bartender acknowledged us while serving a customer at the bar. I continued.

"We all know what today is. That's why we're here—to bring in our first New Year's Day outside prison walls after a long time. Part of that itinerary was for me to relocate out of the country in twelve months."

The bartender arrived to take our orders.

"Divine, we came home a month apart in '97. I myself, on September 17th. You on October 12th. Step one in the plan was made possible when we were in Niagara Falls last December. We met those cuties from Toronto. Well, tryin' to cut wasn't the first order of business.

"Thanks to that encounter, I'm living where I said I'd be within the time allotted."

The bartender returned carrying a tray with our order.

"Nine doubles of Rémy Martin straight. Coke and ice on the side."

We thanked Frank before his departure.

"Let's toast," I said. "You first, T-Rock."

T-Rock looked bewildered, as if truly taken by surprise. His company laughed at him.

"Your turn, Divine," I prodded.

"Man, I'm just glad to be here," he said.

"Good enough for me," I said, raising my snifter. "To being here in the now."

Our glasses touched, and we tossed back the first set of drinks.

"I have a toast," I said, replacing the empty snifter with one containing cognac. "May we prosper in life, in good health, family, and finances."

We touched glasses once more, and I sipped while they drank heavily.

It was my time to be badgered and poked in good jest. They both were aware of my low tolerance for alcohol. Another round was ordered—two doubles this time.

"Fellows, my point is this. Did I not do everything I said I would thus far while in that prison yard?" I asked, looking Divine directly in his eyes.

"You have shown and proved the wisdom indeed," Divine agreed.

"I have another decree," I mentioned in a low, firm tone.

"We will become millionaires soon. Every last one of us. You may not see it at this very moment, but I do. If you still fail to see the path, help me get there. Whatever wall impeding your vision, I'll destroy it from the other side. There won't be a need to climb over or find a way around when you can walk straight through. I'll make it easy—easy, unlike anything you've ever seen.

"It will require three things. One, there must be trust. Two, pay attention to every detail. Three, when it's time to act, we must.

"Cheers."

"Cheers."

***

AUSA Shirkin: What did he say?

Sean Tucker: Preme offered us each a kilo of coke at $21,000 each when they were selling at $30,000. The only way he would give it to us is if we retail the product. He said that, instead of making $9,000 a kilo, we could make $29,000 a kilo each day if we were smart. Above all, selling retail would keep us under the radar longer than someone selling weight. What deterred me from doing business with Preme was the emphasis he put on a statement.

AUSA Shirkin: What statement are you referring to?
Sean Tucker: It was made clear that the men with whom he dealt would give him any amount of narcotics upon request. He said," If my people would give me all of this, knowing how vicious I can be, what does it say about who they are? Furthermore, if any of you take these bricks and think you are going to blow the money. I'm bringing them to your doorstep." That last statement is why none of us accepted the offer.

AUSA Shirkin: That must've been a wake-up call?
Sean Tucker: Yeah, it was.

AUSA Shirkin: Did you ever have an occasion to speak with Supreme further about his business?
Sean Tucker: Yes. He was telling me about the clientele he had and the people he was serving.

AUSA Shirkin: What do you mean by "serving"?
Sean Tucker: Supreme was selling large amounts of drugs to these people; among them were some heavy hitters.

AUSA Shirkin: Do you know the intent of distributing weight to these people?
Sean Tucker: I presume financial gain. We weren't social with respect to juxing anymore. He wanted us to know how well he was doing. I think Preme felt he was better than the rest of us.

Defense Counsel Wolfe: Objection!
Judge Sarasota: Grounds?

Defense Counsel Wolfe: Speculation. Unfounded, Your honor.

AUSA Shirkin: Your honor, can we see you at the side-bar?

Judge Sarasota: Approach.

All Counselors from opposing sides advanced to the bench. There was a conference off record.

Judge Sarasota: After some discussion, the objection is overruled. You may resume, Mr. Shirkin.

AUSA Shirkin: Mr. Tucker, do you recall when you were arrested by the federal government?

Sean Tucker: Yes, I do.

AUSA Shirkin: What was the date and year?

Sean Tucker: April 13, 2003. I've been in custody ever since.

AUSA Shirkin: Have you since that time pleaded out to federal criminal charges?

Sean Tucker: Yes, I did.

AUSA Shirkin: What exactly did you plead guilty to?

Sean Tucker: I copped out to conspiracy with the intent of distributing 700 grams or more of crack, cocaine, and weed. Separate and apart from the conspiracy, I also pleaded guilty to using and carrying a firearm in furtherance of drug trafficking.

AUSA Shirkin: You were indicted for conspiracy to affect commerce by Hobbs Act robberies, correct?

Sean Tucker: Correct.

AUSA Shirkin: Did you accept the plea under the advice of counsel?

Sean Tucker: I did.

AUSA Shirkin: Who did you make this agreement with?

Sean Tucker: The United States Attorney's Office.

AUSA Shirkin: Do you recall which justice accepted your plea?
Sean Tucker: Yes. Judge Sarasota.

AUSA Shirkin: Has a sentence been imposed with regard to your specific set of circumstances?
Sean Tucker: No.

AUSA Shirkin: Are you aware of the sentencing range of the plea agreement?
Sean Tucker: 180 to 240 months.

AUSA Shirkin: In order to be granted this sentencing range, what is required of you?
Sean Tucker: Cooperation with government authorities.

AUSA Shirkin: What is your interpretation of government cooperation?
Sean Tucker: That first, I would enter into a proffer session with the AUSA in charge. If concluded by the prosecutor(s) that any evidence/information I provide may be useful for additional prosecution of certain individuals, it would be recommended that I receive a sentence below the United States Sentencing Guidelines or U.S.S.G. This agreement also included participation in all of my personal criminal activity.

AUSA Shirkin: Your honor, may we have a sidebar?
Judge Sarasota: Granted.

There was another of several off-record bench conferences.

Judge Sarasota: Ladies and gentlemen of the jury. As previously stated, these sidebars amongst the counselors and me pertain to issues of evidence. The significance of whether certain details are deemed permissible is vital. It is consequential to this trial to hear both arguing parties. Doing so off record precludes the court from discharging you, the jurors, each instant an issue arises. You are further instructed by the court not to delineate conclusions, in favor of or opposition to either party, resulting from any ruling I've made. Mr. Shirkin, please proceed.

AUSA Shirkin: Thank you, Your Honor. No further questions.

Judge Sarasota: We'll conclude testimony for today. Trial will resume at 9 AM tomorrow. Ladies and gentlemen of the jury, you are excused. The court is in recess.

***

Judge Sarasota: Good morning, ladies and gentlemen, and counselors. Are we all prepared to proceed?

Several court officers nodded in consent.

Judge Sarasota: Very well. See the jurors in, please.

The bailiff complied with the command. He disappeared through one of the various side doors. Moments later, the jurors were filing into the courtroom. Seven women and five men, all of whom were of European descent. Not a jury of my peers.

Judge Sarasota: Good morning to the jury. Did everyone arrive in a timely fashion? I know rush hour can be unbearable at first thing. Again, I commend your efforts in being prompt in fulfilling this very underrated civil service. Jury duty is one of the primary democratic cornerstones of society as we know it today. Albeit not the most exciting of activities. It's among the most vital. I applaud every one of you. Let's begin, shall we?

Judge Sarasota: Bring in the witness.

Sean Tucker was escorted into the courtroom by a U.S. Marshal. He took a seat on the witness stand, challenging both the chair's structural integrity and audible protest.

Judge Sarasota: Good morning. Mr. Tucker, you are here today to resume testimony. You remain under oath to testify truthfully and as accurately as possible. Before direct examination continues, I instruct you not to mention or make reference to Mr. Murphy ever being incarcerated. Instead, use the phrase, "out of town," so as not to alert the jury to any defendant's previous imprisonment. Are we clear?

Judge Sarasota: Mr. Kent, you're up.

AUSA Kent: Thank you, Your Honor.

The courtroom was jam-packed, so much so, there was a spillover room and a large screen monitor as AUSA Kent approached the podium to direct the examination of the witness.

JAUSA KENT: Good morning, Mr. Tucker. I'd like to refer back to an earlier portion of your testimony with Mr. Shirkin. Do you recall stating that you know someone named Nafis Afrika?

Sean Tucker: I do.

There was a sudden, thunderous outburst from the crowd.

"I CAN'T HEAR ANOTHER WORD OF THIS SHIT. YOU ARE A LYING MOTHERFUCKER!"

It was Emory from Jefferson Ave. He was on his feet with a livid expression on his face.

"WORD IS BOND... SON, YOU A BITCH N*****!"

Before another could be unleashed, U.S. Marshals swarmed him. The lead marshal grabbed his arm, trying to force him down the aisle. Emory fought back with a strength that didn't match his slight frame. Chairs screeched, shoes scraped, shouts cut the air.

Emory's slight build did nothing to foreshadow the inner strength he exuded. If not for the assistance of three additional marshals, the first and largest amongst them was on the verge of being toppled. The skirmish lingered for perhaps two minutes after it began. With each marshal snatching one of Emory's ankles and the third a wrist, little remained of his vigorous resistance except for an unwavering verbal defiance.

The jurors were hustled out in a rush. Silence fell, except for the guttural sounds of Emory's struggle and his raw defiance.

Flat on his stomach, hog-tied, he still spat his last words like fire:

"FUCK THAT SHIT. PEACE GODS! PEACE TO THE GODS!"

They lifted him, carried him out. His voice echoed down the hallway long after the courtroom doors slammed shut.

I had never seen anything like it. The room was frozen—spectators wide-eyed, officers pale. Shock and fear mingled in the air, though I found myself half-amused at their faces as it all unraveled.

Defense Counsel Wolfe leaned close, voice low. "Did you have anything to do with that?"

"Absolutely not," I whispered.

Emory's voice could still be heard in the distance after the U.S. Marshals had carried him off through the double-door entry of Judge Sarasota's court.

Everyone seemed to have a semblance of reprieve with the ensuing lull from such an unforeseen disruption. Even Judge Sarasota, who'd looked one second from bolting off the bench, was left smoothing the chaos back into order with brittle reassurances.

The gavel never fell. The trial was cancelled for the rest of the day. The courtroom emptied into a hush still heavy with Emory's echoing screams.

17

Behind Parker Place

There existed an endearing serenity among those who traveled internationally for the first time in their lives. Everyone had an excellent experience. Even the most reclusive of us. I witnessed those most world-weary in the fold breach their own protective shell. The type of bunkers and walls developed inside the war-torn, neglected, and oppressed neighborhoods within the inner city of the United States of America. Interaction with warm and receptive Canadians dissolved year-round social winters. With them came the sunshine and pleasant rains of spring, promoting growth and evolution. I felt joy on their behalf. Their joy became my own. We returned to Rochester via car service. For all who braved staying awake, the countryside of Western New York would feast their eyes. From the beautiful behemoth of Niagara Falls at Goat's Island to all of the subtle sights along Route 31E in between.

Not only did we all return with an invigorating experience, there were ice coolers of food from "The Real Jerk." Another simple surprise elevated the merriment surrounding our arrival. A few cases of beer were purchased at the government-controlled Beer Stores. Considering the alcohol content by volume, it was arguably the strongest beer in North America. Even though gifts and pictures of time in Toronto were shared, I was seeking a prize of my own.

My anticipation led me to a cozy residence four houses from the corner of West Avenue on Lincoln Street. Stephanie was found upstairs in a customized sitting room she had decorated herself. Employed on a laptop computer, she didn't look up from her work. Easing into the bathroom, I gargled with mint antiseptic. I washed and dried my hands, selecting a men's aromatic musk essential lotion. Rubbing it into my skin left it feeling rich and smooth as strong silk.

She happened to be listening to cordless headphones, unaware of my arrival. I walked into the room, sinking my fingers into the nape of her neck and shoulders. I gently glided an index finger across Stephanie's top lip. My desire to permeate her senses was hearty. Initially taken by surprise at the approach, my touch, however, was all too intimately familiar. The massaging of her temples and scalp was obligatory where time permitted. Intoxicating was the transition of pressure and rhythmic contact. Stephanie closed the laptop. She began slowly, meandering sidelong onto the couch, where she sat. I climbed over the backrest one leg at a time, remaining fluid with her descent.

It was the summer of 1991 when I was first afforded to lay my eyes upon this fine woman. Stephanie worked at a clothing store on the corner of Genesee and Sawyer Streets, Things 'n Things, on the southwest side of Rochester. I was a sophomore at Franklin High School and probably what many would perceive as rather nature. As a result, I usually attracted older females. I presume it's why Stephanie took any notice of me at all. Steph stood about 5 feet 9 inches tall and a solid 160 pounds. Skin like unblemished mocha. With a lean core, every facet of her existence could resonate with self-consciousness in the presence of other females. Since that moment forward, Stephanie has been a queen of queens.

Completing the massage session, I pressed all my weight slowly into her body. She exhaled a moan between both pleasantness and slight discomfort. Stephanie's warmth reverberated upwards through my clothing and into my being. I breathed deeply. My nose set close, nuzzling her neck, right earlobe, and hairline.

"How's my sweet lady doing? I know someone who's been missing you like crazy." I said, raising my torso slightly, not to impair her breathing.

"I'm better since you're here." Stephanie reached her right hand upwards, raking my scalp and face with a brilliant set of one-inch manicured nails. "You give me the chills every time you do that," I whispered.

"That's why I do it," she replied. Hours later, we remained wrapped in each other's arms.

"How long can you stay?" I asked.

"As long as you request, actually," she said through a smile. "Mind you, I do have my salons to operate." I nodded into Steph's forehead gently.

"Of course, I'll grant consideration. As to whether or not to hold you hostage." Holding her hand to my face, I kissed its palm several times, licking swirl patterns.

"I didn't see your car, babe. How'd you get here?"

"Howard brought me. He waited for an hour to see you before leaving."

"I'm sorry I missed him."

"You found a spot in his heart."

"He wiggled his way into mine many years ago. Maybe even before you." Steph hit me broadside in my face with a pillow at the statement. "We used to cruise the city together prior to my abduction."

"I don't know if you recall, but Howard was my greatest and most trusted emissary when it came to you."

"Really? That's news to me. Who else did you have?"

"In all honesty, just Howard. I was exaggerating." Stephanie unveiled that rare bright smile. The kind which caused her beautiful amber eyes to become alit when she did.

"I mean something to you, don't I?" she asked, her hands caressing my chest.

"More than I'm fully aware of myself. Too much to ever grow sick and tired of, like we often hear people complain. So much so that every day I desire to become a better me for us."

I gazed at Stephanie. She was preoccupied, deep within her own private thoughts — a place where the candor of my expression made its summons.

"Your choice of words is very methodical. I'm moved by you, especially now, stirred within more so than I've ever been, perhaps. Sometimes, I just want to relinquish all responsibility and disappear to some beautiful land far from here."

From the cordless headphones Stephanie had been listening to earlier, Sade's voice drifted into the silence — sultry, aching, filled with the weight of a love that refused to be ordinary. The faint melody wrapped around us, becoming the quiet backdrop to her confession.

"You've endured too much and deserve so much better. I want to protect you from all that's bad in this world and surround you with all that's good. To give you all the joy you bring into my life. It lifts me higher by the second. I'll be the first to admit it's not an easy task. But, somehow, you managed and prevailed despite my demure reticence. Beyond family, I've never permitted any man into my emotive domain."

Steph grabbed me by the chin, looking into my eyes.

"Ever. No matter how long the relationship. You, my friend, yes, I said friend, on the contrary, are something...I'll say an enigma. One I instantly knew the answer to, of which is both simple and complex. For starters, you're not afraid to lay it all on the line for me. For any person you actually care about. I've heard too many stories of your Black Mafia vanguarding and loyalty. It pained me to witness great qualities you've bestowed held in such low esteem." She put her nose to my armpit, inhaling deeply.

"I miss the way you smell. I felt that way then and overwhelmingly so now. You were living proof of chivalry, expecting nothing in return. Slowly but surely, prying your way into my heart without permission. Withal, you were really handsome." I chuckled lightly but otherwise didn't interrupt. "Even though you ran with the crew, you weren't a follower. That's the simple."

Steph poked her cheeks out for a moment. She exhaled, remaining silent for a while. I caressed her skin's surface as intimately as possible.

"Now to the complex," she paused. "Things became complex when you began courting a mutual party, shall I say. The potential of what could have been was thwarted by what you'd actually done. At that stage, there was no way I could make myself available to your advances. I received all the messages, hugs, and kisses delivered by your most trusted emissary." My laughter couldn't be suppressed.

"Seriously?" I settled once again.

"Your behavior wasn't easy to disregard. The seed had been planted. It caused thoughts of you to grow inside my head. I couldn't ruminate over your advances. Not on good conscience.

"There was a time when you came to my house. I was curled up on the couch watching television. You came up from behind, covering my eyes with your hand, in the process rendering several delightful kisses onto my cheek and whispering in my ear. The instant my vision was reattained, I turned my head, seeing you hovering over the couch. I next glanced towards the kitchen, in which your eyes followed. Do you recall who was watching everything unfold? I'll never be responsible for breaking another woman's heart by way of her relationship with you. A stranger, perhaps. This, though, wasn't a stranger. Since then, I decided to hold fast and push you out of my thoughts for the sake of everyone."

Steph inched closer, kissing my cheek.

"You're a part of me, Preme. I'm glad you never gave up on me. And, I welcome you like no other ever before."

When I left the seclusion of my secret rendezvous, dusk was fast approaching. The drive back to the scrap yard was brief. I entered with an unwavering determination.

China Doll met me chest to chest as the door closed behind me.

"Preme!" We exchanged hugs. "You snuck away before I could bring you up to speed," she said, pulling out a chair.

"Sit," China Doll ordered. I gave thanks and complied. Her actions brokered my smile. She sat across from me at the kitchen table.

"First, everything went as expected. Everyone has been given water, and their pot chambers exchanged. With regard to feeding, well, everyone was fed. I'll keep things one hundred. If it can't be found in the supermarket, I want no parts. Those items you requested are right over here," she said, pointing.

"Forgive me, I just do not have the stomach for cooking rats, cats, dogs, or whatever else is running through your bizarre imagination. Those suckers aren't deserving of my cooking anyhow. I bought them happy meals instead. I hope you are not upset." China asked more than stated. She seemed to be steeling herself for a response that would never debark.

"What you've done is acceptable. Thank you. As long as you remembered to conceal your identity, great job. At this stage, it would only be routine. He's not telling anyone, anything again." I said, tapping my fingers, tableside, and nodding slowly.

"Depending on your plans tomorrow, God willing, we can go out to Irondequoit Bay or hit Ontario Parkway to see what's biting."

My smile returned.

"I'd love to," I said. China's face lit up like a candle at midnight.

"I'll prepare lunch for us later, just in case it's a sure go," she responded giddily. Standing slowly, I took a long stretch. China met me with another embrace before it was completed. Rarely did I meet someone whose passion is as strong as mine for fishing.

"One more thing," I said before she released me, "let everyone know not to be alarmed by any loud music they hear playing, please."

"Whatever that means. I'll pass it on." Moments later, I was alone in the kitchen.

Those amongst the cipher would understand when it's said, 'Time to show and prove.' Another of several speakers was selected. Strikingly similar to the one presently in the basement next to Sean, positioned at the entrance of the dungeon for clarity of sound. There's this song. Something the world has heard but may have thought inconsequential. Digging, searching, scrutinizing, and perusing hundreds of CDs, I finally found my selection. I pressed play. The percussion was the first sign of music. Slow proved its melody. Induced by a single stroke of a guitar's strings. An electric piano's overtones began their airy float above a conga's rhythm. And yes, it was well trembling loud. I changed into a white jumper. Next to follow was a white cloth tie on an apron. Disposable covers. A clear plastic mop bucket with an assortment of blades, a hack saw, and pliers were all business end down for safe handling. Another five-gallon pail stood adjacent to the other. Its cover was snapped shut, upon which a white towel was neatly folded. Opening the bucket, I peered at its liquid crimson contents. The metallic scent of iron, tin, and zinc was immediate. Finally, I donned a pair of arm-length latex gloves.

I poured perhaps two gallons of blood into the mop bucket and onto its contents. My hands were submerged wrist deep into the blood and retrieved. I rubbed both across the apron and jumper pants twice over. The folded towel was hung halfway into the mop bucket, drawing on its contents. In two minutes, I was heading towards the dungeon, mop bucket in tow.

My gait was slow and steady. Time was on my side. Visibility became more imposingly obscure as I descended the stairs. Shadows morphed eerily amidst the depths of subterranean territory. As every step was taken, there seemed to be a louder pounding within my chest and pressure in between my ears.

Excitement was building. The silent shift within was occurring. Nearing my destination, I walked forward, progressing through the narrow hallway. It opened into a much larger area. The stage was once again where an old pal had been detained with only uncertainty in sight. As I swung into his line of vision, I was not sure what had been noticed primarily. Divine remained motionless in the cage, his mouth agape. Overcome with shock, he steadily absorbed the reality of my presence. One man looked deeply into the eyes of the other. We did not see the same things. I pulled over the chair next to the desk, five or so feet from Sean. Resting the mop bucket at my covered boots, I grabbed the towel, squeezed the drenched portion of it free of blood, and wiped my gloves as clean as possible. His eyes darted from the bucket with its contents to me rapidly. His bed of straw appeared agitated, though he sat unmoved. Music was the only thing stirring the air, heavy and electric. Phil Collins' *In the Air Tonight* poured from the speakers, its haunting rhythm and brooding tone filling every corner of the room. The song carried anticipation and judgment, like a reckoning long overdue.

I stood motionless, letting the track pulse in the background while I studied the man before me. Sean kept his gaze low, unwilling to meet mine. It wouldn't have mattered if he had—his choices were carved too deep to be undone by courage now. As the final notes ebbed into silence, I spoke at last.

"Hey, Sean. Divine? Which do you prefer?" I asked, locking eyes with him. "I doubt you planned on seeing me again. We both know what you've done, so let's skip the pretense. I'll be frank—if you're wise, your affairs are already in order. For now, things stay as they are. The real question for you to consider is this: how would you like to die?"

I let the words hang, giving him time to chew on them. "Think it over. I'll be back at sunrise. Sleep well."

My departure was deliberate, every step slow and steady as I climbed the stairs, leaving The Brown Street Bully alone with his thoughts.

18

Shadow Work

Dawn had arrived. Surpassing its zenith by three hours. To one who had no access to the time or daylight, it was all the same. After refining myself and getting dressed, I was afforded an ice-cold glass of orange juice upon entry to the kitchen. Thanking my host, I began a quiet and steady descent down stairs. Divine was lying sideways. He snored heavily. With very little stealth, I set my drink on the table and took a seat. Small sips of orange juice were taken, appreciating its zest. I closed my eyes in easy anticipation. Processing the variables of approach and angles for accomplishing further opprobrium beyond this setting was a prerequisite. Simply taking Sean's life would not rescind the consummate enmity that's evolved since my incarceration.

For years, I've ardently struggled with debate-filled controversy both externally as well as within. Many people have been conditioned and trained to think or believe certain aspects of reality are justifiable by certain circumstances. The bitter cold irony of this accommodation and precept is utterly fraudulent. Each person knows it, especially when the act or behavior is in direct violation of one's own moral and principled reasoning. Truth be told, it came down to selfishness. It will not be tolerated. I wondered many times if this dude was actually going to become a witness for those government people. Sean proved more than willing. As a result, there hasn't been a day or night since I haven't visualized someone's face or heard another's voice opposing my freedom during this trial of thirty-five days. Quite naturally, all favors must be returned with a high rate of interest.

Divine continued in his snoring state of slumber. He must've been up late, turning my question over and over in his brain like fried potatoes. Normally, time would not be wasted on this pariah. If applied correctly, however, I've learned patience could be the ally of conquerors and kings. Likewise, the lack thereof could devolve me into the master of the oppressed.

During my time lingering in those federal penitentiaries, patience soon became a virtue. At one location alone, over fourteen people lost their lives in less than five years. Life took on a different meaning in such environments. To many, another's well-being carried little value. Just as easily as I could take a life, my own could have been forfeited at the hands of another.

Tolerance levels remained very low, while the respect standard was usually kept rather high. So many had lost all hope—losing themselves in drugs and homosexuality. People would often do things to provoke their own deaths, longing to end their hellish existence. There was an assemblage of cynics, most willing to oblige anyone crossing such a fine line.

The judicial branch that created these environs also helped breed the despair—through its disparity, partiality, and corruption of the entire system itself. Care and discretion made plenty of sense in how one chose his movements. Correspondingly, thinking for others was paramount.

I opened my eyes, and with it arose my thoughts of the present. The itinerary for this morning would be precise and meticulous. Today, Divine would have the wonderful opportunity to have some company other than me to converse with. A heavy object, perhaps a chair, fell to the floor. It sounded with an echoing thud, vibrating through the floor joists to my ears below. Someone spoke, but I couldn't make out their words. It caused the man amongst the hay to stir. A great deal of gas exited his person. Raising his head and taking in the surroundings, he soon realized he wasn't alone. It didn't take long for Sean to find his haunch and posture upright.

"Top of the morning, sport. Feeling pretty gassy, aren't you?" I mentioned in a humorous tone.

"Did you get a good rest? That snoring sequence seems to say so. Anyhow, what conclusion have you drawn to last night's question?" I asked.

"Pills. If I had to go, I'd rather take some pills, overdose, or die in my sleep," Divine answered.

"So, I presume you've given this a lot of thought. Why pills of all the ways to meet your maker?" I asked genuinely.

"Yes. Since death is often painful to others, hopefully, the manner in itself can bring closure by helping them heal versus a gruesome end," Sean said.

"That's an interesting analogy," I countered.

""Based on my recollection, you've never been concerned for anyone's pain or suffering. I surely didn't receive any consideration prior to your testimony. What makes you different now from the person you were in July of 2003, when you pointed me out in court and told your lies on the stand for a sentence reduction?" I retorted coldly.

"You turned on the faucet the moment you set foot in the county. And for what?!" I both asked and demanded to know, still incredulous regarding events from two decades ago.

Sean's eyes were largely diverted to the floor during the discourse. He also understood justice being either one's reward or penalty for chosen ways and actions. This wound had refused to heal and was quite raw.

"I'm sorry, Preme," Sean said in a barely audible voice. Tears were beginning to flow down his jowls.

"Pardon? My ears didn't quite grasp your comment," I told him.

He sniffled heavily, considering whether or not to look me in the eye. "I'm sorry for what I did to you," Divine had spoken louder.

"Do you mean by testifying?" I asked.

"The problem didn't begin there, obviously. You had been harboring ill sentiments far longer than I'd realized to commit such treason." I massaged my temples for a moment.

"Are you sorry for breaking your honor then, or because you're in a pickle?" I asked, posing a catch-22 scenario.

"Both," uttered the caged man. I shook my head in disapproval.

"You shouldn't have gotten back into the streets when you came home in '97 if you knew you couldn't hold water. In open court, those government people were trying to create ways to give me the death penalty plus three additional federal indictments. They even attempted to pursue the arrest of my mother."

I stood and began pacing the floor slowly. "Still, I held firm. Did you know that sometime in March of 2019, two homicide detectives came all the way from Rochester to see me, in Berlin? One was from Gates; the other a N.Y.S. Trooper. They had the nerve to ask some questions pertaining to murders committed during 2012. I'm pretty sure it was. These crimes unfolded some eleven years after my incarceration."

Sean watched my movements with great desperation, holding on to each word. "Come to find out, you were the prime suspect. They were praying I'd be bitter enough to give you a taste of your own medicine, so to speak."

I ceased in movement, facing Divine.

"Needless to say, the help or information they were desperately longing for wasn't available." My pacing continued.

"Would you believe," I said, turning to face him once more, "that the law people asked how I could still show honor and loyalty to someone like you after all you've done to me?"

I took a seat facing the captive, sipped some orange juice, wetting my palate. "It finally shone on me that they would never comprehend the position or stance illustrated. Revenge upon you shall never come through serving the oppressor. I'm not willing to live with that type of self-compromise. 'Tis the very reason you're in this cage and not some U.S. prison." After another sip of juice, I set the glass down and approached him.

"It seems when you were picked up for a robbery and double homicide in Gates you had something else to say. What was it?"

I pondered the thought, holding my chin between the thumb and forefinger of my right hand.

"Something about a code. That it went against the code to kill a white woman with blonde hair. As a result, you could have never been involved. Those lawmen drove so many hours to ask about this code you speak of. I laughed a good laugh while their faces went from pale to radish red with disappointment." I stretched slowly and yawned loudly. "It must've been one of the goofiest statements I've ever heard.

"One thing's for sure. You can't keep your mouth closed. I'll be back shortly. There's someone I'd like for you to meet."

A short time later, I returned with two of my comrades. In our company, there was a man being pushed along in a wheelchair. His face and shoulders were covered by a leather waist-length jacket. His hands rested in his lap and were handcuffed at the wrists. The brakes on the wheelchair were locked into place once it had been parked before Divine. Sean stared at the unknown person now stationed before him. I removed the jacket, unveiling the person beneath. Jerod's eyes adjusted to the lighting. Before long, he was able to realize there was a naked man inside of some kind of cage filled with straw, only a few feet away. I began to share some insight.

"There may or may not be a need to introduce you two. For all I know, you both are having some type of dealings. Lord only knows what you scumbags were out there doing. Something my grandma used to say, minus the scumbag description. You remember my grandmother, don't you, fat man?" I asked with cold eyes.

"How many times have you eaten her food? Too many to recall, right? Don't worry, you won't need to."

Turning on my pivot towards the table, I took an object from my pocket. With my back to the captives, I held the object overhead, commenting, "This is what you two have in common." I inserted a la into the digital recorder and pressed play. The testimony of Jerod Marten began.

***

AUSA Shirkin: When did you first become associated with Luda?
Marten/J.: I'd say around 1988.

AUSA Shirkin: Is Luda present in this courtroom today?

Marten/J.: That's him, wearing a white sweater. He's sitting next to the man with long, straight hair and salt-and-pepper sideburns.

The witness pointed to Luda, seated at the defense table.

AUSA Shirkin: Your Honor, the witness has confirmed the identity of the defendant. May the record reflect.
Judge Sarasota: The record so reflects.

AUSA Shirkin: Do you know anyone who is known as Mateen?
Marten/J.: Yes.

AUSA Shirkin: How long have you been acquainted with this person?
Marten/J.: I'd say 12 to 15 years.

AUSA Shirkin: Do you see Mateen in the courtroom?
Marten/J.: I do.

AUSA Shirkin: Please indicate for the court Mateen's location.
Marten/J.: He's sitting next to the man in a dark blue pin-striped suit, a sky-blue shirt with a matching paisley tie and handkerchief. Mateen's got on a yellow shirt.

AUSA Shirkin: Let the record reflect that the witness has confirmed the identification of Lamont Paige.
Judge Sarasota: The record so acknowledges.

AUSA Shirkin: Directing your attention to the autumn of 2001, were you in contact with Supreme?
Marten/J.: I was.

AUSA Shirkin: Where did this contact take place?
Marten/J.: In Rochester.

AUSA Shirkin: And the purpose of this contact?
Marten/J.: It was drug-related.

AUSA Shirkin: What made this contact between you and Supreme drug-related?
Marten/J.: I wanted to buy some drugs.

AUSA Shirkin: Why did you want to purchase drugs?
Marten/J.: To resell them.

AUSA Shirkin: How much did you pay for the eight ball?
Marten/J.: $150.

AUSA Shirkin: Do you recall whether other people were present during the purchase?
Marten/J.: No.

AUSA Shirkin: Did you have any other drug transactions with Supreme?
Marten/J.: Not directly.

(There was an outburst of muttering from the spectators, both angry and inaudible. Judge Sarasota rapped the gavel twice before speaking.)

Judge Sarasota: Excuse me... Ladies and gentlemen, this is directed to the disruptive spectators in the courtroom. Should you feel it necessary to share in dialogue, please remove yourselves from the trial. Please continue, Mr. Shirkin.

AUSA Shirkin: How were you communicating with others around this time?
Marten/J.: Cell phones.

AUSA Shirkin: Did you ever speak to Luda after having this discussion with Supreme?
Marten/J.: I did.

AUSA Shirkin: How did the conversation come to be?
Marten/J.: We spoke by phone and in person.

AUSA Shirkin: And the purpose of this communication?
Marten/J.: I only called and met up with him to buy drugs.

AUSA Shirkin: What were you purchasing from Mr. Junior Lopez?
Marten/J.: Eight balls of crack cocaine.

AUSA Shirkin: From late 2001 until your arrest in 2002, how often did you see Luda?
Marten/J.: On a daily basis.

AUSA Shirkin: In what area of Rochester were you seeing him?
Marten/J.: Around Jefferson Avenue.

AUSA Shirkin: Did you and Luda ever discuss the activities of other dealers, or who they were supplying?
Defense Counsel E. Baker: Objection—compound.
Judge Sarasota: Sustained.

AUSA Shirkin: What did you do with the drugs you bought from Supreme?
Marten/J.: Broke them down and sold them.

AUSA Shirkin: And the drugs you acquired from Luda?
Marten/J.: Broke them down and sold them, too.

AUSA Shirkin: Where were you conducting your drug activity in Rochester?
Marten/J.: No place specific. I used to move around a lot.

AUSA Shirkin: Have you ever heard of a location called Maxwell's?
Marten/J.: Yeah, I know it.

AUSA Shirkin: Can you tell us about Maxwell's?
Marten/J.: It's a popular bar out on East Ridge Road.

(Defense Counsel Wolfe suddenly sprang to his feet.)
Defense Counsel Wolfe: Pardon me, Your Honor. Sidebar, please?

Judge Sarasota: Approach.
(There was a bench conference off the record.)

AUSA Shirkin: One moment, please, Your Honor.
Judge Sarasota: Certainly.
(There was a pause in the proceedings.)

AUSA Shirkin: Have you ever been to Maxwell's?
Marten/J.: I have.

AUSA Shirkin: How often would you go to this bar?
Marten/J.: I'd say two or three times a month.

AUSA Shirkin: Was there ever a time when you witnessed any defendants present at Maxwell's?
Marten/J.: Yeah.

AUSA Shirkin: Who was it you saw?
Marten/J.: Lamont Paige----Mateen.

AUSA Shirkin: What year did this occur?
Marten/J.: Early 2002.

Defense Counsel E. Baker: Objection—too broad, Your Honor.
Judge Sarasota: Sustained.

AUSA Shirkin: Do you recall the month of this encounter?
Marten/J.: I'd say February or March.

AUSA Shirkin: Were you social with Mateen on this night in question at Maxwell's?
Marten/J.: I was, yes.

AUSA Shirkin: What did the conversation between the two of you entail?
Marten/J.: We talked about doing some business.

AUSA Shirkin: What type of business are you referring to?
Marten/J.: Drug business.

AUSA Shirkin: To the best of your ability, tell us the details of this conversation between you and Mateen.
Marten/J.: Basically, Mateen said he had good weight for sale, what the prices were, and that he would make himself available whenever, if the money was right.

AUSA Shirkin: This conversation took place where?
Marten/J.: Maxwell's, at the bar.

AUSA Shirkin: Did you buy any drugs that night?
Marten/J.: No.

AUSA Shirkin: When did you next come in contact with Mateen?
Marten/J.: I called him. He told me to come through the neighborhood.

AUSA Shirkin: Where was he at that particular time?
Marten/J.: Lennox and Genesee, on the dead end.

AUSA Shirkin: Would this be in Rochester, New York?
Marten/J.: Rochester, yes.

AUSA Shirkin: Did you meet at a residence or some neutral site?
Marten/J.: Mateen was at Science's house, sitting on the front porch.

AUSA Shirkin: Why did you go over there?
Marten/J.: I needed to buy a gun.

AUSA Shirkin: Did you find a seller?
Marten/J.: Yes.

AUSA Shirkin: Who sold you the gun?
Marten/J.: Lamont Paige a.k.a. Mateen.

AUSA Shirkin: Walk me through the process.

Marten/J.: Once I called, he told me to meet him on Lenox and Genesee. Once there, I explained that I needed some protection—that I wanted to buy a gun.

AUSA Shirkin: What type of gun were you looking for?

Marten/J.: A revolver.

AUSA Shirkin: Was anyone present during this conversation between you and Mateen?

Marten/J.: There were two guys on the porch. Our conversation took place curbside. No one was in hearing range.

AUSA Shirkin: At what point did you buy the gun?

Marten/J.: After telling Mateen the type of gun I wanted, he walked between two houses—on the side where Science lived. He came back with a paper bag, motioned toward my car, and we got inside.

AUSA Shirkin: Where were you and Mateen seated in the vehicle?

Marten/J.: I was in the driver's seat, Mateen in the front passenger seat.

AUSA Shirkin: What happened once inside?

Marten/J.: Mateen handed me the paper bag. I opened it, reached inside, and pulled out a black .38 snub-nose. About 20 bullets were with the gun.

AUSA Shirkin: Previously, you revealed being in custody since April 2002, correct?

Marten/J.: Yes.

AUSA Shirkin: For possession of a firearm?

Marten/J.: Yes.

AUSA Shirkin: Your Honor, I'm going to ask Detective Janute to unseal the sealed contents of this bag.

Judge Sarasota: The record shall so reflect.

AUSA Shirkin: Your Honor, I'd like to introduce the following evidence as Exhibit 27, and its contents as Exhibit 27A.

Judge Sarasota: The record reflects.

(There was a pause in the proceedings. A ghostly quiet haunted the courtroom.)

AUSA Shirkin: Detective Janute is opening Exhibit 27.

Judge Sarasota: Thank you, Mr. Shirkin. Please proceed.

AUSA Shirkin: Mr. Marten, I'm showing you what is now recognized as Exhibit 27A.

The prosecutor handed a large, clear plastic Ziploc bag. Inside: a black snub-nosed .38 special revolver. Six live Black Talon hollow-point bullets rested heavily in one corner of the bag.

AUSA Shirkin: Can you tell me what you're holding?

Marten/J.: It's a gun. Specifically, a .38 special revolver. The bullets are at the bottom of the bag.

AUSA Shirkin: What type of weapon were you arrested for in April 2002?

Marten/J.: This very weapon. *(The witness returned the exhibit to the prosecutor.)*

AUSA Shirkin: And from whom did you buy this gun?

Marten/J.: From Mateen.

AUSA Shirkin: How much did you pay?

Marten/J.: $350.

AUSA Shirkin: Who did you give the $350 to?
Marten/J.: Mateen.

AUSA Shirkin: Was this a cash payment or some form of trade?
Marten/J.: Cash.

AUSA Shirkin: Prior to your 1994 conviction on robbery charges, were you having regular contact with Supreme?
Marten/J.: I was.

AUSA Shirkin: Where did this usually occur?
Marten/J.: On the west side of Rochester—Brown, Clifton, Lennox, Jefferson, Genesee Street.

AUSA Shirkin: What was the nature of your contact with Supreme?
Marten/J.: Buying drugs from him.

AUSA Shirkin: How much were you buying at that time?
Marten/J.: Quarter ounces of powder cocaine.

AUSA Shirkin: How much were you paying for that amount?
Marten/J.: $250, sometimes $300.

AUSA Shirkin: Were these purchases frequent?
Marten/J.: About two or three times a week.

AUSA Shirkin: Was anyone else present when you bought drugs from Supreme?
Marten/J.: No.

AUSA Shirkin: How long were you doing business with Supreme prior to your arrest?
Marten/J.: About a month and a half.

AUSA Shirkin: Did you know where Supreme lived during this time?
Marten/J.: On Lennox and Epworth—corner house.

AUSA Shirkin: Earlier, you mentioned buying drugs from Supreme sometime in 2001. Are you certain of the year and what occurred?

Defense Counsel Wolfe: Objection—leading, Your Honor.
Judge Sarasota: Sustained.

AUSA Shirkin: Where did these drug transactions occur?
Marten/J.: I don't recall.

AUSA Shirkin: May I have a brief moment, Your Honor?
(A pause. AUSA Shirkin conferred quietly with government co-counsel.)

AUSA Shirkin: Do you know anyone by the name of Gerald or Duce?
Marten/J.: Yes. Gerald and Duce are brothers.

AUSA Shirkin: Were you in contact with the brothers anytime during 2001?
Marten/J.: Yes.

AUSA Shirkin: Do you recall where you saw Gerald and Duce?
Marten/J.: On Smith and Broad Street, at the corner store.

AUSA Shirkin: Was this in the city of Rochester?
Marten/J.: Yeah.

AUSA Shirkin: Who else did you see present at this time?
Marten/J.: Supreme was there too—he was exiting the store.

AUSA Shirkin: Tell us what happened next.
Marten/J.: We all got into his Expedition.

AUSA Shirkin: Who do you mean by "we"?
Marten/J.: Supreme, Gerald, Duce, and me.

AUSA Shirkin: Who was driving?
Marten/J.: Supreme.

AUSA Shirkin: Was there anyone else in the car?

Marten/J.: Yeah—a young kid, about 13, was already sitting inside.

AUSA Shirkin: Where did you sit?

Marten/J.: In one of the rear seats.

AUSA Shirkin: Where was Gerald seated?

Marten/J.: He was riding shotgun.

AUSA Shirkin: Was this young person male or female?

Marten/J.: Male.

AUSA Shirkin: Do you recall his name?

Marten/J.: Nah.

AUSA Shirkin: And he was seated where?

Marten/J.: Next to me.

AUSA Shirkin: Did anything stand out while you were driving?

Marten/J.: Supreme was questioning the kid about some money he owed.

AUSA Shirkin: What was said?

Marten/J.: Preme was mostly yelling and cursing at him. When the kid tried to answer, he told him to be quiet.

AUSA Shirkin: What happened next?

Marten/J.: Preme stopped talking for a while and kept driving.

AUSA Shirkin: Where were you going?

Marten/J.: I wasn't sure at first. Preme eventually pulled into the Burger King parking lot on Lyell Avenue.

AUSA Shirkin: Did you order food?

Marten/J.: No. Preme got out of the driver's seat and into the back, where the kid and I were. He started beating the kid with his fists.

AUSA Shirkin: Supreme was beating this young kid?
Marten/J.: Yeah. He punched and slapped his face multiple times—split both his lips, busted his nose really bad, even choked him.

AUSA Shirkin: Where were you during the assault?
Marten/J.: In the back seat, next to them.

AUSA Shirkin: Anything else about this assault?
Marten/J.: Yeah, two things.

AUSA Shirkin: Go ahead.
Marten/J.: When we left Smith and Broad, Gerald and Duce were rolling a couple of Dutches. By the time we got to Burger King, the blunts were in rotation. Preme took a break during the beating, grabbed the blunt from me, puffed it until the cherry was glowing, then exhaled smoke slowly into the kid's face.

(The witness paused, voice trembling before continuing.)

Marten/J.: Supreme grabbed the kid by his lower jaw. The boy screamed as Preme's left hand clamped down like a vise. Slowly, and laughing, Supreme pressed the glowing ember of the Dutch into the kid's face.

The courtroom fell silent. When the shock subsided, members of Jerod Marten's family voiced their disgust. Judge Sarasota banged the gavel for order until the room settled.

AUSA Shirkin: Anything else, Mr. Marten?
Marten/J.: Yes. I noticed Preme had a gun on his waist during the assault—a semi-automatic.

AUSA Shirkin: When did you notice the gun?
Marten/J.: While he was beating and burning the kid.

(A pause in the proceedings.)

AUSA Shirkin: In April 2002, during your arrest for possession of a firearm, did you have your cell phone?
Marten/J.: Yes.

AUSA Shirkin: Was it taken into police custody?
Marten/J.: Yeah.

AUSA Shirkin: Did it have a directory of numbers?
Marten/J.: Yes.

AUSA Shirkin: Was Mateen's number in it?
Marten/J.: Yes.

AUSA Shirkin: Who entered it?
Marten/J.: I did.

AUSA Shirkin: No further questions, Your Honor.

Judge Sarasota: Well then, it's a few minutes past one o'clock, and we previously told the jury we'd recess now. Ladies and gentlemen, remember the admonitions: do not discuss the case among yourselves or with anyone else; report any improper contact; avoid all counsel and parties; conduct no research or investigation; and pay no attention to media coverage. Keep an open mind until the case is finally submitted to you. Drive home safely—we'll see you tomorrow at 8:30. Thank you.

(Court adjourned.)

***

15 August 2003

The court was called to order.

Judge Sarasota: Note the presence of counsel and the defendants. Counsel, I had Mr. Wesley get in touch with you, but I received a call from Ms. Beget, who indicated she was from the Monroe County Public Defender's Office and that she represented Mr. Marten. She informed the Court that he may need representation.

Thereafter, Ms. Beget, Mr. Wesley, and Mr. Shirkin appeared in the Court's chambers. At that time, Mr. Shirkin, on behalf of the Government, stated he did feel Mr. Marten needed an attorney. He indicated they had checked the time frame that Mr. Wolfe had brought to the Court's attention at sidebar—and to counsel's attention—and confirmed that Mr. Murphy was in jail at the time. Therefore, the incident Mr. Marten testified to could not have occurred then.

Mr. Shirkin indicated it was the intent of the Government to move to strike Mr. Marten's testimony. At that point, the Court indicated it was going beyond the assignment of counsel and that I didn't want further discussion until all counsel could be present. I then asked Mr. Wesley to notify counsel of what had occurred.

So that's the stage we're at. I should add one other thing: the Court did assign R.D. Thompson to represent Mr. Marten. In thinking about it, several issues come up. Unfortunately, I can't get on Westlaw, so I don't know what research I can do from the bench. Issue number one, Mr. Shirkin, is whether it is still the Government's intent to strike the testimony of Mr. Marten?

Mr. Shirkin: Your Honor, I believe Mr. Thompson is speaking to Mr. Marten right now, and I was hoping to have an opportunity to hear back from him after that conversation. At the moment, I don't anticipate anything that would change the Government's view.

Judge Sarasota: What he is saying is, if the Government moves to strike the testimony, I'll throw the ball to the Defense. Do you want it stricken—or, and again, I'm not saying there might not be other motions—do you want it stricken, or do you want to highlight to the jury the fact that the witness was not being truthful? Mr. Wolfe?

Mr. Wolfe: Your Honor, before we even get to that issue, the first thing I want to address to the Court is that, after the sidebar in which the discrepancy in time was brought to the prosecutor's attention, there was testimony about an incident in 2001 involving this young kid being beaten up by my client. That's the problem I have—the

170

Government, having notice that this witness was not truthful about the 2001 incident, still elicited testimony about it. You can't go back in time, Your Honor, but they were on notice about this and still brought out the testimony.

Judge Sarasota: What you need to think about are the applications to preserve the record. I can't get on Westlaw, so I'm going from memory, but the issues are post-trial issues. To the extent—and again, I can't get online—but I seem to recall the cases are clear: where the Government knew or should have known that the witness was committing perjury, that doesn't necessitate a directed verdict. It's a post-trial matter. We're at trial. What you're indicating is that the Government should have known. I don't think—and Mr. Wolfe, you're not indicating—that the Government did know, but you are indicating they should have known that Anthony Murphy was in jail at the time the witness was testifying about the events.

Mr. Wolfe: Obviously, mistakes happen at trial, and I'm not saying they don't. But my point is that after the fact of knowing—being on notice—that Mr. Murphy was incarcerated at the time this witness was testifying about, ten minutes after starting, it was brought to the prosecutor's attention that this event couldn't have happened in 2001. It was also directed to your attention, and they still elicited the testimony about it.

It's my intention to move for a mistrial because of the inflammatory nature of the testimony and the prejudice to the jury. We could strike the testimony and tell the jury to disregard it, but my issue is that the prosecutor was aware that, in 2001, these two individuals could not have had any contact on the street—and still went into facts that were alleged to have occurred in 2001.

Judge Sarasota: So the record is clear, and either side can have an exception to the Court's ruling. What I want to do is put on the record— to the extent we did not—what our sidebar conversation was, because obviously that is not on the record. Place on the record what occurred at the sidebar, and I'll see if I can get this up.

(There was a pause in the proceedings.)

AUSA Shirkin: I'm going to direct your attention to 2001, late in the year. Did you have an occasion to have any contact with Anthony Murphy or Supreme?
Marten/J.: Yes.

AUSA Shirkin: And where was that?
Marten/J.: In the City of Rochester.

AUSA Shirkin: And how did you come to have contact with Supreme at that time?
Marten/J.: About some drugs.

Judge Sarasota: Mr. Wolfe, that's the point you objected to. So that's the context. There was testimony about late 2001. You objected. Put on the record your recollection of the bench conference.

Mr. Wolfe: My recollection of the bench conference is: I brought to the attention of the Prosecutor and the Court that Marten/J. had been released from prison on October 5, 2001, and that, by that fact alone, they could have had no contact on the street in the year 2001.

Judge Sarasota: And what was your recollection, if any, of Mr. Wesley's or Mr. Shirkin's response?

Mr. Wolfe: My recollection of Mr. Shirkin's response was that he had to check his notes.

Judge Sarasota: I do recall Mr. Wesley... Mr. Shirkin said he had to check—that's my recollection. So I'll toss it to Mr. Wesley and Mr. Shirkin. Did you determine—now, you indicated that subsequent to that, there was testimony about an incident involving...
Mr. Wolfe: ...an incident involving Gerald, Duce, Anthony Murphy, and a young kid, in the year 2001, where I believe it was Gerald, Duce, and/or Mr. Marten who were picked up at Broad and Smith Street.

172

Judge Sarasota: I'm going later in the testimony, so the record is clear, after the bench conference.

AUSA Shirkin: Did you have occasion to be with somebody known as Gerald and Duce in 2001?
Marten/J.: Yes.

AUSA Shirkin: Where was that?
Marten/J.: On Broad and State Street—excuse me, Broad and Smith Street.

AUSA Shirkin: Is that in the City of Rochester?
Marten/J.: Yes.

AUSA Shirkin: Did you have occasion to see Supreme there?
Marten/J.: Yes.

AUSA Shirkin: Where was he?
Marten/J.: At the store on the corner.

AUSA Shirkin: What happened at that point?
Marten/J.: Got in the car.

AUSA Shirkin: Who did?
Marten/J.: I did.

AUSA Shirkin: Anybody else?
Marten/J.: Supreme and Gerald and Duce.

AUSA Shirkin: Who was driving?
Marten/J.: Supreme.

AUSA Shirkin: After you got in the car, was there anybody else in the car?
Marten/J.: Yeah, a young kid.

AUSA Shirkin: And did you know his name?

Marten/J.: No.

Judge Sarasota: Here's the question: "Did you have occasion to be with somebody known as Gerald and Duce in 2001?" Is this any more specific? You're indicating that Mr. Marten got out of jail on October 5—

Mr. Wolfe: 2001.

Judge Sarasota: When did he go to jail?

Mr. Wolfe: 1995.

Judge Sarasota: From 1995 to 2001, he was in jail. So the point is that at no time in 2001 could he have been on the street with your client?

Mr. Wolfe: Correct.

Judge Sarasota: Mr. Shirkin, does the Government agree with that?

Mr. Shirkin: Well, it certainly agrees now, for sure. Let me first say I agree with Mr. Wolfe's recitation of what he said at the sidebar—the original sidebar—and that the Government said it needed to check. There were two things that needed to be checked, Judge. One was when Murphy went in and remained in, and that was, we believe, toward the end of August 2001—which was confirmed after court yesterday. And as of the time we were in court, what we were working off of was the criminal history record from the State of New York—the rap sheet from Mr. Marten—which indicated he went on parole on October 5, 2001. What we were not able to check until we got out of court was to speak to Parole and check the Department of Corrections to confirm that it was correct.

Judge Sarasota: Wait a second. You have a NYSIS. Doesn't the NYSIS indicate when he was sentenced?

Mr. Shirkin: Yes.

Judge Sarasota: When was he sentenced?

Mr. Shirkin: In 1995.

Judge Sarasota: The first thing it shows thereafter is that he was paroled in 2001.

Mr. Shirkin: Right. But the NYSIS reports are not always correct with regard to the release dates.

Judge Sarasota: What does it say he got as a sentence?

Mr. Wolfe: Four to eight.

Mr. Shirkin: Four to eight, and his original release date was January of 2000.

(There was a pause in the proceedings.)

Judge Sarasota: The point is, he was in jail at the time; Mr. Wolfe brought that to your attention. Here's how I see the argument: Mr. Wolfe, at sidebar, brings to the attention of the Government that—listen—this event could not have happened with Supreme because—

(There was a pause in the proceedings.)

Judge Sarasota: First alternate, Jimmy Johnson, has called my chambers this morning. He said he has a swollen foot, is in pain, and went to the doctor's office. His doctor's office is not open yet—he's waiting outside. Can you ask him: Is this a recurring condition? Has he been treated for it before? Is this something that occurred out of the blue? Can he walk? Can he not walk? I assume you can't transfer this to me up here—see if you can.

(There was a pause in the proceedings.)

Judge Sarasota: Let's wait to resolve the Mr. Johnson issue.

(There was another pause in the proceedings. The judge had telephonic communication with Juror Johnson.)

Judge Sarasota: Counsel, hopefully you heard most of my conversation. I'll throw this out—he is our first alternate. The jury looks healthy; he may not sit anyway, but I want to leave it to the attorneys to determine whether he stays. I will note he is the only African-American on the jury panel, and I'm conscious of that. We have had a conference with counsel that, because of Mr. Johnson's condition, he may not—it didn't appear that he was paying as close attention as some of the other jurors. So let's think about that issue, and then we'll go back to the one we have. So, if I understand, Mr. Shirkin, what you're indicating is that from the review of the NYSIS— that's the printout from Criminal Justice Services—it did appear from the NYSIS that this... Let me go back. Was the Government aware when Mr. Murphy was taken into custody?

Mr. Shirkin: I'm going to say yes, because even if I wasn't thinking about it, certainly I should be aware.

Judge Sarasota: It certainly should be pointed out that Mr. Wolfe did point out at sidebar—I think you said August 23?

Mr. Wolfe: I have the PACER report, and he was arrested on August 23. I don't know what time, but—

Judge Sarasota: Here's the issue, Mr. Shirkin, that Mr. Wolfe seems to be raising. Obviously, this case involves a lot of witnesses. While certainly you may have at one time been aware of it, it's easy to forget. However, Mr. Wolfe specifically indicates his client was in custody as of August 23, 2001. From Mr. Marten's NYSIS, which the Government had, it appeared he was released—was paroled—in October.

Mr. Shirkin: Well, we got interrupted as I was in the middle of explaining.

Judge Sarasota: What does the NYSIS indicate?

Mr. Shirkin: 3500-1-C, for robbery in the second degree; he had a conditional release on January 7, 2000, and then the next entry says he went on parole on October 5, 2001.

Now, with respect to the incident he testified about after the sidebar—before the Court—before he testified, the Government independently had obtained information that the incident involving 2G and the beating had taken place. With respect to Mr. Marten's testimony, while I would certainly say I was not focusing at the time on what Mr. Wolfe pointed out at the sidebar, having independently determined that in fact the incident took place, and with the fact that there was some issue—in both the Court's and the Government's mind—about whether Mr. Marten could have been available to participate in it, until we confirmed yesterday afternoon exactly what the release date was, that part of his testimony did not seem out of the question.

Judge Sarasota: Here's what I'm missing. The conditional release date and the maximum expiration date are two dates set when he's sentenced. It appears clear to the Court that this says he was released from the New York State Department of Corrections on 10/5/01. Here's the issue: having known that—and I'm not suggesting you didn't have independent information—but Mr. Marten testified he was present, and he could not have been present. He could not have been present on the date he indicated, and the Defense alerted you to the fact that when he testified to contact with Mr. Murphy in 2001, it simply could not have happened.

So he testified to this contact—whether it was buying drugs with Murphy and Defendant Junior Lopez, or this incident—he said he was present for.
Mr. Shirkin: So the—

Judge Sarasota: Let me ask you this: the information you had that it occurred—when did the other individuals say it occurred?
Mr. Shirkin: Well, the information I had originally was simply, yes, the incident had taken place. When further inquiry was made after court yesterday about it, I couldn't get a specific date. But it was

possible, and it continues to raise questions in my mind about Mr. Marten's participation in it.

Judge Sarasota: Here's the situation the Court has to decide. I'm not accusing you of intentionally doing anything, and I'm making the record clear. But the issue is beyond that—should the Government have known, especially after Mr. Wolfe alerted them, that eliciting testimony from Mr. Marten concerning contact with Mr. Murphy in 2001 would, in effect, be untruthful?

Mr. Shirkin: Well, Your Honor, with respect to the drug transaction— that testimony occurred prior to sidebar—I would say there is no question we should have known that was impossible. Obviously, if I were looking to create false testimony, I would do it in a better way.

Judge Sarasota: I want to set the record straight. I'm not suggesting you were trying to create false testimony. You have 25 witnesses, and most of them are receiving benefits or seeking benefits. If I find—and I think I would have to—that the Government should have known that the testimony concerning transactions between Mr. Murphy, Mr. Junior Lopez, and Mr. Marten, as Mr. Marten testified to, could not have occurred—

Mr. Shirkin: But again, I want the record to be clear, Your Honor— with respect to Mr. Junior Lopez, there is nothing that was testified to that is impossible to have occurred.

Judge Sarasota: You're correct, other than the fact that he indicated that—

Mr. Shirkin: —he was referred to Junior Lopez by Murphy.

Mr. Nappa: Correct. Other than the conversation where Murphy said, *"Go talk to Luda,"* could not have occurred.

Judge Sarasota: Right. I stand corrected. Clearly, he could have had contact with Mr. Junior Lopez, but as Mr. Nappa points out, it may make his entire testimony suspect.

Judge Sarasota (cont'd): Here's the issue before me: If I find that the Government should have known that the testimony of Mr. Marten—specifically concerning his contact with Mr. Murphy, including the testimony that Mr. Murphy referred him to Mr. Junior Lopez—was untrue, now we're at the point of determining the remedy. You're asking for a mistrial?

Mr. Wolfe: That is my request.

Judge Sarasota: So we have a record. Is anyone joining in the application?

Mr. Nappa: Your Honor, on behalf of Mr. Junior Lopez, I would join in the application for a mistrial.

Mr. E. James: Mr. Stinson would join in that.

Mr. Molt: We are not asking for a mistrial, Your Honor.

Judge Sarasota: So procedurally, the posture we're at is this: Mr. Wolfe is moving for a mistrial, Mr. Nappa is moving for a mistrial, Mr. E. James is moving for a mistrial, and Mr. Molt is not.

The Court finds the Government should have known that the testimony given by Mr. Marten was untruthful with respect to his contact with Mr. Murphy, because it simply could not have occurred in 2001 as he indicated. Mr. Shirkin, what is the Government's position on what the appropriate remedy should be?

Mr. Shirkin: Your Honor, as indicated—and as we intended to do yesterday afternoon—we would move to strike his testimony. I would also add that I know Mr. Thompson is now in the courtroom. I haven't had a chance to speak to him, and that might affect things also. But the Government, obviously, in light of what occurred yesterday, is not looking to rely in any way on the testimony of Mr. Marten.

Judge Sarasota: We'll let Mr. Thompson be heard in a moment. The application is for a mistrial; the Government's response is that the correct relief would be to strike the testimony. The Court does not believe a mistrial is called for, but would consider a curative instruction.

The curative instruction the Court would contemplate is simply what the Court has said: that defense counsel brought to the attention of the Court and the Government that the events testified to by Mr. Marten involving Mr. Murphy could not have occurred. I do not want to indicate that Mr. Murphy was in prison. The Government acknowledges that Mr. Marten was untruthful in that regard.

The Court finds that the Government should have known, when they put Mr. Marten on the stand, that these events to which he testified could not have occurred when he said they did. The Court, therefore, upon application of the Government, is striking his testimony. That's one option.

Option number two—I don't know what option two is. Obviously, if I were to assume that any... And Mr. Thompson, this is where you come in: If Mr. Marten were put back on the stand, would it be fair to say that you would—there are two issues—can he purge himself of the perjury, or would it be your advice to Mr. Marten, as his counsel, to take the Fifth?

Mr. Thompson: I want to talk to Mr. Shirkin first, Judge.

Judge Sarasota: Okay. I'm thinking of the option short of a mistrial, and the Court is not inclined to grant a mistrial because I think the instruction the Court would give is certainly consistent with the defense theory—and that is, guess what, cooperating individuals lie to gain a benefit for themselves. That's certainly what the defense commented on in openings, and—

Mr. Molt: Your Honor, if I could be heard, I could have a suggestion.

Judge Sarasota: Yes.

Mr. Molt: Again, at the sidebar, it was made very clear to the Government that Mr. Murphy was in custody at the time these events were being testified to, and the Government persisted in offering the testimony without checking. Then there was a break, and they came back and offered more. My suggestion is that the Government be admonished in the presence of the jury for offering false testimony, which is, at the very least, in reckless disregard for the truth.

Judge Sarasota: No. What I would do, as I said, is tell the jury that the Government should have known—and I'm making that finding. The Government should have known the testimony was untrue.

Mr. E. James: Section 26-3, Federal Criminal Procedure, page 435, first full paragraph—the section on new trial motions—the editors talk about where, and you highlighted this, *"where the Government knew or should have known of the perjury."*

Judge Sarasota: *"Perjury Claims"*—is that the caption?
Mr. E. James: Yes.

Judge Sarasota: What paragraph—first?

Mr. E. James: First full paragraph, second sentence, where it says, *"Where the Government knows or should have known."*

Judge Sarasota: Okay. Here's the issue, though, and that's the point I was trying to make. The *Wallach* case, with which the Court is very familiar, was a post-verdict remedy. The Court feels it can effectively deal with the issue we have here, so it's not inclined to grant a mistrial.

In other words, in all the cases you're going to find where the verdict was set aside—and some where it was not—where the Government knew or should have known there was perjury, those situations were post-verdict. Here, we're in the middle of a trial.

So, for the record, the Court feels it can give an effective curative instruction. The effective curative instruction would be along the lines

I'm suggesting. To the extent that counsel has input, I'm open to suggestions.

Again, what I would tell the jury is exactly what occurred—that at a sidebar conference, Mr. Wolfe brought to the Court's attention that incidents Mr. Marten testified to, and was expected to testify to, regarding contact with Anthony Murphy in 2001 could not have occurred.

Mr. E. James: And that's by way of explanation as to why you're striking Mr. Marten's testimony.

Judge Sarasota: No—and I'm going to continue. The Court has now determined that this is correct: when Mr. Marten testified to contact with Mr. Murphy in 2001, it was untruthful—it was perjury. I find that the Government should have known that what he was testifying to was untruthful.

Now, upon application of the Government—because it is on the Government's application—the Court is striking the testimony. That means you may not consider it in any way. If you want me to, I will strike it. Now, you may not want me to strike it—you may want me to leave it based on that instruction—and I would give you that option to argue. Your theory of the defense is that cooperating individuals lie.

So, I'm offering the defense this: I'm not going to grant a mistrial. To the extent Mr. Shirkin made a motion to strike, if you're joining that and there's no objection, then—let's go on the record.

Let me make this clear so the record is preserved. There is a motion for a mistrial by three defense counsel. That is denied.

The basis for the Court's denial is this: the Court believes that an effective curative instruction can be given. The Court has given this jury instructions throughout the trial, and the jury appears to be following them conscientiously. Therefore, the Court believes that under the circumstances, an appropriate instruction can be given.

Mr. E. James has directed the Court to *Federal Criminal Practice: A Second Circuit Handbook*, section 26-3, which discusses remedies upon perjury. In the *Wallach* case, which is cited and with which the Court is familiar, the witness who perjured himself was the key witness—the centerpiece of the Government's case. The perjury was uncovered after the verdict.

That is not the situation we have here. There have been numerous individuals who have testified. Mr. Marten is hardly the centerpiece of the case—the one key witness upon whom a finding of guilt or innocence would be made. So, the Court does not feel a mistrial is appropriate because of the distinction between this case and *Wallach*, both substantively and procedurally.

However, the Court would be inclined to give a curative instruction. If the defense does not want any, I will not give one. If you want me to give it, but do not want any input, I will fashion the corrective instruction myself. The motion is to strike the testimony. If there are no objections to striking the testimony, the Court will do so and give a curative instruction. I need input from the defense.

Mr. Molt: First of all, Your Honor, I have consulted with my client on the motion to strike, and—whether other defense counsel want to join in the motion to strike Mr. Marten's testimony after you give a curative instruction to the jury—while you're doing that—

Mr. Shirkin: And, Your Honor, perhaps while counsel are talking to their clients and thinking, if I could, I'd like to talk to Mr. Thompson, and then we'll have everything in place.

Judge Sarasota: Certainly.

(There was a pause in the proceedings.)

Judge Sarasota: Counsel, also, when we come back, Mr. Jones is due to call at 10:00, so I would like a decision on Mr. Johnson. Again, it may be in everyone's best interest if we excuse him. If you don't want to, however, I will consider adjourning the proceedings to see if he becomes available on Monday; however, he is an alternate. Our jury seems relatively healthy and has been pretty conscientious in coming in—especially considering what happened yesterday. It's amazing that they made it by 8:30.

Mr. Nappa: Your Honor, regarding the decisions to be made, is it possible we could stand in recess?

Judge Sarasota: Yes. What we'll do is recess for 10 minutes.
Mr. Wolfe: Thank you.

(The Court was recessed and reconvened.)

Judge Sarasota: Note the presence of counsel and the defendants. Mr. Shirkin, has the Government's position changed at all?
Mr. Shirkin: No.

Judge Sarasota: I want to make the record clear. One thing I want to clarify—Mr. Shirkin, you indicated before placing Mr. Marten on the stand that the Government had information that the incident involving the beating of the young boy had occurred, but did not have a time frame. In other words—
Mr. Shirkin: —didn't have a time frame from the independent source.

Judge Sarasota: Right. After court, you talked to your independent source and got a time frame?

Mr. Shirkin: Well, we got a range that didn't give us any further comfort that Mr. Marten could be correct.

Judge Sarasota: Would it be fair to say that the range you received from the independent source led you to come to court to indicate that Mr. Marten committed perjury?

Mr. Shirkin: We certainly believe that Mr. Marten was untruthful in his testimony. And let's be clear, it was in the range that he testified at the meeting.

Judge Sarasota: Well, let's not mince words—he was committing perjury.

Mr. Shirkin: Well, I'm not in his head. From my standpoint, it's untruthful information.

Mr. Wolfe: Here's my problem—it is the defense that alerted the prosecutor to the testimony.

Judge Sarasota: Now, let me indicate where I stand. I've indicated I'm not granting the motion for mistrial. I've explained why and cited the *Wallach* case, both procedurally and substantively. Here's where we stand: There is a motion to strike by the Government outstanding before the Court. The defense, at this point, has joined it. The Court has indicated a willingness to give a curative instruction. The defense has not yet responded. Your exception to my denial of the mistrial is preserved.

The curative instruction—

Mr. Wolfe: I want to speak on behalf of all the defense counsel. We want it clear, in our summations, we want to be allowed to comment on his perjury and the fact that the Court found him to have committed perjury.

Judge Sarasota: Well, here's the situation. If I strike the testimony, counsel cannot comment on it in summation, and the jury cannot consider it.

If you oppose the motion to strike, I will not strike it. In that case, Mr. Marten will retake the stand and undergo cross-examination. If he takes the Fifth, I will allow him to do so in front of the jury because he has already testified. The situations where it is not done in front of the jury are when there is advance notice that a witness may take the Fifth before testifying.

If he takes the Fifth—so, Mr. Wolfe, if you were to ask, *"Isn't it true you lied on the stand when you indicated my client..."* and he takes the Fifth—that would be in the presence of the jury.

Judge Sarasota (cont'd): If his testimony is not stricken, then it is certainly a fair comment. It's not to say the jury couldn't—because I would give a perjury instruction—that they must... I will indicate to the jury in my curative instruction that I found he committed perjury, after his testimony is concluded, and I will include a similar instruction in my final charge to the jury.

Here's what I'm saying, and I want it clear because this is obviously a significant issue for the defense: If you continue to join in the motion to strike, I will bring the jury out, give a curative instruction, and indicate that I have stricken his testimony. I'm telling you, normally you can't comment on testimony that has been stricken. If you give me case law to indicate otherwise, I will obviously consider it; you would have an opportunity to do so before summations. But typically, a jury is told they cannot consider testimony that is stricken, and I don't know that the defense can have it both ways. You can't say, *"We want the testimony stricken, but we also want to tell the jury to consider it as a negative."* In other words, remember all that testimony from Mr. Marten? He lied, and then make whatever argument you want. With the testimony stricken, you can't comment on it.

Mr. E. James: Your Honor, can I make a point?

Judge Sarasota: Let me finish the options. Option 2: You oppose the motion. Mr. Marten is put back on the stand, and you, Mr. Wolfe—I forget where we are—but to reopen your cross, I'll allow certain questions. He can either answer them, or, as I would guess, Mr. Thompson may advise him to take the Fifth, and I will allow that to be done in the presence of the jury.

So, for example, if you said, *"Isn't it true you lied yesterday when you said you were with Mr. Murphy in 2001?"* and he takes the Fifth, that's going to be in front of the jury.

After his testimony concludes—if it becomes obvious he's not going to testify—then I will give the explanation and curative instruction. The explanation will be: *"The Court finds, and all parties agree"*—unless, Mr. Shirkin, you don't—that I make an affirmative finding of perjury.

Mr. Shirkin: Your Honor, I think Mr. Thompson wants to be heard. Certainly, I think the jury should be instructed that the testimony was untruthful, or however you want to phrase it, but— I can let Mr. Thompson speak to it—but I think Mr. Thompson considers it a legal finding that at this stage doesn't—

Judge Sarasota: No, there is case law that would require me to make a finding of perjury. It's not *beyond a reasonable doubt* for purposes of trial; it's upon sufficient evidence. The Government is giving me sufficient evidence. The Government is telling me that, based on your conversations, the event he testified to—not only was he wrong on the time, but you're telling me the only independent information you have is that he could not have been there because he would have been in jail during the time frame it occurred. Isn't that what you said?

Mr. Shirkin: That is what I said.
Judge Sarasota: Okay.

Mr. E. James: Regarding summation—if you grant the motion to strike the testimony and your explanation to the jury is your curative instruction—would we be allowed in summation to comment on your curative to the jury?

Judge Sarasota: I haven't looked at that issue, and I tried, but Westlaw is down. I can only tell you at this point—I'm not sure. I don't think so, because normally the rule is that what I tell the jury is they can't consider testimony that has been stricken. What can you do in summation? You can comment on the evidence and suggest to the jury reasonable inferences to be drawn from the evidence. If testimony is stricken, it is not evidence.

Mr. E. James: But what you said on the record can be commented upon. What you told the jury can be commented upon without getting into Mr. Marten's testimony.

Judge Sarasota: Well, all I am saying, Mr. James, is that I don't really know the answer—but Mr. Marten is no longer part of the case. So again, I'm not sure, but normally you couldn't get up and say—I mean, I won't even be mentioning him in the charge again unless you ask me to.

If you do ask me to, what I would say is: *"Ladies and gentlemen, remember that the Court has stricken the testimony of Jerod Marten. You cannot consider his testimony in any way in reaching your decision."* That's the black-letter law that is usually given when testimony has been stricken. *"Remember my opening instruction—in reaching your decision, you cannot consider testimony that has been stricken."*

So those are the options as I see them.

If I grant the motion to strike and the defense joins it, I'll bring the jury out, give them the curative instruction, and explain that the testimony has been stricken. In my final instructions, I will repeat that since it's been stricken, they may not consider it in any way when reaching their verdict.

If the defense does **not** want it stricken, we'll resume with Mr. Marten. He will take the stand, and I will allow some questioning until it becomes apparent whether he is going to invoke his Fifth Amendment rights. If he does, then at that point I will give a curative instruction. If the defense moves to strike at that point, I would consider it.

Let me explain—on a motion to strike testimony for invocation of the Fifth, the testimony is **not** stricken if the invocation is on a collateral matter, meaning a matter going only to credibility. For example, if you said, *"Isn't it true that on such-and-such a date you were convicted of a* *crime?"* and he took the Fifth—that's a bad example—but if he took the Fifth on a collateral matter, then the testimony is not stricken. In that case, I would give an instruction to the effect: *"You heard him take the Fifth. You may consider that in determining whether you believe the witness."*

If it's **not** a collateral matter—if it goes to the heart of his testimony—then upon application, I would strike it in its entirety.

Judge Sarasota (cont'd): Even then, if the application is made by the defense because he refuses to answer questions central to his testimony as opposed to collateral matters, we're still back to the same point—it's stricken, and I instruct the jury they may not consider it for any reason.

So frankly, because of how and why we got here, and because the Court feels—based on the appropriate law—that a motion for mistrial should not lie at this stage, I am denying the motion for mistrial. Again, I say that both procedurally—we are in the middle of the trial—and substantively—Mr. Marten is not the only witness who incriminates the defendant. This is therefore distinct from the *Wallach* case.

Now, I'm throwing the ball to the defense for what you believe is the appropriate cure.

Mr. E. James: Again, we would join the Government's motion to strike Mr. Marten's testimony.

Mr. Wolfe: That's on behalf of Mr. Stinson. Stinson should oppose that.

Mr. E. James: I want—

Mr. Wolfe: And I would want Mr. Marten to take the stand, and I would like the opportunity to question him concerning his testimony.

Judge Sarasota: I'm going to give the defense a chance to confer so you can discuss the options.

Mr. E. James: Your Honor, we have already conferred, and I don't see—

Judge Sarasota: Again, I wanted to put all the options on the record.

(There was a pause in the proceedings.)

Mr. Shirkin: Your Honor—

Judge Sarasota: Counsel, Mr. Shirkin wants to place something on the record. Please go ahead.

Mr. Shirkin: I'm requesting a twenty-minute recess to go back up to my office and confer before we resolve whatever is going to happen.

Judge Sarasota: I will give you a break; however, let me say that this is not a finding beyond a reasonable doubt. This is not a situation where such a finding is required. Again, I don't have access to Westlaw at the moment, but I believe the applicable citation is *Montaleone*, 257 F.3d 210, at page 219.

The relevant cases include *Wallach*, 935 F.2d 445; *Napue*, 360 U.S. 264; another Supreme Court case, 427 U.S. 927; *Helmsley*, 985 F.2d 1202; and *Montaleone*, 257 F.3d 210.

The instruction I would give—tailored depending on whether the witness claims the Fifth or whether the defense joins the application to strike without the witness retaking the stand—would be essentially this:

"I instruct you that the Government witness, Marten/J., perjured himself concerning portions of his testimony regarding contact he claimed to have had with Anthony Murphy in August 2001. To 'perjure himself' means that the witness did so willfully, and not as a result of confusion, faulty memory, or mistake.

I further instruct you that when a witness lies about a material—that is, important—matter, you, the jury, as the triers of fact, are free to reject the witness's entire testimony on the principle that one who testifies falsely about one material fact is likely to testify falsely about everything. However, you are not required to find the witness totally unworthy of belief. You may accept such parts of the testimony as you deem true and disregard those you believe false. Since Mr. Marten committed perjury, his testimony should be viewed with caution and great care. It is for you to determine how much of his testimony, if any, you wish to believe."

That is what I would give.

In other words, if the defense joins the Government's motion to strike, there is no need for Mr. Marten to retake the stand. I will bring the jury out, give them that instruction, and indicate that Mr. Marten's testimony has been stricken and they may not consider it for any reason.

Mr. Nappa: Your Honor, then why would you read the portion saying they may consider part of his testimony—

Judge Sarasota: You're right. I would strike that portion. I was thinking of the other situation. You're correct, Mr. Nappa.

Mr. Nappa: Thank you.

Judge Sarasota: If the defense objects to the motion to strike, I would direct Mr. Marten to retake the stand. Mr. Thompson could stand next to him and advise him whether to take the Fifth. I would allow more than one question before invoking the Fifth becomes apparent.

If the refusal to answer concerns a matter central to his testimony, and the defense then moves to strike, I would grant that application. I would then give the same perjury instruction and direct the jury that they may not consider the testimony for any reason.

If the defense does not want it stricken, then I would give the full cautionary instruction I read earlier.

So that we are clear—I do not yet know the answer to whether the defense can comment on Mr. Marten in closing if his testimony is stricken. My initial reaction, without research, is "no," since I will have instructed the jury that they cannot consider stricken testimony.

Those are the options.

Judge Sarasota (cont'd): Mr. Shirkin, how long would you like?

Mr. Shirkin: Half an hour, Your Honor.

Judge Sarasota: I'll give you twenty minutes. We will reconvene at 10:20.

Before we break, Counsel, what do you want me to do with Mr. Johnson? If you want him kept, I am mindful that he is the only African-American on the jury. Since it appears he will not be needed—and all jurors, even those traveling two and a half hours, have been punctual—I propose excusing him. However, if counsel insists on keeping him in case of an emergency, I will recess the jury today and allow him the chance to appear on Monday. There is no guarantee he will return, but—

Mr. Nappa: Do we have the 10 o'clock update from Mr. Johnson, Your Honor?

Judge Sarasota: I didn't get it, but I'll call down.

(Pause in the proceedings.)

Judge Sarasota: Mr. Johnson has not called back. I presume he is seeing his doctor. Does the defense have a position?

Mr. Wolfe: I believe we've been discussing this issue, and we are adamant that we would like him to remain on the jury.

Judge Sarasota: Here's what the Court intends to do. Before we reconvene, I'm going to bring the jury back in and excuse them for the day. I will explain that, in addition to a legal issue, we have been waiting for further word on Mr. Johnson. I see no problem in telling them what I told you: he has a recurring problem with his foot, he went to the doctor, and we are waiting to hear from him.

I am reluctant to excuse him because he has been a part of this jury, and, though he is an alternate, there is still a possibility he may sit. I'm going to recess them for the weekend. Let's bring the jury in.

***

Judge Sarasota: Let the record reflect the presence of counsel, the defendants, and the jury.

Folks, as you can see, one of your number is missing. Let me explain. We did have a legal matter, but just as significant, we are missing one of the jurors. Mr. Johnson called in this morning. He told me that when he woke up, his foot was so swollen he could not get his shoe on. This is apparently a recurring problem for him.

You may recall that during jury selection, he said he had sustained certain injuries. On at least one occasion, he was taking pain medication. He explained that he has a valve problem in his leg which causes fluid to pool in his foot. From time to time, the swelling comes on suddenly, and it appears that is what happened today.

He told me that the condition usually resolves itself if he lies down and elevates his foot above his heart. In the meantime, he went to see his doctor. I told him not to take any chances with his health and to call us again after his appointment. He was due to call back at 10:00, but I have not heard from him, so I assume he is still with his doctor.

Even though he is an alternate, alternates sometimes serve. He has put in significant time on this trial, and unless he is incapacitated, I would like to give him the chance to remain. Therefore, I am releasing you until Monday. This will set us back a day, but we will still finish by the 22nd.

If Mr. Johnson cannot return, I will excuse him at that time. But if he is able and willing, I want to give him that opportunity. He has endured discomfort to be here, and I appreciate his commitment.

I had hoped he would call back to say, "The doctor gave me a pill, and I'm fine," but that does not appear to be the case today. So, we will adjourn.

On the positive side, it's going to be 88 degrees today. If you want to enjoy some of the PGA, we won't keep you here.

Thank you for your patience and cooperation. Please remember the admonitions I've given you:

- Do not discuss the case among yourselves or with anyone else.
- If anyone attempts to talk to you about the case or acts improperly, report it to me immediately.
- Avoid contact with counsel or anyone connected to the case.
- If anything appears in the media, disregard it entirely.
- Do not conduct any investigation or visit any locations mentioned in testimony.
- Keep an open mind until the case is finally submitted to you.

With those reminders, you are excused until Monday at 8:30 a.m. Drive carefully.

One last thing—I want to commend you. Given yesterday's circumstances—some of you likely without power and facing concerns about spoiled food or other difficulties—you were all still here on time this morning.

Remember when I gave my "apple pie, flag-waving, and motherhood" speech about trial by jury? You are living proof of that commitment.

Your punctuality, especially today, shows the seriousness with which you approach your duties.

On behalf of all of us, thank you.

(The jury withdrew from the courtroom.)

Judge Sarasota: Mr. Shirkin, I will give you your half hour now.

There's another matter to consider. Investigator Hanus will be unavailable next week. Mr. Nappa, you indicated you want him to testify. My suggestion would be that we videotape his testimony, if possible. I don't see any problem with that.
Mr. Shirkin: We have a stipulation.

Judge Sarasota: You have a stipulation? Okay, thank you very much. We will be in recess for half an hour, until quarter to eleven. Again, I would like the defense's position. It can differ between counsel—that's fine—but I would like each counsel's position on the record.
Mr. Shirkin: Thank you.

(The Court recessed and reconvened.)

Judge Sarasota: Let the record reflect the presence of counsel and the defendants. I want to address the standard of review for abuse of discretion. I'm going to read from *United States v. Moreno*, 181 F.3d 206, at page 213:

"Even if Moreno's claim lacked merit, whether the introduction of perjured testimony requires a new trial initially depends on the extent to which the prosecution was aware of the alleged perjury. If the prosecution knew or should have known of the perjury, a new trial is warranted if there is any reasonable likelihood that the false testimony could have affected the judgment of the jury. Where the government knowingly permitted the introduction of false testimony, reversal is virtually automatic. However, even assuming that the government knowingly introduced the perjured testimony—which we don't have here—where independent evidence

supports a defendant's conviction, the subsequent discovery that a witness's testimony at trial was perjured will not warrant a new trial."

Again, I point out, procedurally and substantively, we're at a—

Mr. Nappa: Your Honor, if I may make a statement?

Judge Sarasota: Yes.

Mr. Nappa: As far as how it affects the jury's judgment on the Luda count, it has to do with the testimony of this witness—that Murphy told the witness to call Luda if he needed to buy more. With the exception of Trisha Thompson, that is the only evidence of the two defendants working together in a conspiracy.

So this is not, in my opinion, cumulative testimony where, even if the jury disregarded it, there would still be a boatload of other testimony supporting Junior Lopez's involvement in the conspiracy. In fact, there are only a handful of witnesses who even mention Lopez, and most simply testify that they knew him from the streets.

This is actual perjured testimony indicating that Junior Lopez committed acts in furtherance of the conspiracy. Under the *Moreno* decision, it is substantial perjured testimony—serious enough to potentially lead to a guilty verdict—not merely minor testimony supporting other, stronger evidence.

Judge Sarasota: Again, the application is denied. I focus on the language in *Moreno*, which also appears in the *Montaleone* cite I previously gave:

"If the prosecution knew or should have known of the perjury, a new trial is warranted if there is any reasonable likelihood that the testimony could have affected the judgment of the jury."

That standard applies in a post-trial situation, where no curative instruction can be given. Here, during the trial, the Court is going to tell the jury that the witness perjured himself regarding the 2001 contact with Anthony Murphy. Therefore, the Court determines that, procedurally and substantively, the facts do not align with the *Wallach* decision. Mr. Shirkin?

Mr. Shirkin: In the section Mr. E. James cited from *Federal Criminal Practice: A Second Circuit Handbook* on perjury claims, the last paragraph on page 436 states:

"Where a witness's perjury is discovered and fully corrected during trial, a new trial is ordinarily not warranted," and it cites the Second Circuit case *United States v. Blair.*

Judge Sarasota: Again, this is during trial, and the Court believes a curative instruction will be appropriate. Mr. Shirkin, you asked for half an hour. Is there any change in the government's position?
Mr. Shirkin: Your Honor, there's no change in the Government's position—we are moving to strike the testimony.

As the Court knows, I had an opportunity to speak with Mr. Thompson before our break. Based on the information he provided, I have requested additional details from his client. From what I've heard so far, there may be other issues we need to explore. Mr. Thompson will need to speak with his client again and get back to me. However, I am not changing the Government's basic position—we still move to strike.

Judge Sarasota: Then I need to know, so we can move forward on Monday, whether the defense has a uniform position or if there is disagreement.
Mr. Wolfe: We have a conflict, Your Honor. I believe Mr. Nappa and I are moving that the testimony be stricken, and Mr. E. James also agrees.
Mr. Nappa: And that the curative instruction, as outlined by the Court, would be given.
Mr. Wolfe: Your Honor, we've conferred for about 20 minutes. I've spoken to my client, and we will join the other defense counsel. We

will not oppose the testimony being stricken, with the Court giving the curative instruction.

Judge Sarasota: So all counsel are in agreement. Here's what will happen: On Monday, when the jury returns, I will give the curative instruction I outlined earlier—removing the portion Mr. Nappa pointed out. I will stop at the point where I explain what perjury is.

I will explain that the Court has found Mr. Marten committed perjury with respect to his testimony concerning contact and discussions with Anthony Murphy in 2001. Based on that, I will state that an application to strike his testimony—joined by all parties—has been granted. I'll prepare it in real time so Mr. Drumgoole can type it up.

Here's the wording I intend to use:

"During the early portion of Marten/J.'s testimony on Tuesday, August 14, you may recall that Mr. Wolfe made an objection and asked to approach the bench. At that time, there had been testimony about events in 2001. Mr. Wolfe indicated that he believed the testimony could not be truthful because Mr. Marten could not have had contact with his client during that time. You will recall that, after the objection, the Government continued to question Mr. Marten about events he claimed occurred in 2001 and involved Mr. Murphy.

Subsequent to court proceedings on Thursday, the Court has determined that Mr. Marten perjured himself in his account of contact and conversations with Anthony Murphy in 2001, and that the Government should have known the testimony was not truthful. In regard to perjury..."

—At this point, I will define perjury, reaffirm my finding, and state that the Court is granting the Government's motion, joined by the defense, to strike Mr. Marten's entire testimony.

"You will recall—and I will remind you again during my final instructions—that you may not consider testimony stricken from the record in any way in reaching your verdict. Mr. Drumgoole will type this up exactly as indicated."

Mr. Shirkin: Your Honor, I'm not entirely clear why the limiting instruction needs to include the sequence of events or what the Government knew or didn't know. But if the Court intends to say the Government should have known of the perjury, then the Government specifically requests that the instruction also note that the Government moved to strike the testimony.

Judge Sarasota: Yes, I made that clear. I included it.
Mr. Shirkin: I'm still unclear as to why that finding needs to be given to the jury.

Judge Sarasota: I believe it should be given because the Government should have known the witness was committing perjury. There is a certain responsibility the Government bears in putting a witness on the stand when it should have known there was a possibility of perjury. To that extent, the Court feels it is appropriate and fair to so instruct. I will also note that the Government moved to strike the testimony. That's the instruction I will give. If anyone objects, you may have an exception.

19

Crowning the King

Once the recording was completed, the tape was paused.

"Well, that raised an eyebrow or two, didn't it?" I asked, nodding.

"Please know you two are not here by coincidence but by design. Now, it's time to experience the design," I said, looking to one of my comrades while giving a hand sign. He nodded and went up the opposite set of stairs leading to the kitchen. He returned shortly with the same mop bucket I had yesterday, along with its bloody contents. The breathing of the detainees seemed to grow shallow as anxiety settled in. I looked from one to the other as the mop bucket was set before me.

"I have a proposition for you guys. It may be your only option to make amends for the sins you've committed against me. Of course, you are entitled to decline the offer. I won't force you to accept. However, know that should you vermin respectfully spurn the proposal, you'll have to live with the result."

Exchanging direct stares into the eyes of both Jerod and Sean, I asked, "Understanding understood?"

Both nodded their consent.

"Jerod, have you ever heard of something called snuff?"

He shook his head from left to right.

"No, unless you're talking about a kind of chewing tobacco," he answered.

"Okay," I began. "Snuff is a type of video found on the black market. Usually not something everyone has access to. These things can be worth upwards of a thousand bucks per video—authentic ones at least. In a nutshell, snuff videos normally consist of live recordings of torture and ultimately killing the victim."

I paused, allowing my words to sink into their hyperactive brains.

"Jerod, you are being propositioned to kill this oversized skunk," I said, pointing at Divine. "You'll do it with one of these instruments."

Jerod's eyes followed mine to the floor. I reached inside the mop bucket and gripped a heavy cleaver. Wiping the dripping blood away with a towel, I held the cleaver blade-side up in between my knees. Demonstrating with a paper bill from my pocket, I slid the money across the blade. It severed the bill instantly and very cleanly.

Next, grabbing the cleaver with my right hand, I stood, nodded to Jerod, and Banks immediately secured him in a rear-naked choke—one that restricts mobility and doesn't harm. Despite Jerod's fearful protests and pleading, I grabbed a handful of mid-length wicks at the crown of his head. Roughly shifting his head left, I warned,

"I'd be very still if I were you."

Pressing the blade at an angle to the temple, I shaved three-quarters of the right side of Jerod's head bald in one clean motion. Locks tumbled onto the floor and onto his lap.

"Clean as a baby's bottom!" I said aloud to no one in particular.

Fearful, the boy complained about his hair and my violating his newfound culture. I open-hand smacked him across his mouth with ferocious power.

"What were you saying?" I asked as blood streamed from his mouth and nose.

Silence prevailed. My right index finger pressed Jerod stiffly into his forehead until his chin tilted upward.

"This is how it's going to happen. We'll string the fat man up on that wall." I pointed. "Next, you'll be uncuffed and given a blade to chop him slowly until his death. Someone will be standing behind you with a loaded firearm pointed in your direction. If you don't comply, you shall die unceremoniously without a funeral or kind words to be remembered.

"You will be recorded on video. Once the killing is completed, the dismembered body will be relocated. At this time, you will be informed as to where. From there, you'll turn yourself in to the law and admit to your crime. The video is what will get you out of a murder charge and down to manslaughter. You'll probably sit for fifteen years maximum. Actually, the same amount of time you were facing before hopping on my case. No one's going to tell on you except you. Are you ready?" I asked politely.

The cowardly lion that accompanied Dorothy would give the answer most befitting his character. Jerod could not bluff, pretend, or fake it until he made it. This arena he found himself in was driven by cunning gumption—something very few could afford the capability of withstanding. Thin is the veil between cowardice and courage. The coward could, one day over time, develop some heart through evolving other facets of his life. It would also take a great teacher for such instruction. But the one who lacks patience erodes internally upon acknowledging another's prosperity rise. He becomes like Judas to Jesus and Brutus to Caesar. Hence, envy is one of four major reasons why so many have gotten into bed with government agencies. There were many things a person may pray to receive. An increase in malice should not be one.

"My friend, let us not dally," I said. "There comes a time in life when decisions must be made with lightning quickness. You gambled and jumped rope on a razor blade. I learned that from Ice-T back in the '90s."

I took an inventory of Divine's nasty and naked form. The fear was thick and prevalent in his eyes. He was sweating.

"Would you consider yourself a time-conscious person, Jerod?" I asked.

"What do you mean?" he asked, seemingly not comprehending.

"Is time important to you?" I rephrased the question.

"I'm unsure how to respond. It depends on the circumstances, I guess," he answered.

"Considering how you concocted a scheme to avoid doing time, I presumed time is of the essence. Speaking of, what is your decision? Ten seconds," I said, counting.

"Eight, six, four, two, time."

"I'm sorry! I'm so sorry! Please! Find it in your heart to forgive me!" Tears—lots of tears—accompanied the words.

"Hey, listen well. By not making your choice, you made a choice. If you keep it up, I'll glue your lips shut."

The pleading ceased, but the sobbing continued.

"By decree... of a power greater than yours... it pains me to give you a slow and unceremonious death without funeral, kind words of remembrance, or closure. Your final destination will be either a vertical hole (because you don't deserve to rest in peace) or the Genesee River."

Before speaking further, I assumed a pensive and almost dismal demeanor.

"The most intimate of times will no longer exist as you once knew them. The roots of trees and creatures that live in the soil shall make love to your corpse until all gluttonous desire is fulfilled."

Shaking my head as if saddened, I explained,

"You will give back to Earth as you've taken. When gravity decides to pull your astral self yet deeper, beyond the crust and into the realm of hell, the devil will spend eternity prodding your anus with his trident—sans provocation. He, of all beings, greatly despises a rat. Why else would the rodent be a snake's most prized meal?

"My poor fellow. Ignorance is not bliss. Falling stars never study. The unstudied never rise like the geysers of ether."

I patted him on his shoulder, firmly displaying earnest compassion.

"I've also learned through various cultures that if a person passes from this world not physically intact, the soul wanders all of Earth until gravity intervenes. It'll be an honor to serve as your intermediary of transition. May your nuts hang in the sand in the next world, for surely you lacked the balls to stand against the government in this one."

Somewhere in the background, Scarface's gravel voice spilled from a speaker, heavy with talk of murder and retaliation — the kind of track that set a grim rhythm to the moment. My attention turned to the skunk in the cage.

"As for you, there will be no pill overdose or dying in your sleep." I paused in thought.

"You don't deserve it," I said, turning to one of my comrades.

"Banks, please string Jerod up to the meat hook. Afterwards, immobilize his feet." Dressed in a one-piece jumper, long latex gloves, and a rain poncho, it was time to proceed.

Dressed in a one-piece jumper, arm-length latex gloves, and a rain poncho, it was time to proceed.

"Good brother Stackhouse, may I trouble you for the stage one kit?" I asked. "Thank you."

"Yes, you may, good brother," he replied.

Stackhouse returned almost instantly. All of our tools of the trade were neatly organized on the shelves of this very room. Access made easy and simple.

I pushed the chair I was sitting in closer to Jerod. He was stretched out, arms above his head and the balls of his feet barely touching the floor. I set "stage one" on the chair and opened it. Contents hung on both sides of the clamshell case. On the upper tier, there were numerous scalpel blades—both rounded and pointed, various in size. The base tier held a selection of scalpel handles, plexiglass rug cutters, Oxford razors, a few filleting knives, bottles of antiseptic, and a small but sturdy pair of scissors.

Jerod had a clear view of the contents. His lips quivered, and a sick moaning was slowly erupting from deep inside his gut. I perused the items. As I did so, I began to hum a tune—one of many that came to mind when getting ready to work.

Scissors were my first selection. I picked them up and began cutting up the side of his pants leg. Before making it up to the mid-thigh area, his pleas for mercy began.

"Preme! Please, Preme! You know my brothers, my cousins! Please! I'm beggin' you! How can I make this right?" Jerod exclaimed.

"You got money? Real money?" I asked twice. I knew the answer.

Jerod began with the crocodile tears. Big, wet droplets escaped his tear ducts. I resumed cutting up to the waist and repeated on the other side. His shirt, not made of jean material, was easier to remove. Laid bare was Jerod's body, with the exception of a pair of undershorts. Pinching him hard on the thigh, calf, bicep, and forearm of the same side, I nodded to myself in approval.

"Hmm," I said. "You've lost just enough weight. There's a separation between your skin and muscle tissue." A smile appeared on my face. "Makes things easier," I confirmed.

"Easier? Easier for what?" Jerod asked through his sobs.

"How about this. I'll talk you through the process. I'm sure doing so will help you remember," I said, selecting a scalpel blade and handle from 'stage one.' I inserted the blade into the head of the security bit.

"Comrades, there won't be any need to hear this one's voice or screams. Will you be kind enough to exercise the gag order, please? Thank you, kindly."

It only took a pair of strong hands to coarsely grip Jerod's lower jaw shut and head in place, while another spread across both lips with a sticky substance.

Thirty seconds later, the room had become much quieter. I smiled at Jerod.

"That's so much better. Since you will not be under any anesthesia for your operation, suppressing any additional noise you'll make in the near future will aid in keeping a steady hand."

I looked Jerod in his eyes.

"Only if those peepers could reveal your thoughts." I chuckled at my own humor.

"Okay, buddy. Let's get to it."

20

Cold as Justice

"I've been going fishing with my grandparents ever since I was four years old. I don't recall the first fish I ever caught. I do remember my first time falling into Lake Ontario, at a place called Point Breeze. The coldness of the water never factored in. Considering I was dressed in a snowmobile suit over other layers of clothing, I'd had the appearance of a buoy or flotsam." An application of iodine was spread around Jerod's wrist and inner forearms, the top of the foot, and ribcage, all on the left side of his body.

"Iodine is widely used amongst medical professionals' pre-surgery to help prevent any type of infections or unwanted bacterial development," I said while waiting for the skin's surface to dry.

The story continued. "I was standing on some large boulders on the pier when the plunge was taken, only feet from my granny. She reacted without thought, risking her welfare to secure mine. Hearing her alarm, a friend of the family by the name of Deacon Gray, glided amongst the maze of stone. He swooped me from the cold water in one swift motion. All of my elders were contrite with worry. I shed not one tear and did not scream. I assured all concerned, in a calm demeanor, that all is well and to continue fishing. The fish were biting. After being taken to the RV by grandma and fitted into dry clothing, I was ready to get back on the water. The scare I'd caused had been too much for the moment. Once everyone's nerves had settled, I would be good to go.

"An hour or so into watching the family reel'em in, the bite slowed." I paused.

"There are many reasons for this occurrence. However, I'll share four that often fit freshwater species criteria. One, an abrupt rise or decline in water temperatures. Two, a change in the direction of the current. Three, a shift in the pattern of the target fish's forage. Four, predators." I walked to the desk and indulged in a drink of bottled water.

"On this particular day, the problem was reason four. Predators. Depending on the waterways, a person's fishing for larger species like salmon, trout, northern pike, muskies, eels, and both blue and channel cats." I wondered if he had knowledge of these river monsters.

"Salmon and trout run upriver to spawn in September through November unless Landlocked. The culprits in this scenario were mature Northerns and really big eels. It became evident when people fishing closer to the surface were catching pike from a seven to fourteen-pound range. Those tight-liners struggled to pull in eels sometimes as large as a man's leg. Those eels, for some reason, struck more fear into fishermen than those toothy pike so willing to take a finger from anyone careless enough to misplace one near their mouth. Eels resemble snakes in appearance and movement, even though it is a fish. Some species have teeth enough to remove an appendage as well. If one were to wrap itself around your arm, let's say, while unhooking it, its slime is so viscous that securing a grip is impossible with bare hands. If left to dry, the slime will tighten until all circulation is prohibited between the two points of contact. The result, a person may be forced to amputate." I took another few sips.

"My family despised eels. On the contrary, my great-grandmother (bless her soul) loved them. So, whenever eels were caught, they were brought home, even if purchased from other fishermen. These creatures are known as a delicacy worldwide by many different names. The flesh is muscular, firm, high in fat, and has a distinctive, strong, full-bodied flavor. When cooked, the meat turns bright white and flaky. Probably the second biggest peeve of the eel was even after frying, blood still often found its way onto the food tray after an hour or so. It had to be cooked slowly or sliced thin for the best results. Now, the hardest part of handling an eel after landing one is skinning it. Unlike you, there's no separation between the skin and its muscle. We'd string one up just as you are now, perhaps with a nail through its skull against some tree or board. What I'd do next is find the point of insertion and begin gently tapping the skin with the scalpel. Fortunately, for you, I can raise your skin to make the incision, avoiding veins."

Retrieving the scalpel, I said, "Okay, here goes nothing. Try not to wiggle and squirm much." I began lancing a sketch pattern at the base of the palm around the entire wrist. The muffled screams still proved moderately amplified, as did the show of tears. Blood streamed lightly down his forearm, off his elbow, and dripped onto the floor. A greater portion dove into Jerod's armpit, traversing slowly and sporadically through its hair, descending the ribcage.

I took a pause in the procedure.

"I'm willing to bet you watched lots of television growing up. All of the scheming and skullduggery obviously adapted became commonplace in your DNA. You expressed a great deal of humor while testifying. Not only was there a smile upon your face, but your eyes smiled as well. Please, find that same humor in this moment. Do that for me. Will you? When I'm done here, you'll have a clean slate; a blank canvas. I give you my word."

This time, I was the one doing the smiling. Another scalpel handle was retrieved from 'stage one'. A skinny bit of stainless steel, approximately one-eighth of an inch in diameter. I inserted the handle a few inches into the incision, moving parallel with the arm itself. Just beneath the skin. I worked my way around the wrist, lifting his hide in the process. Jerod emitted a sound of indescribable agony.

I tossed the handle into the mop bucket on the floor. "This is what I meant about you starting over with a blank canvas," I said while attempting to unsuccessfully fold back the skin at his wrist with my fingers. I used two pairs of lightweight needle-nose pliers to clamp onto the skin. Gently turning downwards, the pliers begin to roll the skin inside out. It exposed the pomegranate-tinted flesh beneath.

Jerod's body began to tremble like some battery-operated dildo. His behavior ignored, I continued an even pull, reaching away from the forearm. Veins lined the exposed area, matching the pulse of an erratically beating heart. There was a gorgeous blue coursing within these avenues. Few things are ever compared to the study of living anatomy.

"If you were dead, I'd skin you faster than a rabbit three days late for supper. Since you're not though, how are you coming along?" I asked, knowing the answer. I began peeling once more. "I'm sure you probably feel you're not deserving of this treatment. You couldn't be more wrong. Remember DJ UNK? Out of ATL? He made that song.

Walk It Out. I bet that's what you had planned when you got your 2 to 4 years, even after being charged with perjury by the feds. You probably danced your way out the door after two years. You'll be dancing before this is over. Just like a stripper." We all laughed at that comment, with the exception of Sean.

I navigated the elbow and eased towards the bicep. "Jerod, my first USP in the Feds was at Lewisburg after getting sentenced. T-Rock was there too. Remember him, don't you? I'm sure you do. Anyhow, there was this Irish dude out of Boston who resided in the same housing unit as me. People called him Billy Kenny. There were three things this guy loved. Robbing banks, good food, and having a hearty laugh at another's expense." I peeled an inch further. He pissed himself. It made me livid.

"You shouldn't have done that!" I said sternly. Setting the pliers down, I grabbed two handfuls of his arm's skin and snatched. Jerod's body went rigid and his spine arched as if daring to snap. His jaws were open, giving way to screaming agony that yielded to a pair of sealed lips.

The skin tore free from his body in a jagged display above the deltoid muscle and midway into the armpit. It had an appearance more like the skin of some hairless cat or dog than what it actually was. I dabbed my hand's contents into the growing pool of blood by Jerod's feet. Without warning, I flung the skin directly at Divine inside the bear cage. The bars caught the bulk of its spreading mass. A splattering of Jerod's blood from the saturated skin streaked across his face and torso. He shrieked like a woman who experienced something really disgusting.

"You'll make an excellent floor mat, Sean. You're large enough in the center that when I remove your pelt, I'll also cut away the arms, legs, and face. After some stretching during the curing process, a nice rectangular finish will result. We can wipe our dirty shoes off on you or leave them on top. At least you'll be some good to someone. What do you think?" Laughter ensued. "I can't believe you cats let the feds trick you into doing their work. Can a devil fool a Muslim?" I asked.

No response came. Jerod couldn't talk even if he desired to. Divine cowered at the far side of his cage. I'd have him singing like the bird he is before long. In the meantime, he'd be suffering the anguish with those before him. Gravity seemed to be gaining an advantage on the skin versus the cage bars. Slowly, centimeter by centimeter, it edged towards the floor like a chameleon. From brown to red, both brown and red, and in no specific order. Jerod hung from his new post in life. Head dangling forward as if defeated and fatigued. The adrenaline coursing through his bloodstream while distressed had ceased. Maybe he just wanted to sleep. Hopefully, when he awoke, it would be all some terrible nightmare. Not this time. At some point, that a rekindling of an old thought crossed my mind. 6395 days; 166,440 hours; 9,986,400 minutes spent inside some cement and iron enclosure.

"No, no, no, no, no, no. Not a dream, Jerod." I said while snapping some smelling salt and placing it under his nostrils. The next skin laceration case was at the base of his neck. Muffled noise of attempted screams followed, as did a few bright streams of blood in various areas. "In all attempts ever made at flaying someone, Jerod, I've never kept the skin in one piece thus far. It's very difficult. I'll manage it, I'm sure, before the grave accepts me." I made another vertical inch-long cut parallel to his spine. "Wasn't your attribute, Jahiem? Ja for short?" Sealed lips. "I'll call you Ja from here on out. Maybe you'll be able to share with us all what you're going to learn about the truth of the mysteries. Hmm, then again, perhaps not. The dead have never been known to return from the grave."

I wrapped a layer of gauze around my hands for grip and plunged my fingers, from index to pinky, on both hands into the horizontal slice. One on either side of the vertebrae until the base of my knuckles made contact. Ja's antics were ignored. I snatched forcefully with both hands. There was a fusion of sound. Sounds reminiscent of varying lengths of duct tape being torn away from a carpeted floor. The skin of his back lay open at the spine like a button-up shirt. It hung grotesquely at the sides, dangling where the *latissimus dorsi* and oblique muscles intersect from the armpit to the waist. Ja squirmed like a fat worm surprised by a sudden and powerful beam of sunlight after bathing in the shade of darkness. I'm sure Ja was suffering in the present. As did I suffer in the recent past. When pain becomes consistent and lasting during prolonged periods in one's life, the despair of another truly deserving proves inconsequential.

Someone upstairs selected another genre of music. It wasn't particularly loud. However, I imagine it would disguise any noises traveling from within the depths upward. There began an accumulation of blood being lost. An amount that could begin to weaken someone of Ja's stature. A pause was given as certain considerations were weighed. Shortly after, I spoke to be heard by the men occupying opposite sides of the room.

"Banks, Stackhouse," I called.

"Did you two finish your training with China Doll and Naja?" I asked, ninety percent sure of the answer.

"Yes, we did," answered one.

"Knows it like the palm of my hand," said the other. It was great to hear. Surely, no one wanted to bother those two women with such an occupation if not absolutely necessary.

Experiencing firsthand, it would take lots of foot rubbing, cooking, and pampering to supplant them from the dark places this type of work often leads. "Great. Since we know his blood type, why don't you give him a transfusion, starting with one pint to slowly replace his loss thus far? Afterward, give him some fluids with electrolytes.

"Also, combine some aloe, collagen, Vitamin E, plant-based gelatin, or glycerin. Once emulsified, put it in an airbrush. Coat his flesh with a few layers to both soothe and maintain the moisture of his exposed muscle tissue. This will give the platelets something to adhere to, and staunch any further blood loss." The two men set into motion. It gave all the confirmation of understanding needed.

All efforts to perform the perfect art of skinning had been aborted. My work, once slow and methodical, was accelerated in its delivery of cold efficiency. On short notice, all were removed except for the skin of Jerod's hands, feet, face, buttocks, and genitalia. He resembled some twisted version of a freshly groomed poodle. In a pile next to his feet lay Jerod's skin. I sat down studying his anatomy for a spell. Removing my gloves, I retrieved the bottle of water I'd half-drunk already. My eyes then found their way to the caged bird. There wasn't much fight remaining in those peepers. He was consumed by something that opposed bravado. Perhaps with all unfolding before his eyes, accepting a new reality for what it has actually become is quite a harsh and sobering pill to swallow.

Sean turned in on himself more by the minute. My expressionless stare seemed to cause him physical pain. If looks could kill. "One, two, I'm coming for you. Three, four feds made you their whore. Five, six, now you're in the mix. Seven, eight pray it's not too late. Nine, ten, I'm coming for your skin." I sang to Divine. Banks and Stackhouse were busy on the Jerod project, keeping him in the game. I watched with keen interest. Help from skillful hands always made less-traveled roads more manageable. It meant times when I didn't need to fret over each detail, large and small. After the transfusion came the hydration issue. Immediately, Stackhouse followed up with the first aloe-collagen application.

The solution was cold and unforgiving. Jerod's body writhed with active nerve responses. He made earnest attempts to scream. I'm sure his lips being sealed saved us all a few headaches. The silverskin and muscle tissue accepted the solution readily. By the second application, Jerod's blubbering and whining had subsided. As did the bleeding. The soothing properties were beginning to have their effect. To Ja, a great relief may have been found in such a small comfort. In my view, however, there was no respite. Just the simple serenity of the calm before a typhoon strikes full strength. Water itself was not enough to curb the hunger of a growling stomach. Deciding not to prolong any further. The comrades and I agreed to refine ourselves according to custom and indulge in some sustenance. In approximately two hours, we'd reconvene and resume the purge.

21

Traps and Triggers

The telephone rang. Only my eyes blinked in response. I inhaled deeply, slowly awakening to Leah's sweet aroma and curvy softness. I was enveloped by warmth and comfort. The comfort is attributable to the woman I've literally spent almost every night with for the past five months. Aiding in this indulgence were the seven hundred and fifty thread count sheets and an underpad designed for targeting pressure points of the body. An airy goosedown quilt, accompanied by my significant other, made such a simple extravagance possible. Our skin merged like the melting of caramel and chocolate. A willful cohesion of one another's anatomy. We seemed unified for Leah's entire expanse. I didn't desire to move a centimeter. After the fourth ring, the call went to voicemail.

Seconds later, my mobile unit began to vibrate on its charger. Instead of rising to my feet, I inched closer, pressing into Leah in hopes of ignoring the caller. While tracing the tip of my nose over the top of Leah's shoulders and nape of her neck with sultry emphasis, the private line next to my side of the bed began to sound. Eyes wide with an alertness not present seconds ago, my stomach began to churn and twist in a sense of foreboding. Good news had yet to come on the private line. Until it did, there was no need to think contrary. In one smooth yet subtle motion, I was at the bed's edge picking up the receiver. I greeted the caller. The voice that returned was rife with panic and extreme duress as it spoke in low tones.

"Family! Where you at?" Tae-dow asked.

"I'm in the Roc. How you?" I inquired.

"Not good!" he said in a worried, low tone." I'm in Sylvia's on 125th right now. Trapped in the bathroom. I need you to fly down asap!"

"I need you! Four cats just came into the spot with hammers. All of 'em are barefaced. I've never seen them a day of my life. One was talking on the phone to somebody. I was in line waiting to have my order taken when I overheard Duke on the jack say, 'I don't see nobody wearing a black leather coat and a grey fitted you described. We're in Sylvia's right now."

I listened intently. The moment he paused, I shot questions his way.

"What does this have to do with you?" I queried.

"I had just hung my coat inside out on the back of a chair and put my hat in its sleeve, barely sixty seconds it seemed, before overhearing the conversation. That's what I am wearing. You gotta get down here! Hold on." Tae-dow moaned. "One of them is coming this way. I think he's about to check in here. P, this might be it. Hold on." I maintained radio silence. At first, I didn't realize I was holding my breath. His fear and anxiety reached through the phone, taking hold of me. My mind was racing. I didn't want to lose my friend. I felt utterly useless not being able to come to his aid when he needed it perhaps more than any other time in his life.

Suddenly, Tae-dow's voice pierced the silence. I exhaled.

"Yo, you still here?" he said.

"Duke ain't see you?" I asked incredulously.

"Nah. I stood on the toilet in one of the stalls. He stuck his head in the door and peeked around. Once he saw it wasn't nobody in here, he went back up front," he answered.

"Can you see any of them now?"

"Yeah, they're standing back-to-back, combing every table. One of them has the exit covered. I'm trapped. I need you! Get here, please!"

"Most importantly, keep your cool. None of them knows what you look like as a person. They only know the description of clothing. If not, your brains would be all over the floor already. Find trust in that wisdom. Is there a window in the bathroom?" I asked.

"Ain't no window."

"There has to be another entrance, especially for deliveries. Find it and use it!" I insisted in a tranquil manner.

"I don't want to risk it, P," he said with much indecision.

"Listen, you gotta let your nuts hang! Walk out the front door. Leave everything at the table, company included. Just keep it pushin'. Get some distance between you and Sylvia's as quickly as possible. Whoever their spotter is, he or she isn't out front. If so, you'll be pinpointed by now." I calmly instructed.

"Nah, fam. I ain't feelin' it," he replied, lacking confidence in my words. "Okay, whoever came wit you call 'em. Instruct them to speak privately with an employee. Let'em know a pipe has burst on one of the restroom sinks. When the employee comes put a nickel or even a stack in his or her palm to get you to a window or another exit. Do it! Now! I'm on my way. Call me when you are out of the restaurant." I said, hanging the phone up and rising from bed.

Leah was resting on her left side, facing me. I turned into a set of beautiful eyes. For how long I've been held under her scrutiny, I'm uncertain. "Did I wake you, my love?' I asked, leaning over to share a kiss. "The moment your BTUs subsided, I became alert. Is your friend going to be okay? Sounds like he's in some real trouble," she said.

"I truly hope so. It depends on how well he listens. The next few minutes of his life will be crucial. Either he will evade his pursuers, or he'll ask for an appointment with your Jehovah. I'm sorry, babe, but I must catch a flight to the city. This is some type of mistake. My man is not going to step on any toes hard enough for someone to put money on his head." I defended in frustration.

"In all my years of knowing Shevar, through the good and bad, ups and downs, I've never heard him sound so distressed. Will you please call the airport to find the two earliest flights on any airline going to LaGuardia? I appreciate you." I said with a smile, lying my head on her stomach while she made the call. With a flight itinerary at hand, the next flight out was in two hours. This meant I had an hour to expend. I stood again and walked into the bathroom, turning on the shower. After inviting Leah to shower, we bathed each other." Before leaving, I must prioritize by being a great husband to the wife I've envisioned." I spoke softly into Leah's ear.

"Hmm. When you write that check, just make sure it doesn't bounce," she responded, succeeded by a kiss and embrace.

"Thank you for flying American Airlines. Please remain seated while the plane is taxiing to the exit gate. Be sure to check overhead storage so that any carry-on items are not forgotten. Welcome to LaGuardia Airport. Again, thank you for flying AA," said a woman over the intercom in a highly polished and professional voice. Time literally did fly. Shevar was waiting patiently at the terminal when I arrived. We shook hands and departed immediately. We didn't share in the usual banter between us, we'd grown accustomed to over the years. Instead, our ride carried on in silence.

"Find a place to park. It can be somewhere to eat. As long as it's outside your neighborhood and you're not preoccupied, I'm not concerned." I suggested. Tae-dow decided on a place called Carnegie Deli in the Theater District of Manhattan. It was a Jewish establishment. This place had been founded over a century ago. Around the time when great waves of immigrants migrated from various lands, many being refugees of war, stepped foot on American soil at Ellis Island for the very first time in their lives. Seeking a new start, many exercised their culture, customs, and traditions that would perhaps lead to persecution during this period in European history. Something took root. As for Carnegie, it had grown into a mountain. Its fame for its towering pastrami on rye, matzo soup, and knishes, to name a few, was not to be underscored by the hundreds, if not thousands, of celebs to dine in its halls. From multiple presidents and diplomats the world over, Carnegie was a major staple within the Big Apple.

After a patient wait in line and having our orders taken, we found a booth out of the way of most other diners. I got down to business without any hesitation. Everything Shevar had knowledge of, thought he knew, and didn't know, I probed. He didn't like it, but that wasn't my concern. My brother requested the security conscious and it has landed. Our food and drink arrived. The question and answer scenario did not subside. As we were reviewing and comparing details, Tae-dow's phone buzzed. I attacked my food as he conversed with the person on the other end. My interest solely appeared to be in the meal. However, my attentiveness is something different altogether. When he concluded the conversation, he set his phone on the table. "That was B.O. and Horse," Shevar said.

"What's good with them?" I asked.

"Out in Coney Island at Horse's Aunt's house. Want to shoot out there to scoop them?"

"Yeah. I haven't been out that way since '94. Has it changed any?"

"You know the saying, 'The more things change, the more things remain the same. I don't go to Brooklyn at all, so go figure," he said. I didn't respond to his statement. I've heard it before on several occasions along the way. 'Who is the author of the quote?' I asked myself mentally. I sat in silence, pondering the oddity of this situation. It was a secret to no one. None of it settled well with me. We took leave of the deli. Before long, we were en route to C.I.. Shevar broke the silence once we were in traffic.

"Horse said he might have a line on those cats up in Silvia's this morning. I just told him I'd come through so we can speak in person. I ain't never trusted a phone in my life," he said.

"That's fantastic!" I said.

"We need all of the information we can get. I know there's no need to say it, but I'll do so anyway. DO NOT...put any of the homies on as to why I'm here or what I've come to do." I shared with emphasis. People, even street people, have a tendency to walk on eggshells around those who have lesser difficulty turning out the lights.

Paranoia tends to get the best of most people when certain knowledge is available to them. If they know not, they think not. Besides, you never know when someone in your circle may violate certain unspoken principles. I'm speaking of rules that apply to all. If they don't break them, not a one would ever figure that you had a hitter in your corner in the first place.

"Come on, family. You know I know," he said, gliding through traffic. I nodded a second time, acknowledging our mindsets being in sync. There could be no room allowed for so simple yet so vital a misunderstanding. It was better to clear the air. Too much is at stake. Once back in Harlem, we stopped on 145th and Broadway. Splitting in three directions, Shevar and Horse venture to the pool hall. B.O. went to the liquor store across the street and I eased into 'Harlem USA' to cop a few nice outfits. The ladies working loved dressing me for some reason. I enjoyed their individual sense of style and company. The fellas reconvened at Harlem USA as I was summing up my purchase. We rolled out, pulling up at the apartment the three of them shared. There's no place like Washington Heights. As Horse and B.O. exited the ship Tae-dow yelled, "Yo, I'll be back in an hour. I gotta stop by Mil's spot. Don't drink up all the Henney and Remi!" he said.

"We'll save y'all a cup each," B.O. responded with laughter.

"Positive K kid!" Shevar shot back.

We eased from the curb towards our destination. After bending one corner, he lowered the volume of the music. "So, what do you think about the spill?" Tae-dow asked. I was studying pedestrians on the sidewalk and passenger side vehicular traffic. My thoughts were becoming more concentrated. I asked, "B.O. and Horse were with you at Sylvia's earlier this morning?"

"Facts," Shevar said.

"So they got a real good look at the cats who came to get you?" I asked. "You heard it yourself. The same dudes was on the block wit' ol' boy I showed you. The one that's chewin' real heavy," he said.

My head swiveled towards the driver. "He must be the sender. The question is why? Think about that for a few." I said, pausing a moment before presenting another scenario that may have escaped worthy consideration.

"Do you recall telling me about a time when you poked your nose into a guy named Jack's business? I guess it pertained to then runnin' down on someone in a white Porsche. Since it took place on your block, I presume you felt the need to lay down the law. In retrospect, you said your decision may not have been very wise. Think this could be a backdraft?" I wondered.

"Negative. Jack is the type to keep his thumb on the pulse of Harlem. He'll come himself. This is unrelated." Shevar said matter-of-factly.

We slowed to a halt, unable to beat the yellow light turning red. Pressing Shevar to think deeper I questioned.

"If you and ol'boy are on good terms as you say, why would he put money on your head?"

"It has to be a misunderstanding, P."

"Are you willing to live with that? Because I'm not."

"What would you do?" he asked. I laughed.

"On impulse, I'd transfer everything inside his skull onto the sidewalk. After that, leave town and don't come back. A much better option is to catch him where he lays his head. This way, three things can take place. Once you have the mark secure, interrogate him, get the bag, and part his wig like Moses did the Red Sea." I iterated with certainty.

He shook his head in vigorous opposition as the red light turned green. " Gotta keep it one hundred. I disagree with your approach," he said.

"Why am I here? Why did I get on a plane and put some men on the road within the hour of being made aware by your distressful phone call? I'm here to make your problem go away. Simple." Silence followed my statement. He drove for a few minutes, unsure how to respond. Shevar wanted to salvage whatever was possible from this conversation. I began cleaning my cuticles with a small knife retrieved from the car's center console. My mood was beginning to darken. Even the clear blue sky seemed to be developing a tint by the second.

"P, your light switch is out of this world. I'm not wired like you. When we were up north together, you had a wild side. Ever since I've been coming up to the Roc, I could see y'all made rules for others to follow. I called you because there's no one alive in my memory who'd respond properly to a real-time situation like what happened. You're shy. I'm here talking to you, fam. Without you on that line this morning... I don't even want to speak the words." Still rattled, he said, Shevar was still rattled.

"You're still processing everything. I get it. You have my support, obviously. That's why I'm here. Learn this lesson from me. Be clear about what you want done before you cry wolf! If my men get here and see you freeze, they will probably dispose of you for wasting their time. For your own safety, don't ever do something like this again, unless you mean it. Fortunately, we have some business in need of fixing in both Albany and Boston. Pull over. I need to make a call. Once I inform my people of the change in plans, I'll fly up to Beantown and meet them in Albany." Shevar pulled curbside. Exiting the vehicle, I said over my shoulder, "After this is taken care of, you may want to meet me in L.A. We could go see your people, and I'll know you are safe if nothing else." I closed the car door and hit speed dial on the throwaway phone in my possession.

22

Deal with the Devil

With the exception of people eaters (dogs), I was not much of an animal lover. Liked them well enough, just wasn't infatuated. On the contrary, I had known people in the past for purchasing properties solely to create a black market vet operation and nursery. At any given time, an individual, if invited, would come across anywhere from seventy-five to one hundred and fifty pit bull terrier puppies from various breeds and bloodlines. Swollen mothers lying to one side or the other, trying to find comfort from what seemed to possibly be contractions. It was not easy to witness. The animals found comfort in the caress and words of their human caretakers. Some were nursing pups whose eyes had yet to open. Many more were six to eight weeks old.

People were arriving as if going grocery shopping. Several puppies were sold in an hour. Papers and shots included. There were a couple of guys who sought to have their puppies sired from certain bloodlines within the kernel owner's possession. Dog breeding, it seems, is a lucrative business. On top of it, there were those who made a living from gambling on dog fighting. Personally, watching animals fight never actually piqued my interest. I did not meet to parley with anyone in these environments. Something much better could be done with the time. People have always indulged in what they've enjoyed. As a result, I sought the path I'd found most agreeable.

"That meal was excellent. *Hum-du-Allah*," Stackhouse said. "I've never had Ethiopian cuisine before. I can't wait to take my daughters there." He maintained a mile ever since first tasting his meal.

"I know it has to be a few spots like this one in the Chi. Most likely it would be out North. The African community is stronger there than anywhere else in the city. You pulled my cost to something good," said Banks.

"Stackhouse, did you acknowledge the customs employed while dining? The menu?" I asked.

"Indeed, I did. More reason to return and support their establishment." Stackhouse said.

"Speaking of which, I have to feed my newest acquisitions."

Banks and I both looked at Stackhouse with curious eyes.

"What do you speak of?" Banks asked.

"Today is just as good as any to let you see for yourself." Stackhouse nodded.

"Pound for pound, I think these jokers are ten times worse than pit bulls. You'll see," he said, smiling and rubbing his hands together. We walked at our leisure through Village Gate Square. Formerly known as Peddler's Village, it has come a long way. It was a place quite foreign to Banks and Stackhouse. I took turns answering Banks' and Stackhouse's inquiries. After taking the scenic route, we found our way to the car, heading toward the destination and purpose ahead.

Jerod was asleep when we returned. I'm sure his shoulders were on fire like the rest of his skinless portions. At least he was no longer bleeding. The guys did a wonderful job. I congratulated them on their efforts. Divine was looking terrified. He had known that things weren't going to improve in the least. As he looked at me, I wondered if he still saw light at the tunnel's end. While detaching the plexiglass wall panels lining the room, I asked a question.

"Stackhouse, did you take Banks through Scio since we've been back?"

"Not at all. Everything has changed. Too many have been compromised to risk exposure. Excluding family, anyone worth mentioning is up north doing forever. Never know who might pass something along to the feds. Forbid anyone from seeing us together," he answered flatly.

Nodding my consent, I continued, "I'll say this much. Guys like Almightly, his brother Gerald, and Tin Dog Loc from your block."

Looking in Stackhouse's direction, I asked," What's this acquisition you mentioned earlier?" My work proceeded with the plexiglass walls. Each eighty-by forty-eight-inch segment was carefully placed into its own foundation track. Once connected properly, Jerod was completely surrounded, and Sean still had a full view of the goings on. "I'd rather show you than tell you." Stackhouse disappeared. In the meantime, Banks and I took a seat and relaxed.

Ten or so minutes passed before Stackhouse returned. When he did, along with him was a push cart occupying eight midsize kennels. The noises, a growling of sorts, were quite unfamiliar and very disturbing. I had no intention of being curious. The manner in which these creatures attacked the metal cage of each kennel's entrance revealed their large teeth, sharp claws, and tenacity. I made sure to maintain my distance, should one of those things break free.

"These," Stackhouse said, are Tasmanian Devils in the flesh. At least one of a few species. I have to keep them separated. They don't tolerate each other well unless its plenty of food present. For some reason, I'm someone who is countenanced." Stackhouse donned some of the thickest leather gloves I had ever seen as he began to manipulate the kennels.

He looked in my direction while opening one of the kennel cages. As the gate opened, one of the most hideous animals I have ever seen jumped into Stackhouse's arms. It bit, chewed on, and snapped at his gloved hands, clothes, and apron. Stackhouse talked to the creature as he handled it. At around twenty pounds, a Tasmanian Devil could pass for a genetically mutated rat. Its head and jawbones were massive, as was its black-haired body. The Devil's tail was a thick, hairless cord of bone, skin, and gristle.

"This is Paul. Are you ready to start the feeding?" Stackhouse asked.

My demeanor displayed some reluctance.

"You sure this is a good idea?" I responded by answering his question with a question.

"Been through it enough to know. I even know their individual personalities," he said.

I nodded, stood, and went into the area where Jerod was enclosed. A durable sheet of transparent plastic covered the entrance. As he set Paul down onto the floor to open the other gates, it darted towards

Divine, growling loudly. It began immediately chewing at the arm skin of Jerod's lying at the base of the cage. Soon, another arrived, ramming Paul. Both clamped down powerful jaws on mouthfuls of the bloody prize during a tug of war.

The instant the battle had begun was like a dinner bell for all the others in the kernels of the bottom row. If Stackhouse didn't do something soon, these things were on the brink of pandemonium. Those of the bottom kennels charged teeth first into the faces of Paul and his opponent. Suddenly, it became four against two as the newcomers fought to pull skin from the mouths of the others. Holding smelling salt under Jerod's nose had awakened him. Once I had his attention, I lifted the heavy plastic to one side of the plexiglass wall.

The last two Stackhouse set on the floor advanced towards the frenzy but stopped short. Sniffing the floor and the air, they both looked on in my direction, growling, baring teeth, and nostrils flickering. With no time to spare, the creatures were upon me. Following the scent of fresh blood, the other six devils converged. Jerod's fear was prevalent in his eyes. I, too, felt discomfort. He watched as the animals literally ate the skin off his back. Immediately, I'd come to the conclusion that Jerod's pile of skin would not suffice in appeasing the appetite of even a single Tasmanian Devil.

As Stackhouse cordoned the animals into a corner with a floorboard, Banks brought over the sand blaster as discussed. It was ready for use. I tied two lengths of strong latex above Jerod's knees to serve as tourniquets. The sand blaster awaited on the same table 'stage one' had occupied prior to lunch. I donned my gloves once more and told Divine, "Watch me work."

Quickly becoming comfortable with gripping its handle, I entered the transparent enclosure. Jerod had no success in his verbal communication. The superglue held those lips together like a disgruntled clam. However, the tears didn't subside. The Tasmanian Devils began turning against one another. Stackhouse seemed to be trying to console the savage creatures to no avail. Jerod's eyes followed mine to the corner where sounds of pure chaos reverberated. I turned back to him. "This is going to sting a little bit," I warned.

Covering my eyes with goggles, I aimed the sandblaster, braced myself for the recoil, and pulled the trigger. As the spray of pressurized water was released, the flesh of each foot and toenails was torn away up to the ankle in seconds. Where Jerod's feet once existed, only pearl white bone remained. He jerked and squirmed as if possessed by an ominous poltergeist.

Releasing the trigger, I reached into the right pocket of my overcoat. I retrieved one of three syringes that held a measured amount of morphine. The top was removed. Jerod received the injection in the right quadricep just above the tourniquet. His body abated as if nothing ever happened. That would soon change. Flesh chunks lay on the floor behind Jerod. A bright salmon colored mist adorned the lower portions of the plexiglass walls. Stackhouse struggled to contain the collective strength of one hundred sixty pounds of hungry rage. I picked up the sand blaster, aimed, and squeezed. Once the bones were completely showing to the knee of both legs, I backed away, speaking to Stackhouse.

"Turn 'em loose."

The minerally content of blood was still quite noticeable despite the deluge of water. The animals feasted noisily with disregard for anyone or anything present. Every large chunk of flesh was not relegated to one set of jaws. It was forcefully shared, much to the dislike of the initial possessor. Paul and company sloshed back and forth through the blood soup at my feet. In two minutes' time, only small particles of edibles remained. More were sought after. The hunger subsisted. The devils had begun to stand on their hind legs in order to reach towards the fresh blood slowly streaming down the shin bones. They licked at the red flow while nibbling on any ragged edge of meat available to their powerful jaws.

Jerod's muffled screaming indicated the sensitivity of nerve exposure. There were some pains even morphine wouldn't nullify.

"Stackhouse, your boys are still hungry. Move them to the side, please?" I humbly asked. I didn't feel comfortable trying to handle these savage beasts. Besides, one of them could get injured if contacted by the water pressure.

"I got you," he said, herding the creatures into the corner.

Just as quickly, I began my process. Jerod's legs were stripped up to his groin. Unfortunately for him, he bled to death during the process.

There were no farewells, goodbyes, or kind words. He departed the physical realm as he deserved. In fear and pain. Despair had branded its face into Jerod's last moments. One that I hoped would travel with him for the rest of his journey. Dark arterial blood began pooling as the water receded. That strong metallic smell had returned and was unrelenting. Paul and the company recognized it as well. They were becoming more unruly by the second. I returned the sand blaster to the table where Banks had initially placed it and grabbed a clean towel. I wiped splatter from my face and goggles.

Seemingly in the same shake, those devils burst forward in a frenzy. I waited patiently as they gorged themselves. With their bellies dragging across the floor, I sensed these monsters would be as close to content as at any other time. The nausea which haunted me a few minutes prior abated as I watched three of the animals devour Jerod's genitals. Another lay on its back, wrestling with a shredded pair of boxers. One by one, Stackhouse returned each devil to its kennel without rebuke. He told them how good a job they'd done as he scratched their sides and necks. I laughed at the sight.

"Time to reward these babes with a warm bubble bath," he said.

My work wasn't done. There remained half a human hanging before me. Fortunately, on-the-job training could be conducted in the process.

"Banks! What's up, my g? How are you feeling?" I asked.

"I'm soaking everything up. That's about it. You have peculiar methods of handling business I must say," he said.

"Yeah." I nodded.

"This is dancing to a different tune. The music's playing right now. The DJ's spinning your song. You're up." I said, waving Banks forward to stand at my side.

"We are going to need an empty bucket and a blunt-nose hawkbill knife. A three-inch blade, please." I humbly requested. Divine looked on helplessly. He appeared as if on the brink of being overcome by sickness. Banks returned. I accepted the five-gallon pail and placed it between the skeletal remains of the cadaver's legs. I grasped the hawkbill firmly in my right hand. Its blade curved downward mostly into an extremely sharp point. The cutting edge was on the innermost side of the hook.

I grabbed the corpse around the right oblique muscles and probed the abdomen forcefully.

"Repeat my actions," I said to Banks. He complied.

"Do you feel how thin the muscle tissue is in this area?" I asked. Banks nodded.

"Due to its thinness, little effort will be needed to puncture through to the stomach lining." Looking towards the big boy in the cage, I said,

"Someone his size may be a different matter altogether. A smaller blade actually would have sufficed for this one. You'll see soon enough."

I turned to the corpse and pressed into its lower abdomen, just beneath the navel, until my finger found the ridge of bone. I held it there. "See this?" I asked Banks. He nodded.

"On humans, I start every incision here, running down the center line. Aside from detouring around the navel, I prefer cutting through soft tissue rather than wrestling sinewy muscle. The torso is built to shield and anchor the vital organs — beyond that, little else in the body matches its purpose."

"I was about five years old the first time I held a hook knife. My grandfather, bless him, took me to a slaughterhouse. It was fully operational. I'm going to minimize the details so as not to bore you. There were hundreds of pigs hanging everywhere on meat hooks. Just like this." I said, pointing at Jerod's body.

"Empty buckets were strategically placed about the floor. When I asked, 'Why were the pigs hung up in such a fashion?' he explained. I then asked to try it. My grandpa consented, and the man walked me through each step. I'm going to pass on this knowledge to you." I shared wholeheartedly.

"The tip of the hook knife is sharp enough to pierce flesh, but wouldn't cut anything. Once pushed completely through into the stomach cavity, the resistance subsided. With the tip of the hook resting on the interior lining of the stomach, an upward motion is made to begin an incision. As you reach the navel, cut around it and proceed on the center between the left and right abdominal muscles. Your incision should conclude at the sternum bone of the chest cavity." A stream of blood, though not much, dribbled into the bucket.

"Now cut along the pelvis using the same method, both east and west of the primary cut. Once done, set the knife down and grip both the left and right abdominal wall. Afterwards, pull apart."

My hands were busy working while explaining the steps to Banks. The moment I yanked in opposite directions, Jerod's innards collapsed into the bucket. He appeared displeased with the scenery. Working with cutlery has always had a different effect on people who may be used to handling firearms. It's said the act is more personal. I explained the purpose of removing the entrails. If ruptured, the stench would be unbearable and deprive one of all the subtle pleasantries this work offers. I slit the corpse's throat to the bone and turned it around, spreading its buttocks to cut around the posterior opening of the alimentary canal free. The next stage would be to rid the cadaver of its remaining flesh.

I employed the sand blaster once more. Instead of goggles, we wore full-face shields for the next course of action. The process was expedient. Since Banks was standing on my right, I aimed the jetstream at Jerod's right eye. The result was an expulsion of brain matter erupting from his open mouth, nostrils, and left eye, shooting from its socket. The eyeball struck Banks' face shield, as did brain natter to follow. I didn't cease until the skeleton was bare. Banks left the dungeon without a word and wouldn't speak to me for the rest of the night.

23

The Last Move

One day, a seed of doubt had grown into suspicion. Continuing on in its weed-like growth, it reared its head into my blossoming relationship. I recall a time Leah consciously acknowledged, "I've never seen anyone leave before sunrise and return after sunset to go fishing. The strangest part of the scenario is you don't come home with any fish," she said.

Even though I downplayed her inference of the possibility of carnal indulgence elsewhere, her point of view was reasonable. With no desire to fuel such an inquiry, I decided to plan a surprise excursion for just her and me.

We made lunch that Friday evening and turned in early. On Saturday at five a.m., we were close to departure. Leah slept a while longer during the drive. Twenty or so minutes into the journey, she was rejuvenated and had the opportunity to see the sun rise over the horizon.

"Good morning. For the second time," I said, smiling.

"I needed that," Leah replied. Looking around, she asked, "Where are we?"

"We are on the Ontario State Parkway heading west. Have you ever been out this way?" I asked.

"No, babe. Not besides going to the Charlotte Beach," she answered.

"Well, I'm glad you're awake. This is some very beautiful

countryside. Almost as fine as you," I said.

"Thank you. I appreciate this," Leah said.

Traffic wasn't very dense traveling westbound. Mostly, the thick of it headed east into the city. I did not have to watch the road exclusively for other drivers. However, wildlife did abound in the area. I accepted the role of tour guide to Leah, pointing out each body of water I've fished and the species that school there. She wore a continuous smile.

"This stretch of road takes you all the way to Niagara Falls. We're not driving up that far today. Something we can do come autumn, though. You should see the trees," I said.

We took the Kendall exit. After stopping for gas, refreshments, and tackle, we were on our way once again.

Thirty minutes later, I pulled over into a small parking space. We'd reached our destination. It was a clear sunny morning. Clouds were sparse overhead, and an impressive blue canvas could be seen for miles. Upon exiting the vehicle, a roaring thunder could be heard. One loud enough to force a person to speak over its volume to be heard. The source wasn't visible. It, in fact, is where I planned to take Leah. We walked along a concrete path. The Erie Canal bordered us on the south. To the north was a drop-off in the depth of the canal at approximately 25 feet. On our right, we looked down onto an impermeable, lush green canopy crowded with trees. A rolling mist lay at its center, billowing visibly skyward, followed by more forest. The seven-foot-thick structure beneath us hardly seemed capable of keeping such vast sums of water at bay. I was used to the surroundings. However, Leah absorbed it all with fresh eyes.

Across the canal, houses and civilian activity could be seen. The farther we walked, the drop-off to our right began steadily ascending. As the woodland elevated, visibility through its trees was permitted. There appeared to be a gorge not far beyond. The rumbling sound of thunder was less intrusive. Perhaps one third of a mile into the walk, I slowed as we came towards a large tree. It was growing two or so feet from the side of the canal. Someone many, many years ago had nailed two-by-four sections to its trunk, constructing a makeshift ladder.

The air was cool upon our skin and crisp to the lungs. I ducked underneath the metal railing onto its opposite side.

"This is the place, babe," I said, extending my hand, beckoning that she hands me the fishing poles. With all that I could carry, I scurried down the ladder. After a few trips, all of our belongings were at the base of the tree. Leah climbed down. I assisted her, though she didn't require it. The ground was barren and uneven, protruding with large tree roots and stones. We were now enveloped by the shade of the canopy above.

Worn paths could be seen leading in several directions.

"Watch your step, babe. The terrain is rather rough down here."

"I see," she responded.

We collected our items and proceeded onward. Within a minute's walk on the trail, we arrived at one of several steep declines at the top of the gorge. The river, its water dark and translucent, was reminiscent of sun-brewed tea infused with fresh cinnamon bark at its base. On the surface, foam in infinite supply bobbed and danced to the river current's rhythm. It probably would be unnerving to the person who has never seen this water type. The mysteries of what lies beneath and its actual depths weren't easily presumed.

"I'm going to bring our gear down first. Pay close attention to my route. The ground on the decline will shift under your weight. Since I'm used to it, I know what to expect."

I began my descent without hesitation. On the second trip up, I escorted Leah down the ragged slope.

"Should you fall, I won't let you get past me to the bottom. That's my word. Trust me."

She took my words to heart, her confidence growing instantly. We made it to the shore, moving a few yards from where our climb took place. I began to immediately set up the rigs for each rod.

While I worked, Leah soaked in her surroundings. The river stretched close to thirty feet across in this section. To the right, she saw white water rapids. On the left, the river could be seen meandering a few miles into the distance. Once more, we either had to stand close to talk or raise our voices considerably to counter the returning thunder.

Leah was the first to make a cast. She used a medium-action graphite rod and a slip bobber on ten-pound test braid. Her double hook rig was set eighteen inches apart. For bait, she used a shiner and a softshell crawdad.

"Whatever you do, love, keep an eye on your float. If it disappears, reel in the slack and set the hook like we've practiced."

She nodded as I continued.

"It's normal to catch very large fish here. I've caught fish bigger than one of my own legs, especially now, when the water levels are high. When this happens, the predators migrate further inland from the lake to feed."

"What's causing that sound?" Leah asked.

"It's a waterfall. I'll take you to see it. We have to go around that bend," I said, pointing. "There's a whirlpool at the base, and it's rather deep. You're going to love it."

There was a certainty in my words.

Five minutes hadn't passed when Leah hooked and landed a two-pound yellow perch. Instructing her of the dangers of this species of fish—its sharp dorsal fins and razor-like gill plates—I demonstrated how best to avoid getting injured. With the first keeper in the bucket, I went to rebait Leah's hooks. She stopped me short and did it herself. I was impressed.

We caught several fish over the next hour and may have lost just as many. We were totally embraced by nature. In our togetherness, we were oblivious to time or the concerns of the world beyond this gorge. She was falling in love with something I've loved my entire life. To share this experience meant so much to me, especially after seeing her joy.

As Leah continued fishing with live bait, I began casting large spoons and plastic grubs. I hooked into something that knew how to use the current to its advantage. Drag was being pulled for long runs at a time. My rod was doubled over.

"Babe, reel your line in, please."

Leah complied. Once the rod was set to the side, I handed her my pole with an angry fish at the other end.

"Time for you to feel a big fish's power," I said.

Wrapping my arms around her waist in a loving fashion, I instructed Leah on how to fight the fish to shore over time, as well as when not to fight and be patient.

Leah held the rod in her right hand and reeled with the left. As the battle ensued, her right arm began to spasm. Requesting my assistance, I refused, suggesting she transfer the rod to her left hand. I did begin to massage her bicep and forearm as the fight continued.

"Thanks. That feels much better," she said.

"My pleasure. I'll explain why I wouldn't take the rod from you later," I replied.

"You are doing great, sweetheart. My heart is swelling with joy."

She flashed me a radiant smile, and I offered up a quick kiss.

Half an hour into the skirmish, the fish went airborne for the fourth time, trying to throw the hook. Each time, Leah immediately lowered the rod tip. Finally, the fish was coaxed out of the main current and closer to shore. I readied the net while delivering commentary on what to do next. She was visibly afraid of the creature attached to the other end of the line. It was an understandable fear.

With the fish only a few feet away, it remained obscured, hidden by the dark waters. It haggled at the bottom, refusing to give in. I had an idea.

"Babe, lean away from the river with your rod. Let's see what some extra pressure will do."

My choice proved poor. The fish, a large rainbow trout to be exact, erupted from the water. It began a series of tail dances across the surface. Too many for Leah to parry. With so much pressure on the line, it finally succumbed to the wildness of the rainbow and the river.

There was a loud snapping of the line. It now hung limp at the rod tip. I was dumbfounded by the sudden chain of events. Leah faced me and said, "I'm sorry."

Rallying out of my stupor, I smiled. "Can't win them all," I responded.

I reached for the rod, and she handed it over. Her fingers were trembling. Giving Leah a big hug and lower back massage, we held the position for a measure of time. We talked and laughed in each other's ears. Her nerves settled. Once calm, she said, "I understand why you stay out on the water for so long. It's like a drug."

"Yes, it is, and I'm hooked twice over. On fishing and you," I answered.

"I bet you say that to all the girls," she said in good jest.

"Only you. Let's take a walk to the waterfall," I insisted. Before heading off, I tied on a diving stick bait.

"Did you get a good look at your fish?" I asked.

Her excitement returned instantly as she described it in detail: deep forest green on its back; its belly a milky silver with a pinkish hue; a large blood-red bar stretching across its gill plates to the tail, along the lateral line on both sides. It was covered with hundreds, if not thousands, of black speckles, just like freckles on humans. Its nose was hooked, and it had several pointed, curved, bone-white teeth. This trout had large eyes suited for sharp vision.

I'd estimate this landlocked rainbow in the fifteen-plus-pound range. I shared in her enthusiasm.

We navigated the bend upriver. The waterfall loomed before us. The sound was deafening. A constant mist remained in the air, adding moisture to our clothing by the second. In between rocks and boulders to our right and raging rapids to the left, I held on to Leah, lending comfort and support if she wanted it.

Leah looked upward for some time, absorbing nature's power and beauty. The whirlpool, literally at our feet, was alive.

"I used to walk from my grandma's house to this place all of the time growing up," I commented. "I'm going to share a thing or two with you when we leave here today. For now, let's enjoy some fishing."

I pointed out our path along the canal as someone walked by far above the waterfall. In all, Leah caught six different species of fish. We were having a splendid time. At noon, I'd decided for us to move forward to our next destination in order to maintain the itinerary.

Once safely back at the car, I made way to where I'd grown up within Medina on Orient St.

"That stream," I pointed into the backyard, "is what feeds the very river you were just fishing."

Turning around the vehicle, I stopped at the corner of Oak Orchard St. We made a left turn and drove until reaching the cul-de-sac at its furthest point.

"This is where I went to school. Oak Orchard Elementary. I presume the school's named after the street," I said.

From there, I brought Leah to the hospital where my mom had given birth to me and where my grandfather passed away. We chatted for a moment about life in the area.

Pulling into a park not far from my grandma's home on Orient Street, it astonished me how crisp memories of old were. It was a scenic place to have lunch.

South Main Park was at least one square mile in size. Its border to the east and north was a wider expanse of that same tea-colored water. The park hosted softball and soccer games. It had a family-friendly touch, though it wasn't frequented by large numbers of people. I glided to a halt on the shoulder of the paved roadway winding through the park.

Ten yards from the shoreline, enormous oak trees stood mightily. Many were spaced out strategically along the entire expanse of the park bordering the stream. It performed as a windbreak and to prevent erosion. Shade abounded amongst the trees. A total contrast to the openness of the stretching landscape on the opposite side of the road.

We exited the vehicle. As I opened the trunk to retrieve our cooler, comforter, and pillows, I said,

"You lead, and I'll follow."

Leah found a well-manicured patch of grass that she felt was suitable. It was on a very subtle slope. The breeze was gentle and warm.

Traffic could be seen in the distance. We had the entire park practically to ourselves. After indulging in the light lunch prepared the previous evening, we spent time feeding each other grapes, strawberries, and fresh-cut fruit. There were only our voices and the gentle wilderness echoing the vibrations of sound.

Eventually, we dozed for a while beneath the canopy until mid-afternoon. As we awakened to one another's smiles, I said,

"There's at least one more thing I'd like to show you."

We exited the park, taking Sixty-Three South to Thirty-One East. Around ten miles later, we turned left onto Wood Road. This was rural Medina. Only four residences had this address. Michael and his parents' home stood alone on one side. Three homes occupied the other. Mike's dad could be seen close to the barn on a riding mower, wearing goggles and ear covers.

I came to a complete halt once in front of the second property we encountered.

Its front yard stretched three hundred feet from the road to the front porch. The driveway was just as long, with mature pines and oaks lining both sides. Additional yard reached across the driveway where a pond, a large chicken coop, two gardens, and a pig pen barely stood erect. I used to dread landscape duties.

I pulled into the gravel-strewn driveway.

"This is where I was raised since the time my mother brought me from the hospital. On this land with my grandparents is where so many of my core values were deeply instilled."

I exited the vehicle once I'd honked the horn a couple of times. No one came outside. After a time, I climbed back into the SUV.

"It would mean the world to me to acquire my grandparents' lost property and keep it in the family. I'll show you where the property line ends."

Turning the vehicle around, we eased our way to the road and continued our journey.

As we traveled east on Route Thirty-One, I explained, "Should we decide to stay on course, this route will lead us directly into Rochester. It turns into Monroe Avenue, to be precise. The highway running parallel to this one at the moment is called Old Thirty-One. It turns into Lyell Avenue."

Leah and I held hands during the ride. We were mostly silent, contemplating our own intimate thoughts.

For some time during the ride home, Leah took inventory of me. I kept my eyes on the road as if oblivious, smiling inwardly. She squeezed my hand. I responded with an embrace of my own and smiled.

When I looked into her eyes, she said, "Thank you. I had a really wonderful time today."

"You're welcome. There will be many more to come."

24

Beneath the Surface

Divine had been spending too much time alone. Under the circumstances, I'm sure it wasn't good for his mental health. No matter who I asked, each person seemed to have a greater priority. Some were online college students. That was totally understandable. Besides the bare necessities provided along the way, Sean would not be privy to anyone's empathy. Out of respect for the fat man, I appointed some accompaniment. I set Jerod's skeletal remains in a chair, tying it in place next to the cage. For now, it would have to suffice. Not long after, "The Bully" could be heard bawling loudly like someone extremely lost and forlorn.

The sublevel area that held Sean cleaned up quite well. I couldn't iterate enough how functional the plexiglass walls are. I'd cleaned each section and tract just as easily as I marred them. With the floor thoroughly scoured, it was as if Jerod's purging had never happened. Actually, from this point on, Jerod who?

Sean had visibly begun to show his weight loss. Since diminishing the calorie intake of his diet, the proof was in the pudding. One day, while exchanging the hay and blanket in his cage, Divine asked, "Why haven't you killed me yet?"

I looked at him with uncaring eyes. My answer wasn't immediate.

"You're not the first to ask that. Some feel that you being in this cage like so, is inhumane. The mistake they're making is that they're trying to put themselves in your position. When no one has done what you did, your circumstances will never prove befitting." I paused for a moment before continuing.

"Do you recall my asking how you would like to die?" I didn't wait for a response. "Sleeping pills are out of the question. Besides, why rush the surprise?"

I stared into his face. The eye contact seemed longer than it was. He diverted his eyes toward the skeleton.

"You were out here living by the sword even when you didn't need to. Desperate to make a name for yourself. On the contrary, I suggested you make money. As long as your foundation is secure, who cares if anyone knows the name? One thing was for sure: if anyone decided to test you properly, only failing grades would result. But you didn't appreciate that motto. In fact, you didn't regard many of the jewels I brought to the table. So, when I decided on keeping you at arm's reach, you didn't respect that either. You must've fathomed entitlement to what I worked to accomplish."

I drank from a bottle of water that I had brought with me.

"How many people do you know of who are foolish enough to intentionally break into one of my residences?" I asked. I looked at him with a knowing expression. "None that I'm aware of. However, a smart person—or one who thinks he's smart—may give it a go. Especially if he knows when I'm not in the country."

My laughter was sudden and on the loud side. "I bet you thought I didn't know all of these years, huh?" I laughed some more. "Oh my goodness. You're such a silly little rabbit. After twenty long years, I've not forgotten. All there was for me to do was reflect. And, of course, make plans. If you're unable to decide your own fate, I may keep you for years on end, naked and afraid."

I stood and went upstairs in the middle of our conversation without warning or pardoning myself. My absence was brief. I returned, a file in hand, sixty-three pages in total. Getting comfortable, I allowed the file to rest on my lap.

"This is a copy of my sentencing minutes. I'd like to read a few things to you that the judge had to say," I said calmly. Fingering my way to one of the pages I had dog-eared, I stopped. Skimming over the contents of the page unsatisfied, I moved onward.

"Okay, on page eleven, we have something interesting. Ms. Rosa had a lot to say, even though she wasn't called as a government witness. Listen carefully, Sean. She says the following verbatim.

Ms. Rosa's Statement (read aloud):

My name is Mary Rosa, and I can say that this has affected me in a way where I can't live my life in peace. I am scared of life itself. I seek help. I don't let my kids play out with people. He may have stopped me from hustling and dealing drugs out there, because I wasn't the perfect person, but this does not mean he can beat me up and stab me and cut me and beat me for so long and then to beat my mother—to beat my mother in a way that they did, and I was hopeless. I don't know what they came after. I don't know what he wanted.

I hope to always be breathing the air that he will never breathe in his life. I hope he goes to hell. I hope he rots, and everybody who follows him, because he deserves to die in the worst way ever. God forgive me for wanting him to die in this way, but he has hurt me in a way that I will never, ever forget. I can't even trust any man to be sexually with me because of this man. I don't trust anybody—nobody in the world—because of what this man did to me and my family. I'm dealing with it to the best of my ability. I'm really angry. It took a long time for him to get captured, but he's caught. He's going to rot in hell, and that's all I want to say. Thank you."

"Are you aware that, according to statements given by Ms. Rosa, a Jamaican cat approached her on Smith Street? It pertained to some necklace, specifically a medallion she was wearing. This man had told her it belonged to his people and he wanted it returned. If not, it would be taken by force. Sometime later, a few weeks down the line, ol' girl's house was invaded by what witnesses say were Jamaicans. The irony of it is that the uninvited visitors kept demanding the location of a gold medallion."

The expression on Sean's face indicated he didn't know how to properly respond.

"With all this being said, how is it that I became involved with this specific home invasion with you? Not just this one, but Da'Quan and Hot Rod as well? If I helped, when did I get my cut?" I asked frankly.

Truth is, the fat man had begun talking on the day he was taken into custody and charged as a co-conspirator. On May 13, 2002, the very day my trial had been set to begin, I was arraigned on a second superseding indictment charging eleven counts in total. This strategic move by the government forced my trial to a halt, even after being ready to proceed into battle. After fourteen months, I'd seen the evidence and was aware of the witnesses. I presented a genuine plea to those now charged with many of the same crimes.

I began with the following. "Divine, T-Rock, Mateen, and Luda. I need you all to pay attention very closely. We all know that this case is thrown together. There's not a man here who is doing business with the other. On my last court date, April 23, 2002, a trial date was set for today per the request of the defense. I've combed this case many times. Even neglected and lost a true relationship over it. They hope to build a case while we're incarcerated.

The prosecutor stated in open court, "Your Honor, I'm not ready to proceed to trial. It's the very reason you all are here. You want to go home?" he asked, knowing the obvious answer. Every man concurred.

"We all need to push for a speedy trial. By law, it must be provided within seventy calendar days. Weekends and holidays are not included. If not honored, we can move to dismiss the indictment. Chances are, the judge will deny the motion to dismiss. If he did, though, it would be without prejudice. From there, the government could reindict, which it surely would. That's neither here nor there. He's going to help the prosecutor in every way possible.

The judge himself was a New York State District Attorney for his entire professional career prior to being assigned a seat in Federal District Court. He's never lost a case—with the exception of Bazz on that triple homicide trial.

The Seven got acquitted. Unfortunately, Be Luda got slayed with the help of Adrian testifying. That was the only blemish to the judge's fifty-eight-and-zero trial record at the time. We ain't got nothing coming in his courtroom. It'll be two prosecutors to each lawyer every time. Those aren't good odds.

If he wasn't ready for trial against me alone, he'll never be ready in seventy days now that there's an additional four alleged co-conspirators. All we need to do is press for the trial. Reserve the right for counsel to submit any pretrial motions in the future. Also, have your lawyers file for a joinder with any and all motions I've submitted. In this manner, should there be a need for them to file anything additional, it won't be much."

I paused to rest my vocal cords and get a drink.

"As of right now, there are only four witnesses on the government's witness list, not including law enforcement. There's no evidence. No undercover sales of drugs, video surveillance, drugs, or weapons recovered. Besides my phone counts from a previous indictment and the gun charge against me alone, there's nothing.

We need to press the gas, beat this case, and get in the wind. Y'all wit it?" I asked.

Apprehension and reluctance were written over their fearful faces.

"Man, I need to see what my lawyer's talking about," said one.

"We don't even know what's going on," said another.

"Everyone's gonna at least need to file motions to suppress evidence," exclaimed the third.

"I'm scared to death and don't know what to think," uttered the last.

I held my tongue until all had finished speaking. Their words were quickly digested for review. When my response came, it was clear, concise, and cut sharply like a *katana*.

Pointing towards the first man who spoke, I said, "Your lawyer's not going to know anything close to what I do anytime soon. I've been pressing hard on the government these past fourteen months."

I went down the line. "I'm sharing with you what's going on. They have no case and are trying to construct one. They have a set amount of dudes on something called a 'Blacklist.' Believe it or not, the protocol is to get them off the streets by any means."

My gaze wandered over to T-Rock. Our eyes met and locked.

"You mentioned motions to suppress. Where were you when you got snatched?" I asked.

"I was driving and they pulled me over," he answered.

"Did they find anything on you or in the car?"

"No."

"So, what is there to suppress? Unless these devils were issued warrants to search your residence or somebody made a statement when he came in, motions to suppress are a waste of time. Did the feds run up to anyone's house?"

Each one answered in the negative.

"Has anyone talked to them people since the arrest?"

No was the collective response.

"Men, let's not make this matter harder than what it is. I'm seeing the situation clearly simply because my life has revolved strictly around this matter for more than a year. There's no physical evidence. Every motion you can think of, it's probable I've submitted. Everything was denied. He's gonna do the same to you, dragging the proceedings in the process.

Pressure bursts pipes if applied correctly. Play chess or poker, it's your choice. Either way, we have to call the devil's bluff."

Settling in on the last talk, "Fearing this situation is understandable. If you are unable to rally your fear into courage, though, you'll do something stupid and probably live to regret it. Strap your boots up tight, fellas. Real talk, the only problem I see is with you three," I said, speaking to T-Rock, Divine, Mateen and Luda. "Somebody was out there dealing with those rats, Dut and Jason. All along, they were offering grand jury testimony against you. The first time was in April 2002 and again in early May 2002. It seems a couple of you cats were doing some pillow talking with these cocksuckers. Did you know the feds have something called the hearsay rule? Unfortunately, unlike the New York State Penal System—where hearsay is not admissible—in federal court, it is permitted. So, in this arena, words alone have weight. Just as fingerprints on a murder weapon or a suitcase full of money connected to a heist found in your bedroom closet may have, if the details are woven together properly enough by the AUSA."

Thirteen additional long and miserable months passed before we were finally able to proceed to trial. My severance from the other co-defendants was long denied by the judge despite being trial-ready on May 13, 2002. Jury selection would begin on July 22, 2003. Further compounding my burden, on July 21, 2003, the day before trial, I was indicted on eleven counts of firearms trafficking throughout the United States. The complaint even went as far as to suggest involvement of shipping weapons internationally.

Prior to the trial, the judge said, "Note the presence of counsel and the attorneys. First, a couple of housekeeping matters. I understand the defendant has been charged on a separate indictment as of yesterday afternoon. Has there been any negotiation between the defense and the government on the possibility of resolving both matters?"

"No, there is not, your honor," The defense counsel answered.

"Very well, I would like to strongly urge an agreeable resolution at the behest of all involved," said the court.

My lawyer shared that after the court proceeding, a third federal indictment was being sought for Racketeering Influenced and Corrupt Organization (RICO), coupled with the prosecutor seeking the death penalty. I asked myself, "What's it going to be next?" During this time, I could feel the harsh grasp of the devil's embrace, like a five-hundred-pound constrictor becoming overly acquainted. Its coils piled high one upon the other. From my ankles to my ears, it overlaps, blotting out the light of day. It hindered the ability to breathe freely and think clearly as duress struck my physical vessel. The struggle ensued as the burden became more unbearable with each instant. But sparks are flying. The war has begun not to become overrun or overwhelmed. I resisted the oppression of life by an imposing U.S. Government. Despised is the majority of a unified urban minority. The Nixon Administration made that quite clear.

However, there is an exception. The strings of the puppet are at its master's disposal. To control by folly and whim. A life not to be mourned if torn asunder or lost. Puppets are conveniently expendable to their master whenever the decision to replace one is desired. Hence, the host of the doll danced the mechanics until there were several in motion. Sean and company did the devil's bidding. Accordingly, it's why we're here today.

25

Righteous Wrath

The flight out of Logan Airport was pleasant enough. I had a slight throb around my temple area, presumably from a lack of rest. There would be a two-hour layover at O'Hare Airport in Chicago, IL. I'd often wondered if enough time existed in between delays to visit a few folks. I reconsidered, figuring there's no need to cut corners so closely. I ventured into the Airport and seated myself at one of its several bars. Two doubles of Remi Martin were ordered. I drank very little. However, an exception could be made on long flights.

Time moved slowly. A mental note was made to bring some reading material or a " nice book of maze puzzles along to entertain my thought process. In the meantime, I soberly listened to the elevator music playing lightly through speakers perched somewhere overhead. There weren't very many people occupying the bar. It wasn't exactly empty either. More women than men passed through. My thoughts often wandered about where these people were from and where they were heading. It has always been a simple curiosity. Thirty minutes to the layover's expiration, I made my way closer to the boarding gate. Before long, we were in the air heading over the snowcapped Rocky Mountains. Window seats have always been a preference of mine. The sights from this elevation were beautiful and quite unique. It would've been nice to have a quality camera for capturing each moment.

It was a very sunny day in Los Angeles. LAX was a sprawling airport alive with activity. Despite it being somewhat windy during the month of April, the climate and weather were acceptable. It was a major contrast to the consistent cold rains and Canadian cold fronts pressing in from across Lake Ontario. Just past the light perpendicular to LAX, I crossed Sepulveda Boulevard onto Imperial Highway and contracted a midsize vehicle from Hertz Car Rental. Along the same avenue, slightly adjacent to Hertz's entrance side, I secured a suite at a nice hotel.

Once settled, I made a few calls. Shevar was the first to answer after a few rings. With the confirmation of his arrival later tonight, I informed him of my whereabouts. With time to spare, I found the way to the hotel's gym and indulged in a good workout. Ninety minutes later, I went back to the room to take a long, steaming shower. I ordered a late lunch while watching a pay-per-view movie. There was a knock on the door.

"Who is it?" I asked standing outside the door frame.

"Room service," a woman replied.

I received my meal, rated my appreciation with a tip, and sat down to enjoy some sustenance.

Three hours later, I awoke to the sound of my cellphone ringing. It was Shevar telling me he'd arrived. I came downstairs to the lobby to greet him. Shevar was on the phone, reaching out to family before we towed his luggage up to the room. Within the hour, his first cousin Ced, along with his good associate Cris and I, were shaking hands in greeting for the very first time. The Kumbi-Yah was brief. Our departure onto the streets of LA had begun. Ced and Cris accepted the role as hosts of their city. In an effort to accommodate Shevar's nutritional needs, we landed on Crenshaw Boulevard at a place called Harold and Belle's.

This restaurant was very much in the heart of the city. A place where lives have been lost under previous ownership. Located on the side of the building was a freshly paved and blacktopped area for valet parking. A gentleman in a suit at a podium waited to be of service. It caught me by surprise. I enjoyed the idea that this establishment held such consideration for its customers. Located only a matter of blocks away from where portions of 'Boyz in the Hood" were filmed, the reality of our surroundings didn't go unnoticed.

Harold and Belle's was a restaurant that mainly focused on, according to its menus, Creole and seafood cuisine. We were very warmly greeted upon entry by a beautiful hostess. She led us past a highly polished wooden bar and to a table for four. The place wasn't crowded just yet. After ordering our entrees and drinks from the bar, we'd have time to quietly discuss the specifics of this visit. Doubles of Henessey with sides of ice and Coca-Cola were brought for everyone. Before long, the food arrived, and we enjoyed ourselves sharing food in between.

With all of us coming to terms and having the clearest understanding, all there was to do was enjoy the City of Angels. During the conversation, while en route to Hollywood, Shevar used the "n" word a couple of times. Cris firmly and respectfully expressed his distaste for the use of the racial epithet.

"I do not like that word, brother," he said. "Are you not aware of the self-destructive nature a poor vocabulary has on one's own mind? I'd appreciate you would not refer to me in such a manner. Thank you in advance."

The light-skinned brother with the long ponytail, slanted eyes, and broad shoulders was a quiet but conscious storm. He reminded me of someone I had read about named King Tremain in a book titled *Standing at the Scratch Line* and *Echoes of a Distant Summer* by Guy Johnson.

As rare as it is, I recognized a parallel in Cris similar to the inner qualities of my own. Instantly, I took a liking to him. It became quite clear in that moment that if I asked a question, most likely the answer would be either sincere or nothing at all. While we cruised the city the following afternoon, I sought enlightenment.

"You ever see *Colors*?" Ced asked me.

"Yes, I have. Several times, actually," I said.

"Take a look to your left," he said, indicating. "Does it look familiar?"

"That's where the Crips crashed during the car chase after putting in some work at a funeral. They smashed a few police officers too, before the vehicle rolled and burst into flames," I responded, looking out the driver's side window past Cris.

"Where are we right now?" I asked.

"We're in Watts. Those towers you see are called the Watts Towers," Cris said.

I nodded. "Did the person who made *Colors* create scenarios of violence to try and portray an image of gang life?"

"No. It's the opposite," answered both Ced and Cris. They took turns sharing the history of Los Angeles.

I couldn't help being reminded every time I looked at Ced of the artist Nate Dogg—albeit a darker version. He was wearing a navy, black, and white flannel, black jeans, and Lugs. I wasn't from Cali, but still, it was obvious what it was hitting for.

"The director based the movie on real-life events. He figured out a way to bring our everyday reality of the inner city and format it to fit the big screen. What made it so authentic was eighty percent of the cast really came from the hood," Ced shared.

"The soundtrack from the movie was a wild one," I said. "I bought it and used to listen to it regularly while serving time in prison. It's actually where Shevar and I met and built our bond. People thought my music selections were crazy. What they couldn't see was the realness in the words of those songs. Taking heed of the messages and warnings could save a life. Disregard may result in a loss of it."

We pulled up at the Slauson Swap Meet. It was easily discernible this place made for an intense environment. Blue and red could be seen all throughout the parking lot on this cloudless sunny day. The Latino presence didn't go unnoticed. People were socializing amongst their own parties. I didn't see Blood and Crip—or either of—mingling with the Latinos at any given time. I'd walked into a world where realness was to be expected. The magnitude of which, however, was admittedly unanticipated.

"You said you wanted to see the hood," Cris said.

One thing is certain: Ced and Cris surely delivered. It was a great deal of movement up and down Slauson Street and inside the parking lot.

"Yeah, I did ask for this. Now, I'm going to ask for something else," I said. This was a jungle environment. A place where prey succumbed to predators, and predators just as easily became prey.

"I need a strap, fellas. Preferably a compact .40 or a .45."

I could see the concern in both Ced and Cris's demeanor. They both observed me for a while and seemed to have an unspoken communication amongst themselves. As one spoke his decree, the other nodded.

"Should you have a problem or find yourself being disrespected, go into the offender's mouth with your fists. Just make sure y'all get our attention. If circumstances worsen, we'll clean it up. What we can't have is one of you firing at the wrong person. An apology is not going to cut it. It will start something that we'll have to finish while y'all are on the East Coast laid back."

I nodded in confirmation. The manifesto given was powerful and deserved no reproach. We eventually strolled into the swap meet in order to see the people and their wares. The place was bustling with both merchants and shoppers. Observation immediately revealed the increase in ethnic diversity. The first person I spoke to outside of my party of four was a man of Middle Eastern descent. He wore transitional lenses. and stood three inches above my six feet. He had an airy but full mid-range curly afro. His unique features and bronze complexion reminded me of several Sudanese brothers I've met in my travels.

He initiated the communication. Something a savvy and smart businessman must be able to do when in the sales industry. If not for his address, I would've carried on, lending no more than a side glance at his products. The banter between us was good, as was his English. After fifteen minutes of vibrant conversation, I purchased two pairs of suede K Swiss. One was a lovely chocolate brown, and the other a beautiful cobalt blue, both of which I'd never seen before on the East Coast. We departed with sincere smiles and laughter. I regret not learning the merchant's name and contact information.

Ced and Cris did not immerse themselves in the conversation whatsoever and declined offers to select any items of interest. The two of then navigated Shevar and me through the shopping area. Immediately, we were directed to a stall where a woman sold large paper shopping bags. With coarse twine handles. Cris purchased four and began snapping each one open. He passed them to Ced. In turn, Ced dropped each of our bags into the paper bags. I was bemused as a result of the actions taken. Shevar and I looked at each other questioningly, trying to silently solve the conundrum.

We didn't need to troubleshoot for very long.

"I'll answer the question before you ask. Normally, when you enter the hood of any major city, different rules apply. It's like learning to crawl before walking, and walking before running. You see what I'm wearing?" Ced asked. His navy blue and white flannel spoke for itself. No explanation was needed.

"Anyone, even the civilians, knows what they see when they see me. You must learn the same, but on a deeper level. There's been a truce between the Locs and Damus for a few years now. Every now and then, something kicks off. Overall, though, the truce remains intact. Not long ago, the streets used to run red with blood, no matter your set.

"If you two were out here by yourselves and happened to put on those sneakers right now, and you came across the wrong person or people, you're gonna get approached. The instant one of these serious Damus hears your accent, he'll know you ain't from around here and may give you a pass. Most likely, the conclusion would be that you don't know any better. Albeit, the pass may entail getting jacked under a gentleman's pretense, of course."

Shevar and I exchanged glances. Neither of us said anything, for it wasn't a wise time to speak. However, it was a great time to listen.

"Now, add Cris and me to the scenario. Everything changes. We might all get our caps peeled. Why? Because even though you two don't know any better, we do. Forbid any of them from being dusted on PCP. Despite the truce, such a declaration shall be answered with deadly violence. Threats usually result in the loss of life out here. So, you must pay attention at all times. Don't worry—we'll school y'all along the way," Ced assured as we delved deeper into LA's hood tourism.

On a separate occasion, I requested going to East Los Angeles in order to experience some authentic Mexican cuisine. The desire was the result of a favorite show of mine called *Epicurious*. It revealed the specific but little-known location in this particular region of the city. I'd never forget the response.

"I know just the place," Cris answered.

Ten minutes later, we pulled into the parking lot of Taco Bell. I figured there had to be some humor involved before heading to our intended destination. Cris turned off the ignition, retrieved the keys, and opened his door on the driver's side.

"Come on, Preme," he said.

Reality hit hard in that moment. That wonderful chronic euphoria that existed seconds ago was a thing of the past.

By the time I opened the passenger side door, Cris was already inside the franchise. Acknowledging my disappointment, he returned eye contact.

"Authentic Mexican cuisine," he said.

There seemed to be a gap in need of bridging between my initial request and what I'd actually received.

"Is this how you treat your guests, my brother?" I asked.

"Let's grab something really quick to hold us over until nightfall," Cris insisted.

Everyone ordered something light. Two soft tacos later, a conversation arose while sitting at a table nursing soft drinks.

"I'm pretty sure you two have heard of something called 'the voice of reason.'" Both of us concurred. Cris proceeded.

"The voice you're listening to is coming from that conscientious little devil sitting on your left shoulder whispering, *Why not?* East LA it is. Also, you have an angel sitting on your right shoulder, suggesting sound advice. I'm that angel. For your own sake, I must protect you from yourself. Since Slauson Street and Crenshaw Boulevard didn't help you see it thoroughly enough, I'm going to take you into my hood."

We rode in silence. After twenty minutes on the 405, we exited. Shortly afterwards, we pulled in front of a white house.

"I live in the heart of Inglewood, where Crippin' is good. None of the Ten Deuce. Unfortunately, there's a war going on this instant, and it's Crip on Crip. Monster's mom lives right down the street, about twelve houses, on the other side. See that gas station up there on the corner of Imperial?" Cris asked. "I can't tell you how many lives have been taken in that parking lot over the last six weeks. If either set of Locs caught a car full of Bloods up there versus the Crips they're fully engaged with, they'll give the Bloods a pass and blast on the Crips."

I couldn't believe my ears.

"Crips are supposed to roll together," I stated with disappointment.

"Not when a loc is kidnapped and held for a million-dollar ransom. The ransom was paid, but they killed cuz anyway," Cris said bitterly. "That's why it's a war."

We stood on the curb, soaking in the gas station and all of the passing vehicles at the busy intersection. A slight tint to the sky was beginning to take hold. It was the first sign that night was soon approaching. Elements of a different kind were beginning to rise from their slumber. In the world around, there has always been the fear of darkness—or that which lurks within. One could only wonder which held the greatest concern for those most weary.

Nightfall held no particular effect for me. Life's experiences had shown and taught the very things that come at dusk, will, if necessary, rise when the sun is at its zenith for any undertaking. Locals began emerging from their residences. Observations of the unfamiliar weren't subtle. Considering all of which we were just informed, if not for Cris and Ced, the two of us probably would have been taken just as quickly. Two strangers trespassing in novel territory, now another grim statistic. Several people in the area greeted our guides. We were then ushered into the house. Cris needed some time to get himself refined. In the meantime, I relaxed mostly on the porch with a cold drink.

From time to time, I'd call someone back east to share how beautiful it is in California. My opinion on why they'd enjoy the state followed. Most people I know, the seemingly pessimistic, asserted several reasons why such enjoyment was less likely.

There had been a consistent sound of barking since walking out onto the front porch. I imagined the unfamiliar scent of an intruding human was the trigger. Further inspection revealed a brutal-looking white pit bull adorning a massive chain on the right side of the house. It was muscular and generally large for the breed. Its eyes were cold. If any love existed in this creature, it wasn't available to me as the stranger.

Ced had come outside and joined me. He brought two Coronas, freezing cold to the touch. I thanked him. Even though my alcohol consumption was pretty much non-existent, I chose to accept and indulge his hospitality.

"When we roll out, we're gonna bring you by my man P'Loc's restaurant. Literally, anything Mexican one of his cooks can most likely make." I nodded once Ced had finished speaking.

"Cris never got around to sharing why we couldn't go to East LA," I said.

"Well, I can explain it easily enough," Ced answered.

"Relationships between the Black and Mexican communities were not always this fragile. All things considered, we used to get along well enough. Some years ago, the East Coast homies jacked those fools for a shipment. Rumor has it that it was a semi carrying at least a ton of snow. There were similar incidents between them and us that gradually increased tensions."

Someone close by was blasting the radio. While Ced took me to school, a heavy rotation of E-40, Warren G and Nate Dogg, Dr. Dre, 2Pac, DJ Quik, Snoop, and others made their vibes felt.

"This, however," Ced continued, "broke the levees to hell more so than any other time. It became an all-out war against anyone within our communities who wasn't deemed a civilian. When it rained out this way, it was with lead. So many people have died and still do. It's just as bad in our state prisons. Even in the county, soldiers were catching fades. Usually, when it's serious, the spillover is statewide, prisons included."

We sat in silence for a while, sipping the Coronas. In the early '90s, some of my favorite rap artists hailed from Cali with the exception of Scarface and the Geto Boys. MC Eiht, Spice 1, WC, Ice Cube, Lynch Mob, CPO, and N.W.A. were giving up the gospel as far as I was concerned. Now, being here in the heart of the city and listening to the history gave concrete substance to all of their music.

Ced continued. "East LA is the type of place where you may not return from. Any given gangster may decide the four of us will be suitable sacrifices for the past sins of others. Not today, we won't. So, you must understand—we will protect you even from yourself."

I nodded, fully understanding, and extended my right hand in appreciation. He accepted.

"Thank you both for everything. Forgive us both for our ignorance," I said.

We spoke a while longer. Eventually, Shevar came from inside the house out onto the porch.

Darkness had settled in. It was here to stay until dawn made its presence known. The streets around us had become alive with voices and activity. Perhaps it had something to do with the hot California sun. It could also be a military tactic of moving under the cover of shadows. Certainly, any potential target becomes greatly obscured by nature itself.

I decided to indulge in a deeper dialogue. "Basically, was it between all Blacks and Mexicans in Cali?"

"No. The South Siders vibe with the Bloods for the most part, but it too has its limits, I imagine. On the other hand, there are the Northerners, or Norteños. They reside in the northern parts of Cali, like San Fran, Oakland, etc. Every last one of my men who has been through Folsom, Chino, San Quentin, Pelican Bay—the list goes on—has told me how those guys stand side by side and back to back with the Locs in both times of peace and especially in war. I have love in my heart for them and have never been through the system or met a Norteño yet."

My silence lingered, and my thoughts swirled. I was in awe based on the lessons being taught, never to be forgotten. Deeper was the fact that Ced felt the way he did about those he didn't know directly or share any experiences with. It defined a great deal of who he is as a man.

"So, in retrospect, I made a poor decision by approaching those Mexican women dressed in all black in South Central?" I asked. "It wasn't the wisest choice. The balance is so fragile out here. People in this life look for any reason to kick something off. Most of the time, it's because they've lost a loved one along the way and will be itching for any opportunity at revenge," Ced patiently explained. "When the higher-ups call for a ceasefire, normally, all parties acknowledge it despite their pain. So yes, I'd say you made a dangerous move. It's very likely that half of the females you were around are killers. I could see it in their eyes. Fortunately, you cleaned the situation up well enough. The best places to meet Latino women are in neutral zones where their guards won't be up so high from danger in general," he assured.

Humbly apologizing for my mistakes, I made a mental note not to repeat such carelessness again.

26

A Reckoning at Dawn

The city was in an uproar. A wave of fear had struck at its heart and taken a firm grip. An unprecedented number of missing persons reports had gone out over the past few weeks. Eleven adult males had vanished. There were no clues to their whereabouts. No witnesses were forthcoming, or leads to any potential motive. However, family and friends told authorities foul play was suspected. Public outcry demanded answers from the Rochester Police Department. Flustered by the pressure of their superiors, additional units were put onto the streets in hopes of finding a lead. Any lead that may shed some light on the most recent disappearances.

Frankly, it baffled me. When people were getting decapitated and buried in shallow graves within the inner city, there was little to no publicity. Perhaps it was the unknowing that frayed law enforcement so. If there were ever a trail to pursue worth following into the maze of mystery surrounding the city limits of Rochester, New York, it consisted of bread crumbs. The headlines read, "HAVE YOU SEEN ME?" Detective John Barnes was the leading investigator. He implored the community to speak up. Via televised live conference, the following was stated:

"Fellow citizens of Rochester, I thank you for your time and consideration. We are here today concerning a string of missing persons reports. Due to the lack of information and the few details that have been gleaned from family and friends, the department is leaning towards foul play. We will be looking into every possible angle of each case. It's unclear whether or not any of the missing may have had connections with each other in the past or present. Our department will not allow for any stone to go unturned. Please, anyone within the upstanding community who may have seen something, heard something,

"Please contact me at 585-773-2818. Or if you wish to remain anonymous, call 1-800-458-TIPS. You may also log on to our website address at ..." Detective Barnes recited all avenues of contact. There was a host of reporters shouting a plethora of questions.

"My apologies to the press, I will not be accepting questions at this time. A post media conference shall take place briefly, which may address any questions and concerns by our Chief Spokeswoman and D.A.R.E. Program Director Lieutenant Cheryl Franks."

As Lieutenant Franks stepped forward to the podium, Barnes began his immediate departure. He had a meeting with a potential source. Exiting one of the City Hall's several parking lots, he avoided the crowded press fair on Church Street by heading in the opposite direction. Merging with traffic, Barnes eased onto the inner loop traveling eastbound. Choosing the Clinton Avenue exit, he made a left turn at the light. Clinton Avenue extended for miles on end. From North Clinton, he headed east onto Ridge Road, where Barnes pulled into a well-known burger establishment. He parked his Crown Victoria, took the keys from the ignition, grabbed a Popular Science magazine off the backseat, and began reading while waiting.

The instant the 'Missing Persons Address' became public, I didn't like it. I'd known there weren't any leads in the case. However, any undue heat was unwanted attention. That very evening, arrangements were made for a relocation process. Ten full-size kennels, ones large enough to hold fully mature Great Danes or Saint Bernards, held each of the missing. Sedatives were given to the guests. Once the effects were noticeable, each individual was transferred to a kennel. After loading the kennels into a moving truck, it was taken west beyond city limits and Monroe County. Primarily, anything connected to the string of kidnappings was uprooted if not permanently grounded. Gone without a trace.

I thoroughly observed each sublevel section of the scrap yard/recycling plant. A meticulous acid washing had scoured each concrete wall. Sealant was reapplied to ensure the foundation's integrity. The Hazmat and OSHA training was an excellent class to attend. As a result, certain services could be catered to in-house. Keeping outsiders at bay was key. The floors were now good to serve another purpose.

As each day passed, flyers were posted. On supermarket walls, telephone posts, and in one section of the city close to the Public Safety Building, a billboard read "Have You Seen Me?" with large face shots of every last person in my ward. I smiled. No amount of billboards, flyers, or reward money would save the lives of the wretched within my care. Their stories in the annals of history shall be written differently. The final sentences on each person's page would be narrated by me with a grim certainty. Forceful would be the hand holding the quill.

Several things struck me as odd in the following days. Innocent missing children did not receive anywhere near the same attention as these quislings. Someone in the political arena had to be pressing the issue, but why? Upon turning it over in my head several times, only one conclusion resulted. Some of the captives, if not all, were still working as informants. And whoever's pressing for the whereabouts of the missing may have careers on the line. If it were up to me, those in question would never use another's shoulder as footholds to success.

Pieces were moving all over the city like the gears of a pristine conditioned grandfather clock. The media had become another part of the maze to be navigated. Eager to keep my appointment, I departed the recycling plant. I took Buffalo Road to Mt. Read Boulevard and merged onto the Interstate. I continued west on 490, veered onto 390 South to 590 South, and exited at the suburb of Irondequoit, just above the bay on Empire Boulevard. I loved this area. It reminded me of how life was meant to be. Scarcely a vehicle would ever be heard in passing once off the main thoroughfare. It was an area of extreme beauty.

In winter, the snow was a pristine white and gave the appearance of being busy with animal tracks. Each driveway had been thoroughly cleaned of snow and ice, several of which steamed in the dead of winter. The heated blacktop attracted wildlife both large and small. Spring rains and warm breezes promoted a scenery of bright greenery sprouting above head and below foot.

The people within this community, by appearances, were mostly retired. Those I encountered were warm and friendly. Whether by bike or car, memories of slowly cruising these wide, meandering streets resisted exhaustion. Each repetition brings a fresh brand of some new detail previously unnoticed. My appreciation increased internally. I thought to myself how a mandatory cycling itinerary of both Irondequoit's and Webster's hiking trails on opposite sides of the bay would prove most exhilarating. We could bring food, all of the dogs, and make a full day of it.

I tapped the brakes of my Cherokee as I descended the steep slope from the manicured ridge above. China Doll was waiting patiently at the launch, her hair blowing slightly in a light breeze. She looked warm enough while adorning a North Face outfit. At her feet was a canine. As I pulled up to park, I realized it was Onyx. She was one of the more aggressive pit bulls raised from eight weeks old by either China Doll or me. Onyx gnawed upon an old leather football long ago perforated by her constant chewing.

I turned my SUV around, shifted gears from drive to reverse, and guided the boat trailer just short of its wheels breaking the water's surface. Once the emergency brake had been employed, I exited the vehicle. Catching a familiar scent, Onyx trotted over to greet me, gnarled football in tow. She surrendered it to the ground only to nip at my hands while scratching behind her ears, neck, and muzzle. Onyx's muscle content was amazing. Jaw muscles the size of baseballs protruded from both sides of her face. She resumed standing on all fours, leaving muddy paw prints as evidence on my thighs.

The soft, moist earth sucked at the soles of my hip wanders. Spring was apparent this afternoon. Irondequoit Bay beckoned us receptively. China Doll made her way towards the boat with a bucket in one hand and a tackle box in the other. Onyx reclaimed her football. She met China Doll in stride and escorted her to the boat. I accepted the payload, even though to her it wasn't a burden. She thanked me just the same.

While prepping the boat for launch, I asked, "So, how is the most precious resource of the planet doing today?"

China Doll flashed a bright, and what I considered to be a perfect, smile. "I'm all wise and civilized. Keeping my nose to the knowledge. By doing so, I'm destined to thrive," was her response.

"As we strive, like helium we rise. You, being the kinetic manifestation of knowledge, the anointment by direct sunlight sustains our chakras, inclining us towards the heavens," I shared.

"Knowledge must navigate wisdom to acquire understanding, which is the best part. The root, being just like the rib, it's long established she is most necessary to expanding the culture, likewise civilization. After all, knowledge breeds wisdom," China Doll remarked.

"Actual facts. In Genesis, from the rib of Adam came forth Eve. Flesh of his flesh. As you have said, it is certain. I enjoy stimulating life and matter with your company, both in the form of mind and matter. We shall make this day great, for we have dominion over the elements."

We were both smiling while setting out on the task of becoming closer to departure. China Doll seized an attachment of rope connected to the bow. I hopped inside the vehicle, released the emergency brake, and backed the trailer into the water. As China Doll leveraged her weight against the rope, the watercraft floated outwards. While she secured the boat dockside, I parked where plenty of space was afforded. Being the last in our company to enter the launch, we donned our life preservers. I untied both bow and aft, pushing away from the dock.

Acknowledging the no-wake zone, the bass boat did little more than idle out towards the center of the bay. The three of us sat comfortably in bucket leather seating. I steered in a northerly direction towards Lake Ontario. Once satisfied that I was far enough from shore not to disturb nearby fishermen, I said, "Hold on to your football, Onyx." I pressed my feet steadily upon the accelerator. The twenty-foot craft was powered by a one-hundred-fifty-horsepower outboard motor. It's bow lifted. In less than six seconds, we were exceeding forty knots and increasing.

A black Chevy Tahoe pulled up next to Investigator Barnes. Its front and rear door windows were tinted just enough to disguise its occupants. Three antennae adorned the roof. There was only one person inside. The driver. When he looked up, Barnes closed the magazine and tossed it onto the backseat just prior to exiting his vehicle. He hopped inside the passenger seat of the Tahoe. Without warning, the driver reversed the SUV and departed the parking lot in an instant. Finding its way onto 104 East, the Tahoe soon took the

Culver Rd/Sea Breeze exit.

Before long, the truck pulled into a parking lot at the tip of a peninsula. An impenetrable windbreak paralleled an expanse of beach leading to the lakeshore and pier to their north. To the south, two boat ramps, each with separate docks, were bayside. Large boulders and stones lined the embankment. The parking lot was desolate. The east revealed a semi-wide, deep channel adjoining the bay and lake together. Just on the other side of the canal was the town of Webster, NY. There, on the opposite side, was a small metal swinging bridge. It was designed for two-lane traffic. Every winter, the bridge would connect both Irondequoit and Webster at this point, making for an easier commute.

Knowingly, the driver had come from the west. Only one road could be taken to their location. Culver Road. Since Sea Breeze Amusement Park had yet to open for the summer, fewer and fewer people were going to frequent the area. The driver picked up a pair of high-powered binoculars. Observation was taken in all directions. All that could be detected were two men working at the boat yard across the channel and a couple with their dog fishing out on the bay. Satisfied with the surroundings, the binoculars were set aside.

"Ever so cautious, aren't you?" Barnes asked.

The driver looked at him and smiled. It was beautiful. Fitting for such a striking and lovely woman. He'd get lost in her eyes each instant he peered into them, but would immediately check his emotions.

"There's wisdom to be found in being environmentally conscious," she said. "You of all people know this."

Her scrutiny of him was long and thorough. She made no further comment but did take note of Barnes being cleanly shaved and his wearing of that favorite after-shave of hers, which roused her carnal energy buried deeply within. The crypt of self-deprivation. Longing to caress the skin of his exposed forearm, she refrained. Instead, she looked across the lake as if trying to locate something far, far away.

Victoria (Vikki) Olgelson had solidified a promising career in cross-analysis of international data with Interpol. Her ambition and ability to surmount male bias and egotism in the workplace excelled her career. Vikki had made history. She became the first woman with Interpol to act as liaison between England and the Federal Bureau of Investigation. Detective Barnes sat in silence as she continued to stare. Her eyes, the color of a richly aged Scottish single malt, were alit. As was her hair. Rays of light pierced the Tahoe's windshield. The sun, playing a game of hide and seek amongst bunches of cumulus clouds, had the feel of an overhead disco ball.

He caressed the back of Vikki's hand affectionately. Involuntarily, her eyes closed at the memory of his touch. She flinched as if shocked by static electricity. However, she didn't withdraw. Sinking into the driver's seat, she found the headrest and leaned as it began to recline. Memories flooded her mind. Memories attached to emotions, which presently were fracturing Victoria's polished self-discipline. Image meant both absolutely everything and nothing to her, depending on who you were. This woman was rare, unique, and very comfortable in her own skin.

In the eyes of Detective John Barnes, everything mattered. She wondered how much longer the fissures of her protective wall might endure. One thing was certain. It wouldn't be for long. It had been roughly three years since she'd been intimate with anyone. Just so, that person did happen to be Detective John Barnes. Victoria understood the perils of being overly abstinent. Her thoughts swirled and reeled like the walls of an F4 twister. The blinking of an eye hadn't passed. Vikki found herself astride John, her lips pressed hard against his.

There were no thoughts in this moment. No contemplation or judgment calling. Pure instinct and longing had seized them. Their tongues performed a sacred dance of passion as billions have before them throughout the millennia. Her sharp nails combed the surface of his shaved head. She fought to remove his shirt and tie as he attempted the same. With no time to spare, Vikki was without a blouse, and John was shirtless.

Finding herself antsy to remove the tailored, silk-laced brassiere, the detective captured her hands in his. Rebuking both with a smothering of tender kisses, his decree was delivered huskily in full baritone.

"Leave it on," he said. By then, his long fingers were gripping and massaging her thighs. Steadily, her skirt had risen higher and higher, eventually bunching together just above the hips at the waist. His investigation deepened as he palmed her bum with both hands, firmly spreading her soft flesh apart. She moaned and dug her nails into his shoulders, kissing him wildly.

John smacked her cheeks full on and pulled the thong she wore away from her body, suddenly releasing it. Snapping onto her skin, the panties stung slightly, immediately triggering a climax. She broke off their kiss, wailed like a banshee, and trembled uncontrollably.

He began exploring Victoria's neckline, collarbone, and eventually her full breasts, whose hard nipples defied the silk lace. She reached her apex a second time.

As the investigator struggled to unbutton his slacks, Vikki not only obliged but fully exposed him. She stroked his hardness gently, within her closed hand. John pulled the thong to the side, raising her hips a few inches. She guided his hardness inside her. The feel of her heat and wetness triggered John's member to pulsate and throb with the rhythm of his hammering heart. She climaxed as he inched her ever so closer to his thighs. The woman from Interpol resisted the delightful pleasure. he tenderly overpowered her, entering deeper, centimeter by slow centimeter.

John reached both hands in between Victoria's thighs, cuffing her legs. Effortlessly, he curled her one-hundred-forty pounds. She squirmed, wiggled and pleaded ambiguously, as he touched portions of her being that hadn't been explored since they were last intimate. Overwhelmed by memories of a glorious past and wonderful present, she realized the terrible mistake of not allowing this man to love her these last few years. Tears rolled down her cheeks. despite the display, she became more alive and respectfully demanded his seed. In the melee of fulfilling his task, they both collapsed sidelong.

Vikki dabbed beads of perspiration from John's brow. There was an existing bashfulness beneath the smiles shared between them. They became lost in one another's eye for an eternity. Words alone failed in description of anything to what the couple was experiencing emotionally, socially, mentally and physically.

"I've longed for you so much, my darling. Please forgive me," she said. Her voice barely audible. Barnes embraced Victoria, for her into the enclosure of his arms.

It was the totality of unspoken indication needed. In that instant, a weight had been lifted from Vikki. One she'd been burdened with since last seeing John at St. George's Hospital, 3 years ago. Her spirit was ripe with elation. The couple didn't want this moment to end. They both wanted it to endure eternally. When hunger surfaced, it would indulged as each dined upon the intimate passion of the other, until its initial wave was abated. Tender caresses were traded. John slowly ran his fingers across her scalp and hair. She traced his eyebrows, ears and chin with her own.

Vikki took her sweet time delivering soft kisses to John's bare chest. When she next spoke, Vikki shared,

"Eh, love. I may have some information related to your Missing Person's case. You should take a gander," she said. Her English accent prevalent.

About the Author

Anthony Murphy's story took a sharp turn on August 23, 2001. After a 35-day federal trial, he was convicted on six counts—charges spanning from a ghost drug conspiracy to firearms offenses. Though some of the conduct was never formally charged or indicted, it was used to impose a natural life sentence. Since then, Anthony has refused to surrender to despair, remaining steadfast in his fight for freedom and committed to seeking a correction of his sentence.

Faith has been his anchor. He calls "The Creator" his shield and strength, the constant presence guiding him through years of adversity.

Born in Medina, New York, Anthony was raised on the water's edge by his loving grandparents, who nurtured his love for the outdoors from the time he could walk. A fisherman at heart, he also cultivated passions for fitness, reading, learning, and crafting culinary creations.

Today, he is incarcerated at FCI Berlin in Berlin, New Hampshire. You may send him an email @ a.murphy@linkedup.vip.